HELENA DIXON
MURDER
at the
PLAYHOUSE

Published by Bookouture in 2020

An imprint of Storyfire Ltd.
Carmelite House
50 Victoria Embankment
London EC4Y 0DZ

www.bookouture.com

ISBN: 978-1-83888-067-5
eBook ISBN: 978-1-83888-066-8

MURDER
at the
PLAYHOUSE

Murder at the Playhouse *is dedicated to the memory of my Great Uncle Joe, who worked in the music halls as a young lad, teaching me the songs and telling me the tales.*

Torbay Herald (Early Edition) 29th August 1933

Murder at Churston Golf Club

The body of a young woman was discovered shortly after ten o'clock this morning in a bunker on the eleventh tee at Churston Golf Club. The woman, believed to be in her early twenties, had been strangled. The terrible discovery was made by the captain of the Churston Ladies' team, Mrs Millicent Craven, former Mayoress of Dartmouth, and her golf partner, Mrs Loveday Jennings. Mrs Craven said, 'It was extremely distressing. The poor girl must have been there all night.' The police are reported to be conducting house-to-house enquiries in the area to discover the identity of the unfortunate young lady. A local man, Captain Matthew Bryant, is reported to be assisting the police with their enquiries at Torquay police station.

CHAPTER ONE

Late Summer, Dartmouth 1933

'Well, and what do you make of this?' Mrs Craven, doyenne of Dartmouth society, placed a folded early copy of the *Torbay Herald* in front of Kitty Underhay and her grandmother and stabbed at a tiny front-page article with her forefinger. It was late afternoon and they were gathered in Kitty's grandmother's drawing room at the Dolphin Hotel. Sunlight streamed in through the large bay window with its leaded panes, which afforded a view of the river and embankment.

Mrs Craven had telephoned her friend, Kitty's grandmother, only a bare thirty minutes before her arrival. Kitty, whilst eager to leave her columns of pounds, shillings and pence until a later occasion, was somewhat nonplussed by Mrs Craven's demand that she be present. She was well aware that she was not one of Mrs Craven's favourite people. It seemed balancing the books of bar receipts would have to wait.

'You discovered a body?' Mrs Treadwell peered at the article through her pince-nez. 'Today?'

'Yes, this morning; it was most shocking. I was with Loveday Jennings. You must remember Loveday, terrible posture, her mother used to make her walk around the house with a book on her head when she was a girl. We had just played the tenth hole and as we approached the green, we spotted the body in the bunker. Obviously, I would have called you earlier, but the inspector had to take my statement and speak to Loveday. When the wretched journalist asked me about the murder, I was unaware that they had arrested Captain Bryant. I am astonished it made the papers so quickly – except the reporter was at the club as swiftly as the police. I expect there will be more detail in the later edition.'

'Oh, my dear, how terrible. Who was she, the girl? Do we know yet?' Mrs Treadwell passed the newspaper to Kitty. Kitty's heart raced as she read the scanty paragraph, scarcely listening to the conversation continuing around her. How could Matt be under arrest? Was that what the article meant?

Mrs Craven dropped down into a nearby armchair and began to pull off her pristine white cotton gloves. 'Well, that's the problem, no one knows. A little common piece, if you ask me. She was dressed in a rather flimsy evening gown. These modern girls wear them much too short, no back and not the first quality. She'd clearly been out for the evening before she met her end.'

Kitty's grandmother took the padded, chintz-covered chair opposite her friend. 'She hadn't been interfered with, I hope?'

Mrs Craven pursed her lips. 'I couldn't say. The eleventh tee is the furthest from the clubhouse, so Loveday and I immediately abandoned our match and returned to raise the alarm. I confess, once it was obvious that she was beyond help, I did not care to look too closely.'

'It says in the article that Matt is assisting with the police enquiries?' Kitty frowned. 'I know his house backs onto the course, and he told me a while ago he had taken up golf, but it reads most strangely.'

'That's why I'm here. They have arrested Captain Bryant. That's what it means.' Mrs Craven said. The dainty plume of feathers decorating her summer hat bobbed indignantly.

Kitty stared at Mrs Craven, scarcely able to believe her ears. 'Why on earth would they arrest Matt? That's ridiculous. Are you certain?'

Mrs Craven bridled. 'Please do not doubt my veracity, Kitty. I quite agree; it is preposterous but nonetheless it is true.'

'Who is in charge of the case? Why do they think Matt is the culprit?' She knew it to be impossible. It was beyond impossible, it was ridiculous. She and Matt had been caught up in two horrible murder cases in the last few months. The first case had centred around her home at the Dolphin Hotel, and the other had occurred at her aunt and uncle's home, Enderley Hall, near Exeter. Matt now had his own private investigation business based in Torquay. His character was above reproach.

'The man in charge is Inspector Greville. The same man who solved the crimes here and at Enderley Hall,' Mrs Craven said. 'I spoke to him myself. He took my statement. Apparently, Captain Bryant approached the police himself about his involvement in the case as soon as he heard about the discovery of the body.'

'That makes the matter even more curious.' Kitty's grandmother looked at Kitty. 'When did you last see Matthew?'

She flushed under her grandmother's gaze. She and Matt had parted on bad terms when he left Enderley. They had quarrelled and harsh words had been exchanged on both sides. 'Not for several weeks, Grams.'

Mrs Craven sniffed and raised her eyebrows. 'The point is, what do you intend to do about it?'

Mrs Treadwell looked at her friend. 'I shall telephone Patience, Matthew's mother, and establish what is happening. It is clearly a grave mistake. Matthew's parents are old friends of mine as you know, and I would wish to offer my support and assistance.'

'I cannot believe Inspector Greville would suspect Matt. He must have some piece of evidence that connects Matt to this girl. And for Matt to approach the police about the body and then for the inspector to arrest him; it's ridiculous.' Kitty frowned. She didn't like to think that Matt had any kind of friendship with another woman, let alone one who fitted the description Mrs Craven had given. No, something was wrong, very wrong.

Kitty's grandmother called down to the kitchen for a tray of tea to be sent to her salon then immediately placed a telephone call to Matt's mother. 'There is no reply. Even if they are away from home one of the servants would surely answer and take a message but it's just ringing.'

There was a tap at the door and one of the hotel maids wheeled in a tea trolley. After Kitty's grandmother had dismissed the girl, she set about serving refreshments.

'How did the woman die exactly?' Kitty asked as she accepted a cup of tea. She wished the cup contained something stronger.

'Strangled, as the report says but with a bootlace of all things. It was still around her throat.' Mrs Craven declined a biscuit and shuddered dramatically.

'And no one has any idea how she came to be there?' Kitty couldn't see how a girl in an evening gown – and presumably evening shoes – could have walked so far onto the golf course at night, in the dark.

'There were tyre tracks on the grass. Luckily, they didn't damage the green. I suppose someone brought her by motor car along the track running through Lord Churston's estate which borders the course and then dumped her, or killed her there. The eleventh tee is a long way down the course. It's the point when you begin to start back towards the club house.' Mrs Craven settled back in her seat and took a sip from her cup.

'Most extraordinary. Why then arrest Matthew? He doesn't have a car; he has that motorcycle that he rides around on.' Mrs Treadwell looked at her friend.

'I have no idea. It's very strange.' Mrs Craven tapped her finger thoughtfully against the side of her cup. 'That's why I came over as soon as I saw what had happened in the newspaper. You must go and sort it out, Kitty. This sort of thing cannot be tolerated.'

'Me?' The same thought had already begun to form in her head.

Mrs Craven raised a carefully pencilled eyebrow. 'Well of course you. Who else?'

Matt's steady pacing inside the small six-foot by six-foot white painted cell was halted when he heard the scrape of the key turning in the dark green metal door. His shirt was clammy and stuck to his back and he thought he must go mad if not released from this sweatbox soon. He resisted the urge to check the time once more on his wristwatch.

He hated confined spaces. His time in the Great War, with the constant threat of being buried alive in a tunnel collapse in the narrow, muddy labyrinth of battlefield trenches had scarred his psyche. The conflict might be long behind him, but the memories remained. He had smoked almost all his supply of cigarettes in an attempt to remain calm and clear-headed about his current situation. Surely Inspector Greville should have enough information to clear him of any involvement and release him by now.

'Visitor to see you, you've got five minutes.' The constable said as he opened the door and Kitty walked in, her trim, petite figure smartly attired in a pale green two-piece and her short blonde hair carefully coifed beneath a small beige felt hat.

'Kitty, what on earth are you doing here?' She was the last person he expected to see after their quarrel. He had come to sorely miss her company over the last few weeks but had convinced himself that she would not wish to renew their friendship. He especially didn't expect to see her strolling into his cell, placidly removing her gloves as if she meant business.

'I've come to try and get you out, of course. Whatever has gone on?' She perched herself on the edge of the narrow bunk and looked with distaste at the worn grey blanket which covered the thin pallet mattress and at the earthenware saucer full of cigarette ends.

'I'm really not sure that you can do anything to help. This whole thing is like some nightmarish mix-up.' He took a seat beside her and tried not to think too much about how pleased he was to see her again. From her demeanour he couldn't judge if she had come willingly or if she merely felt obligated to offer her assistance.

'Mrs Craven has dispatched me here. She discovered the body of the girl on the course and insisted I come to your aid when she learned you had been arrested. She even paid for the taxi,' Kitty explained.

'I see.' He wasn't sure why Mrs Craven would request that Kitty try to help, and he couldn't tell from Kitty's body language if he was forgiven for their quarrel at Enderley. Or if she had come willingly. 'I didn't think you were speaking to me after we parted on such bad terms.'

She gave him a look that reminded him of her grandmother. 'We both, I think, said things in the heat of the moment that perhaps with calmer minds and temperaments would have been more moderate and considered. Anyway, that is by the by for now. We have to get you out of this pickle.'

'Thank you for coming, I'm glad to see you.' He smiled at her, relief rushing through him when she smiled back.

'And I you, although not in these circumstances. We don't have much time. Tell me what happened and how you came to be involved in this thing. Start at the beginning. Did you know this girl?' She fiddled with her gloves and avoided his gaze as she posed her question.

'No. I saw her and her companion briefly when they called at my house.' He raked his hand through his hair, aware he was explaining badly. 'My neighbours, the Davenports, the ones who use their house as a holiday home, were giving a party.'

Kitty's brow cleared. 'The theatrical people?'

'Yes. It was late and apparently there was some kind of scavenger hunt set up by the younger members of the party. I was at home and about to retire for the night when my doorbell rang.' He paused, feeling as if he could recite this story in his sleep, he had told it so many times now.

'Go on,' Kitty urged, glancing at him.

'I went to the door. There was jazz music coming from the Davenport house so I guessed the party must be in full flow.' He wished now that he had ignored the door.

'What time was this?'

He frowned. 'About eleven. There were two young women in evening gowns on my doorstep. It was obvious that they'd been enjoying the Davenports' hospitality. They were rather loud and giggly. The dark-haired woman in red was quite vampish. The smaller blonde one in the green dress did most of the talking.' The scene was branded in his memory. 'That was when they told me they were on a scavenger hunt. They begged for a bootlace as one of the items on their list. So, I found one to get rid of them.'

Kitty nodded. 'Which girl was killed?'

Matt sighed. 'The blonde one, apparently, according to Greville. She was strangled with the bootlace that I gave her. I must have been one of the last people to see her alive. When I heard at the club that something had happened, I approached Inspector Greville to tell him what I knew.'

'So, that's why the Inspector has you here. Surely the other girl, the one with dark hair, can clear this up?'

He slumped back against the wall of the cell. 'No one can find her. There's only my word that there was another girl. According to Greville, everyone at the party is denying ever seeing these two girls and no one seems to know who they are.'

'That is most suspicious, don't you think? She may be implicated in the affair or in danger herself.' She frowned, a thoughtful expression on her face.

'I'm glad you, at least, believe me, Kitty. I'm beginning to think I imagined the whole thing.' He scrubbed his face with his hands, suddenly aware of how unkempt he must appear in his current state.

The key rattled once more in the metal door of the cell and the constable reappeared. 'Time's up, miss.'

Kitty stood and fumbled in her bag. 'Thank you, officer.' She turned back to Matt. 'Here, I brought you another pack of cigarettes and a bag of peppermints to be going on with.' She showed them to the constable before handing them over. 'I'll speak to the inspector and see what I can discover. Chin up, you'll be out of here soon, I'm certain.'

The door clanged shut behind her and he strained to hear the click of her heels tapping away from him along the concrete floor of the corridor.

CHAPTER TWO

'Good afternoon, Miss Underhay.'

Kitty was following the constable back towards the reception area and turned at the sound of Inspector Greville's greeting. The officer raised his hat and she nodded to him. 'Inspector.'

'I take it you were here to see Captain Bryant?' His expression remained bland, with his moustache appearing as depressed as usual.

'Yes. I was extremely concerned when I learned you had him in custody. You know Matt very well. You must know he has nothing to do with this woman's murder?' She was annoyed that the tremor in her voice betrayed her anger. Seeing Matt in the cell had affected her deeply. She knew how much he was struggling with the confined space.

'If I might have a word in private, Miss Underhay.' Inspector Greville opened the door to a small office and Kitty followed him inside. 'Please take a seat.' He lifted a pile of manila folders from a wooden upright chair in front of his desk so she could sit down. The office was cluttered and the window grimy. It smelled of old tobacco and damp.

'What is going on? How could you possibly suspect Captain Bryant?' Kitty asked as soon as the inspector had removed his hat and taken his own seat behind the battered wooden desk piled high with papers.

Greville leaned back in his seat and surveyed her with a level gaze. 'I do understand your concern, Miss Underhay. You may rest assured he is being treated well. As you say, Captain Bryant has been of great assistance to the police in the past—'

'Well then,' Kitty interrupted. 'You must know him to be innocent. He doesn't even know this girl. He came forward to you to give information.'

The inspector sighed. 'I dislike this situation as much as you, however there are certain lines of enquiry, Miss Underhay, that must be followed. Captain Bryant is the only person who seems to have seen this young woman and the bootlace used to kill her belonged to him. There is also no trace of the other girl he mentioned, if indeed there was another girl who could corroborate his account of events.'

'Matt would not have said there was a second girl if she didn't exist. He wouldn't fabricate her,' Kitty protested.

The inspector frowned. 'I have never had cause to doubt Captain Bryant's veracity in the past, but no one we have questioned so far recalls this other girl being seen with the victim.'

'From what Mrs Craven has told me, it sounds as if the body was moved to the green by motor car. Matt has a motorcycle. He has no motive. There is nothing to connect him to this crime except his own admission that he met the girls and gave them a bootlace for the scavenger hunt.' She sat upright in her chair; her cheeks hot with indignation on Matt's behalf.

'It is precisely because Captain Bryant is known to us that I must be seen to be especially thorough in this case. There must be no hint of collusion or favouritism. The case has already begun to attract attention, and whether we like it or not, Captain Bryant is the only person connected to the victim at this moment in time. If there is so much as a hint of favouritism, then there will be allegations of corruption and all sorts of nonsense.' Inspector Greville sounded resigned. 'Mr Davenport is also something of a celebrity, with friends in high places. He is being considered for a peerage.'

'I see. When do you think it might be possible to release Matt from custody?' Kitty hesitated for a second. 'I know he will not thank me for saying this, but since the war he struggles a little with confined spaces. It is already early evening and he has been here for several hours.' She shot the inspector an anxious look. She knew that he too was a veteran of the Great War.

Greville sighed again deeply, making his moustache quiver. 'I very much hope that we may find some evidence that will allow us to release him soon. In the meantime, I have asked that he be allowed out from the cell regularly for exercise breaks.'

'Thank you.' Kitty stood and offered the inspector her hand before turning towards the door.

'Miss Underhay, it would be pointless, I'm sure, to ask you not to involve yourself, but please be circumspect in your activities regarding this case. Mr Davenport is a man of influence.'

Kitty smiled. 'Of course, Inspector. I wouldn't dream of being anything less than circumspect.'

Kitty puzzled over the information she had been given all the way back to Dartmouth. She chose to return via the bus and ferry rather than take a taxi. She needed time to think about what she should do next.

The Davenports were well known in Torbay society. They came to their large house at least three times a year, staying for several weeks at a time. She knew Genevieve, the Davenports' daughter, by sight from her involvement with various local charities. Genevieve was a stout, plain young woman of about thirty, a most unlikely offspring for the ebullient Mr Davenport and his charismatic former actress wife.

Genevieve's younger brother, Peter, was also known to her; he had attended some of the social events at the Dolphin with his friends. He often brought a large, gay crowd of friends with him from London. They usually came to the balls and entertainments. She knew the family, but not well enough to go snooping. There had to be a way she could get to talk to them and see what she could discover.

The bus chugged its way around the bay, passing near the golf course and Matt's house. He'd never invited her to his home and she wondered which one of the attractive, white modern square houses was his. She guessed it had to be the one nearest to the Davenports' much larger residence. They had joked about her visiting him before they'd had their horrid quarrel.

She released a sigh as the bus crossed the common to head through the leafy country lanes down the hills towards Kingswear and the ferry to cross the Dart. Matt had been putting on a brave face when she'd entered his cell, but the collection of cigarette ends in the saucer had told its own story. She knew he rarely smoked unless he was stressed. His haggard face and the strain lines around his dark blue eyes had told their own story.

The bus pulled to a halt at the stop outside the station and she collected her leather handbag from the seat beside her, ready to disembark. A familiar female figure was already at the embankment, waiting for the ferry to return.

'Hello, Alice.' Kitty went to stand next to one of the chambermaids from the hotel.

'Hello, Miss Kitty.'

Alice was clearly returning to Dartmouth from a day off. The skinny red-headed sixteen-year-old wore her best dress and a perky straw hat. Alice had accompanied Kitty to Enderley Hall as her maid when the unfortunate series of murders had occurred.

'Had a nice day off?' Kitty asked.

Alice blushed and giggled. 'Yes, miss. I've been to the pictures with one of the other girls, seen a lovely film, Gloria Swanson and Laurence Olivier.'

The young girl loved attending the cinema, she knew, and tended to believe that everyday life should reflect what she saw on the big screen.

'Is it true what's in the paper, miss? About Captain Bryant? I got a copy from the seller for my dad when I come out the picture house and heard the cry.' She had a copy of the early edition *Herald* tucked under her arm.

'He's helping the police with the case.' Kitty fudged the truth, relieved that the ferry had clanked to a halt and the crew were lowering the metal gangplanks so that the foot passengers and the vehicles queued on the road could board.

The maid's brow cleared, and she blushed again as one of the crewmen took her hand to assist her onto the gangplank. Kitty followed her on board, declining any offer of assistance with the shake of her head and a smile. She stood at the rails side by side with Alice as a couple of motor cars and a horse-drawn cart rumbled their way onto the ferry.

'So, is Captain Bryant and you friends again?' Alice glanced at Kitty.

'Alice!' She clutched the rail as the ferry chains lifted and the boat swung out into the deeper water.

'I'm glad for you, miss. You make a good couple, him being tall and dark and you so blonde. Got a bit of a look of Randolph Scott about him,' Alice mused.

Kitty bit back a smile and stared out across the sun-dappled water of the river as the black and white timbered façade of the Dolphin Hotel drew closer on the opposite bank. Mrs Craven would no doubt expect her to telephone and report any information. She had been somewhat surprised by the older woman's insistence that they try to assist Matt, but her grandmother had explained that Mrs Craven felt indebted since he had undoubtedly saved her life earlier in the year when she had been attacked in her own home. Mrs Craven had also taken it as a personal affront that the body had been dumped on the green.

'Wonder who that girl was, what they found on the golf course?'

Alice's question cut into her thoughts as they approached the Dartmouth jetty a short walk away from the Dolphin.

'I don't know. Matt told me she was with another woman when he saw them, but no one is admitting to knowing them.' She waited with Alice for the ferry to be secured and the gangplank lowered to let them off the ferry.

'My cousin, Betty, was a waitress at the party at the big house over there by that golf course that night. She said there was lots of young ladies and gentlemen there doing some kind of treasure hunt. She dursen't tell my auntie or my mum about the goings-on.' Alice glanced around her as they prepared to disembark and lowered her voice. 'Half naked, some of the ladies and drinking like you never seen. Not a respectable house, miss.'

Kitty followed Alice off the ferry and onto the cobbled paving. This could be a way to gain some information to help Matt. 'Do you think Betty might have seen the young lady who was killed? It seems she was a participant in the treasure hunt.'

Alice pursed her lips. 'I dunno, Miss Kitty. I can ask her if you like.'

'Thank you, Alice. Matt and I would be very grateful.' She gave Alice the description of the girl that she had been given by Mrs Craven and Matt.

'I'll likely see her later, miss, but I'll have to make sure Mum doesn't get wind of anything. Being involved with the police is vulgar, she says, and she thinks our Betty is a bit fast anyways, on account of her wearing red lipstick all the time.'

Kitty reassured the girl that it was quite all right if she had to wait for the right moment to quiz her cousin and they parted company outside the front door of the hotel.

The smartly attired girl on the reception desk greeted her as soon as she passed through the oak and glass doors into the wood-panelled lobby of the Dolphin. 'Miss Kitty, your grandmother said to ask you to go to her salon when you got back.'

'Of course. Could you have a tray of tea sent up please?' She desperately needed to sit down with a drink. It had been a busy afternoon and it would be time for dinner soon.

'Yes, miss, Mrs Treadwell has just sent down for tea, I'll order an extra cup.'

Kitty eschewed the stairs in favour of the elevator, an elegant polished wood and brass contraption that had been added to the ancient building when they had modernised some of the rooms a few years ago. She slid the brass cage closed and pressed the button for her grandmother's floor.

As she left the elevator and approached her grandmother's suite, she could hear the subdued hum of conversation from inside the room. She pulled off her gloves and tapped on the door before pushing it open at her grandmother's command.

'Kitty darling, come in.' Her grandmother rose to greet her. 'There is someone here you must meet.'

An older woman in her late fifties was perched on the edge of the armchair nearest to the fireplace. She was dressed in a smart grey two-piece with a pale pink silk blouse and there was something vaguely familiar about her, yet Kitty was certain she had never seen her before.

'Patience, my dear, this is Kitty, my granddaughter. Kitty, this is Mrs Bryant, Matthew's mother. She's just arrived in Dartmouth; they drove straight here as soon as Matthew telephoned them.'

The woman rose and shook her hand.

'Oh, delighted to meet you.' Kitty wished she'd had time to freshen up before meeting Matt's mother. She was conscious of her flushed cheeks and untidy hair beneath her hat, from where the breeze on the river crossing had ruffled her appearance.

'Have you seen, Matthew? Is he all right?' Matt's mother resumed her seat, her expression creased with anxiety.

Kitty removed her hat and attempted to quickly smooth her hair with her fingers as she took her seat opposite Matt's mother. 'Yes, I managed to see him for a few minutes.'

There was another tap at the door and a uniformed maid appeared, wheeling a trolley set with tea things and a plate of scones with butter, jam and cream in small glass dishes. Conversation ceased while the tea things were set up and the maid left.

Kitty's grandmother sat on the sofa and presided over the silver teapot, pouring a cup for her guest first. 'Go on, Kitty, tell us what happened.'

She accepted a cup of tea from her grandmother and took a reviving sip, conscious of Patience's eyes, so much like Matt's, watching her every move. 'Matt is coping quite well under the circumstances.' She quickly told both women all she'd learned from Matt and Inspector Greville.

'Oh dear.' Matthew's mother pressed a small lace-edged hand-kerchief to her mouth, her hand trembling.

'I hope that the inspector will be able to locate this other woman soon and identify the poor girl who was killed.' Kitty took another draught of her tea, the warm liquid reviving her spirits.

'My husband has gone directly to meet this Inspector Greville to demand Matthew's release. We came as soon as we heard what had happened.' Patience twisted her handkerchief between her fingers. 'I was concerned that being incarcerated would be difficult for Matthew. It's a… a hangover from the war.' She glanced at Kitty.

'I know he struggles with enclosed spaces. I took him more cigarettes and some sweets to help him. He was coping fairly well.' She tried to reassure Matt's mother.

'Thank you, that was kind of you. I'm glad he has friends here.' She pressed her lips together as if trying not to cry.

'Now then, Patience, my dear, I'm sure Edward will be able to get Inspector Greville to see sense.' Kitty's grandmother offered her guest a scone.

'I saw Alice on the ferry. Her cousin Betty was a waitress at the Davenports' party. Alice has offered to see if Betty has any information which might assist us.' Kitty applied jam and cream to a scone, the rumbling in her stomach reminding her that it had been a long time since her lunch.

'Alice is one of our maids. Well done, Kitty,' her grandmother explained to Matt's mother.

Patience looked slightly perturbed. 'But surely the police should speak to this girl?'

'I'm sure if she has any information, we will be able to persuade her to come forward. I would not wish to bother the inspector unless I were certain I had something of value to aid the investigation.'

'Oh yes, of course. Let us hope that Matthew will be released and cleared very soon so this will not be necessary,' Patience murmured.

Kitty raised an eyebrow but a look from her grandmother prevented her from voicing her thoughts that this might not be so simple aloud.

'Let us hope so,' Mrs Treadwell soothed.

Patience departed in a taxi to return to Matt's house, leaving Kitty and her grandmother in the suite. As she left, Patience promised to telephone if there was any news and said that they intended to remain until Matt was released and exonerated.

Kitty helped herself to another scone. 'Do you think Matt's father will be successful in securing his release? Inspector Greville seemed very determined.' She licked some strawberry jam from the side of her thumb.

'Edward is not accustomed to being disappointed.' Mrs Treadwell removed the dish of jam from Kitty. 'Dinner will be served soon, Kitty. Save your appetite.'

Kitty suppressed a smile. 'Matt's mother did not appear keen that I had asked Alice to speak to Betty. Or, indeed, that I was investigating the case.'

'Patience may be a dear friend, but she can be a bit of a ninny. Sadly, I fear, a consequence of being married to Edward. He is somewhat opinionated, especially on the roles of women.'

Kitty chewed and swallowed the last bite of her scone. 'Hmm… then he and the inspector may well butt heads. This doesn't bode well for getting Matt released from custody.'

'Let us hope that Betty may have some information which can be of assistance. Millicent knows Genevieve Davenport quite well, I believe. They are on some of the same charitable boards together,' her grandmother sounded thoughtful as she collected up the tea things. 'I shall telephone her after dinner and inform her of your progress. Now, run along and change, my dear.'

'Thank you, Grams.' Kitty stifled a yawn; investigating crime was turning out to be quite a tiring activity.

Matt heard the commotion from his cell. He sat up on his bunk where he had been lying, staring at the ceiling, sucking one of the peppermints Kitty had left for him. The sound of a stentorian male voice echoed along the corridor. Matt groaned.

'I demand you allow me to see my son.' The voice was closer.

Matt's spine straightened and he tucked in his shirt as keys jangled in the lock of his cell door.

''Bout time too.'

Matt stood as the door opened and his father entered the cell. Despite being slightly shorter now than Matt and with a slight stoop to shoulders that had once been ramrod straight, it was clear from his bearing that he was a military man. 'Matthew, my boy, what is going on here?' His father nodded dismissively at the constable still standing in the doorway with a worried expression on his face.

'I don't think that…' The man's voice tailed off. 'Um, five minutes.' He closed the door with a loud clang.

'Well?' His father demanded. 'This is a pickle. What happened? I've been on the telephone to the chief constable and I'm trying to get hold of this Greville chappie. Your mother is worrying herself sick. You know what women are like. Dash it all, Matthew.' He spluttered to a halt.

Matt gave his father the abridged version of the information he'd shared with Kitty. 'So that's it, Father.'

The older man paced about the cell, his walking cane tapping against the floor, bed and wall as his stride was interrupted by the confined space. 'What is this Greville chap doing to find out who this dashed woman is, and her friend? That's what I want to know.'

Matt sat back down on the edge of the bed. 'It's difficult for me to discover much of anything while I'm incarcerated in here. Everything happened very quickly. Kitty – Miss Underhay – is following up some ideas, I expect.' He knew she would be bound to be up to something.

His father snorted derisively. 'I doubt if some air-headed young popsy is going to be of much use. We need to speak to this Greville. Get you out of here.'

The sound of keys jangling at the cell door brought the conversation to a halt. The constable's round, apologetic face appeared. 'I'm afraid you have to go now, sir. The inspector would be happy to see you in his office before you leave.' He stood to one side for Matt's father to pass by.

'We'll have you out in a jiffy.' He glared at the constable. The cell door clanged shut once more, leaving Matt alone with his thoughts. He sighed and lit another cigarette.

CHAPTER THREE

Kitty slept badly that night. Her thoughts kept returning to Matt, unjustly incarcerated in a police cell in Torquay. She joined her grandmother for breakfast as usual in her suite, still feeling muzzy-headed, and helped herself to toast at the breakfast table.

'I telephoned Millicent last night after dinner and she has arranged to properly introduce you to Genevieve Davenport. I know we know them slightly, of course, but Mrs Craven has a closer connection. Anyway, there is a charity matter she needs to discuss with her, so you can accompany her to the Davenport house this afternoon.' Her grandmother eyed her over the top of the teapot. 'Please be careful, Kitty dear, the Davenports are very influential and of course there is a murderer on the loose.'

'I promise I shall be charm itself. I simply want to get an idea of what went on at the party and see what the Davenports' reactions are to the murder. Someone must know the murdered girl, and her friend.' Kitty took a bite of toast and tried to look innocent.

Her grandmother raised an immaculate eyebrow. 'I shall telephone Patience after breakfast and enquire if Edward has made any headway with securing Matthew's release. I fear we can assume not, or we would surely have heard.'

'The inspector must release Matt soon. I can't see that he has sufficient evidence to charge him with anything and his enquiries must surely unearth some new information. I wish we knew who the girl was.' She had been pondering this and numerous other aspects of the case all night.

Her grandmother took a sip of tea. 'I'm sure Edward will have arranged a solicitor to sort things out if he didn't manage to persuade the inspector to release Matthew yesterday. He has a great many connections in high places, as you know.' She set the delicate china cup back on its saucer. 'Speaking of connections, have you had any word from your father lately?'

Kitty tried not to smile at her grandmother's expression. There was no love lost between her father and grandmother. Edgar Underhay had only recently re-entered her life, having been absent for many years. 'Yes, I received a letter last week. He seems to be well and was in New York on business.'

Her grandmother snorted and helped herself to more tea. 'Humph, and what kind of business? Funny business, no doubt.'

'Grams, please.' Kitty smiled at her grandmother.

A knock at the door interrupted their breakfast. Her grandmother placed her napkin on the table and walked across the room to open the door.

'Alice, come in, my dear.' She opened the door wider and Alice entered the salon. She was dressed ready for work in her black chambermaid's dress and white apron. Lagging behind her was a tall, thin, brown-haired girl dressed in a faded cotton-print summer dress and slightly worn pale blue knitted cardigan.

'I'm so sorry to interrupt, miss, but this is my cousin, Betty. She's come to tell you what she knows from the party.' Alice glanced nervously at Kitty.

'Oh, please, come and sit down.' Kitty rose and showed the two girls to the chintz-covered armchairs and sofa near the fireplace. Betty perched on the edge of her seat as if about to take flight.

'Shall I ring for more tea? Betty, would you like a cup?' Mrs Treadwell asked as she came to join them.

'No, miss, thank you.' Alice answered for her cousin as she seated herself on the sofa.

Kitty thought Betty didn't seem to be too pleased to be there and she wondered how hard Alice had pressed her to get her to come forward. She knew Betty was not much older than Alice, but it seemed to Kitty that she had a harder, more worldly edge to her appearance.

'Thank you for coming, Betty. It's very good of you. Alice tells me that you were waitressing at the Davenports' party on Monday – the night the young woman was killed?' Kitty sat opposite the girl while her grandmother joined Alice on the sofa.

Betty fidgeted in her seat. 'Yes, miss. I often do jobs like that, parties and suchlike on an evening. I've worked for the Davenports before.'

'Are they good to work for?' Kitty asked. 'And you can be frank, anything you say here is in confidence.'

Betty picked at a loose thread on the hem of her cardigan sleeve. 'They pay all right. Mr Davenport isn't too bad, flashy, like. Mrs Davenport is a bit fond of the bottle.'

'What about the rest of the family? The son and daughter?'

Betty screwed up her face. 'Genevieve is a proper old maid. Dead boring, doesn't stay long at the parties, goes back to her room and complains about the noise. Moans about everything she does.'

'And the son, Peter?' Kitty asked.

'Oh, he's the complete opposite. Good-looking bloke. Always up for a lark, brings a big crowd with him usually when he comes. His friend, Sebastian, is usually with him. He's one with the patter, Sebastian is. One of them sarky, wicked types.'

'Was there anyone else in the party staying at the house?'

Betty's face lit up. 'There's a famous actress and her husband. Laurence and Tilly Tilney. He makes films in America. She had a lovely frock and a massive diamond on her finger.' She cast a triumphant glance at her cousin. 'There's also some old colonel and his daughter, Saira. They used to live in India, and I heard as

Mrs Davenport is fixing Peter up with this girl. She's pretty, with her dark hair and skin but not very lively. Her father looks proper poorly.' She sniffed. 'Oh, and they had this singer called BeBe and her husband there as well. Local, they are, but they've been working in London. She sang and danced at the party and her husband played the piano while she frolicked 'bout a bit. Bit risqué that was, thought the old colonel was going to have a turn. It was proper busy, must have been a hundred people at that party at one point.'

'Goodness!' Kitty's grandmother exclaimed. 'It sounds very lively.'

'Gracious, it sounds very exciting. Whose idea was it to have the scavenger hunt?' Kitty asked. It certainly sounded like the type of affair where people could have attended on the loosest connections to the family.

Betty's forehead creased in thought. 'They had the lists of things for people to find all prepared. I think it was Mr Peter and his friend who suggested it.'

'The girl they found on the golf course was there with her friend. She took part in the hunt.' Kitty gave Betty the description that Mrs Craven and Matt had given her. 'The other girl was taller with dark hair wearing a red dress. I don't suppose you noticed her at all?'

'I dunno, I was busy handing round the champagne and canapés, so it was hard to keep track, like.' Betty's face took on a sly expression.

'Betty!' Alice glared at her.

Her cousin tossed her hair. 'Well, I might have seen them.'

'I think if you know anything about those girls, young lady, then you had better speak up.' Mrs Treadwell fixed Betty with a hard stare that Kitty knew all too well from her childhood.

Betty's cheeks pinked under the layer of foundation and she glanced at Alice. 'I reckon information like that should be worth a few bob.'

Alice turned puce. 'And I reckon your ma would be havin' the backs of your legs with the hairbrush if she heard you talking that way to Mrs Treadwell and Miss Kitty. You'd best say what you know, or you'll be for it.'

'The trouble with you, Alice, is you've had a right bob on yourself ever since you went to that big house as a lady's maid hobnobbing with your betters.' Betty glared at her cousin.

'Ladies, a young woman has been murdered. Betty, if you know something, you need to tell us so the miscreant can be caught.' Mrs Treadwell's tone was severe.

'All right. I saw the two girls talking to Peter Davenport and his friend, Sebastian, at the party. The taller one had dark hair and a red dress, the other one was short and blonde wearing a green frock. I dunno what they said. I was giving out champagne and the row from the music was something fierce. She was laughing though; the one in green as was killed. Peter looked a bit angry but then they moved on, and I didn't see them again for a bit.'

'Can you recall what time this was?' Kitty asked.

'About ten, maybe. I saw them again after and that's why I remember them. Peter announced the scavenger hunt and people was collecting the lists of things to find and there was a great hustle and bustle about. The dark-haired girl reached over where I was making up a tray of drinks and pinched one of the bottles of champagne. I went to say something, but she must have seen the look on my face because she laughed and said, "Don't worry, it'll save coming back for top-ups", then she disappeared into the crowd.' Betty sounded sulky as she relayed her story.

'How much later was this?' Kitty could picture the scene clearly from her description.

'It was just after half past ten, because I'd been in the kitchen a bit before then to take the empties and I caught sight of the clock.'

'I think you need to tell this to Inspector Greville. Did you see the girls talk to anyone else besides Peter Davenport and his friend?' Kitty asked.

'They might have spoke to BeBe's husband. At least, they seemed to be near him when he was playing the piano. And they was hanging after the Tilneys for a bit as well. Especially Mr Tilney; Mrs Tilney weren't too happy about it.'

'Well, thank you, Betty, that's been most helpful. I shall telephone the inspector. The sooner you tell him this information, the better,' Mrs Treadwell said.

'I don't want no bother with the police,' Betty protested.

Alice scowled at her. 'Don't be silly. You have to talk to them. Captain Bryant needs assistance.'

Betty pulled a face but sat quietly while Kitty's grandmother made the telephone call.

'The inspector is sending a car for you, Betty.' She placed the receiver back on the handset.

'We'll go downstairs to wait, Mrs Treadwell, if that's all right with you?' Alice asked.

'Of course, Alice, and thank you, both of you.'

Alice nudged Betty with the toe of her shoe and the two girls departed.

'Did the inspector say anything about Matt being released?' Kitty asked as soon as Alice and Betty had gone.

Her grandmother sighed. 'No, he merely thanked me for the information and said he was sending a car straight away for Betty. I'll telephone Patience and see if she knows anything.'

Kitty wandered over to the window to stare out at the river whilst her grandmother telephoned her friend. The day had been overcast earlier during breakfast, but the sun was attempting to break through the clouds now and the embankment outside the hotel was busy with day-trippers boarding the paddle steamer.

She shivered despite the faint warmth of the sun on the glass and tugged the edges of her crimson cardigan closer together. She couldn't tell from the low murmur of her grandmother's voice if there was good news or bad. She hoped Matt had been released but surely he would have called her if he were out.

They may have patched things up temporarily after their quarrel but until he was released from the cells and they were able to meet up freely again to talk properly, things simply didn't feel right between them. There were still things she wanted to say.

Presently her grandmother replaced the handset.

'Well?' Kitty asked.

Her grandmother shook her head. 'No, Matthew is still in custody. Edward has engaged a solicitor and they are to see Inspector Greville again this afternoon. Patience sounded hopeful but she said Edward was quite enraged when he returned yesterday evening. Apparently, he and Inspector Greville did not see eye to eye.'

Kitty walked back over to her grandmother and resumed her seat. 'Did she say why they wouldn't release Matt?' She'd really hoped that Matt had spent the night back in his own house.

'No. I expect Edward may have told her, but Patience doesn't always listen.'

'Perhaps having Betty's statement may help matters.'

'Perhaps. Anyway, my dear, you had better finish those accounts you were working on yesterday before Millicent comes to collect you this afternoon. You may learn more when you visit the Davenports later. From what Betty has said, it seems they have not been entirely frank with the inspector, and one cannot help but wonder why.'

CHAPTER FOUR

Kitty changed her clothes after lunch, ready for her social call. She wasn't looking forward to spending time with Mrs Craven even though she did appreciate that the woman was assisting her with an introduction to the Davenports.

She swapped her cheery print dress and red cardigan for a more formal pale green suit with a pastel pink blouse, and had just finished adjusting her hat when the black, candlestick-style telephone in her room rang and reception informed her that Mrs Craven was awaiting her. Kitty took a deep breath, pulled on her gloves and hurried down to the lobby.

'Good luck, darling,' her grandmother called as she stepped out of the hotel to find Mrs Craven waiting for her in the back of Mr Potter's taxi.

Mrs Craven was, as usual, smartly attired in a navy suit with a cream blouse. A diamond brooch glittered on her lapel and a navy felt hat crowned her iron-grey curls. 'Now, Kitty, I shall introduce you as my assistant. I take it you have a notepad and pencil in your bag?' She scanned Kitty's appearance through a narrowed gaze.

'Yes, Grams suggested it would be useful to take notes.'

Mr Potter set off into the traffic towards the ferry.

'Genevieve is on a number of committees, but she is very involved at present with organising a theatrical event at the Pavilion theatre in Torquay to raise funds for St Vincent's orphanage for boys. The local amateur dramatic society suggested it I believe and of course the Davenports can bring the stars to make it a success.

She is keen to recruit volunteers to secure raffle prizes, assist backstage and front of house.' Mrs Craven settled back in her seat and looked at Kitty.

'You are suggesting I should volunteer?' Kitty asked. This struck her as a good way of gaining access to the family.

The motor car rocked from side to side as Mr Potter steered it aboard the ferry to cross the Dart.

'I shall leave that up to you, but I suppose it may be a useful way for you to get the information you require to assist Captain Bryant in clearing his name.'

'Do you know the rest of the Davenport family?' Kitty settled her handbag on her lap.

'I've known them for years. Stanley Davenport is a dreadful little man. Made his money from the music halls in London, thinks he is about to get knighted. Celeste, his wife, was an actress of sorts, I believe, in the music halls. She is too fond of the bottle. Peter, the son, is a wastrel. Never held down a proper job in his life. He's supposed to assist in running the family business, organising shows, managing the theatres, that sort of thing. Whenever I have seen him recently he has had that disreputable friend of his, Sebastian, hanging around. Genevieve is the only respectable one. Her brother got all the looks, but not I fear, the brains. Genny is as plain as a pikestaff, poor soul, but with a good heart and much brighter than her brother.'

The taxi rumbled off the ferry at Kingswear and set off up the hill towards Churston. The grey dullness of the morning had been replaced with a bright, fresh sky, lighting up the green fields and the gathered hay bales. Cows grazed peacefully in the countryside.

Within a few minutes they were at Windy Corner, at the edge of the common. Kitty noted that the entrance to the golf course lay on the opposite side of the road to Churston station. The Davenports' house was along a small road with a few other homes, including

Matt's. The lane afforded views of the bay and she could see boats bobbing on the water in the distance.

The Davenport house was somewhat grander than the others, having been much extended, and was set behind a fine set of wrought-iron gates. It was finished in white render, with a simple porch above the dark blue front door. The taxi drew to a halt at the front entrance and Mr Potter sprang out to open the rear door of the car for Mrs Craven to exit. Kitty scrambled to follow her.

'Come along, Kitty, don't dawdle.' Mrs Craven dismissed Mr Potter with instructions to return for them in an hour. She rang the bell, sending a sonorous note inside the house.

Kitty bit back the retort hovering on the tip of her tongue and took her place at Mrs Craven's side. A smart young maid, immaculate in white frilled cap and apron, opened the door to them.

The maid led them along a white-walled hallway with a black and white chequerboard marble tiled floor to an elegant, modernist lounge.

'Please take a seat and I'll let Miss Genevieve know you're here.'

Mrs Craven took a black leather-covered chair near the glass-topped coffee table to await their hostess. Kitty wandered over to the side table to study some of the black and white silver-framed photographs displayed there. There was a family portrait of the Davenports, clearly taken in a garden somewhere when Peter and Genevieve were small. Stanley was dressed in the attire of a country gent, with his wife wearing a fashionable ankle-length frock, fur stole and large hat. Genevieve, stolid and unsmiling even as a child, stood next to an attractive small boy.

'Do sit down, Kitty,' Mrs Craven hissed.

Obediently, Kitty abandoned her survey of the pictures and took her place on a seat beside Mrs Craven. The sitting room door opened, and Genevieve entered the room, followed by the maid who had let them in pushing a tea trolley. Even twenty years after the photograph had been taken, Genevieve was still easily recognisable, dressed in a plain blue serge frock and her hair scraped into an unfashionable bun. She appeared much older than Kitty, although she knew they had to be of a similar age.

'Good afternoon, ladies. Oh, I'm so sorry. I was sorting out the papers I wanted you to see.' Genevieve took a seat, fumbling with the manila folder she had in her hands.

The maid parked the trolley and left when Genevieve dismissed her.

'Genny dear, this is Kitty Underhay. She and her grandmother own the Dolphin Hotel in Dartmouth. She's been assisting me with some of my committee work and I wondered if she might be able to help you too. She has a great deal of experience with organising entertainment,' Mrs Craven said.

Kitty's mouth dropped open and she closed it again quickly. The brass neck of the woman!

Genny peered myopically at Kitty. She fished out her spectacles from her pocket with her free hand. 'Oh, could you? That would be so lovely. Any help at all would make a difference. I've so much on at the moment with this concert.' She opened the file and dropped some of the papers on the floor. Kitty bent and retrieved them, giving them back to her hostess.

She took the opportunity to discreetly peep at the contents as she handed them over. Most of the pages appeared to be covered with columns of figures relating to the orphanage fundraising. However, she was certain she caught a glimpse of a pencil sketch of a man's face sandwiched in between the account sheets.

Genevieve shuffled the documents back into the folder before extracting the ones she wished to show to Mrs Craven. 'Could I trouble you to be mother while I check these with Millicent?' She blinked at Kitty from behind her black-framed spectacles.

'Of course.' Kitty dutifully poured the tea from the art deco-style china teapot while the two women discussed the minutiae of the expenses from a recent event and Genevieve sought advice on some purchases for the orphanage.

The sitting room door opened as Kitty was dispensing the cups and a good-looking young man in his mid-twenties sauntered in. Dark-haired with hazel eyes, he was dressed in flannels and a blazer.

'Tea, how marvellous! Is there a spare cup?' He smiled winningly at Kitty and ignored the flustered glare from Genevieve.

'Seb, I thought you were playing tennis with Peter?' Genevieve blushed an unbecoming shade of crimson.

'Your mother has commandeered him to play nicely with Saira and her father, so I am at your disposal, Genny dear. Now, introduce me to this lovely young lady.' He dropped down on the sofa opposite Kitty.

'Kitty Underhay, this is Sebastian Prior, one of my brother's disreputable friends.'

'Charmed to make your acquaintance. You appear very familiar. Have we met before?' He winked at Kitty.

'I'm delighted to meet you. I think you may have seen me at the Dolphin Hotel in Dartmouth at one of our functions. I presume you already know Mrs Craven?' she couldn't resist asking, knowing the older lady was probably silently bristling with indignation at Sebastian's rather brash behaviour.

'The lovely Mrs C, of course, please forgive me. And yes, I believe it was the Dolphin. A masked ball with a terribly good American jazz singer.' He bestowed a smile upon Mrs Craven, and she simpered under the force of his charm.

'Mr Prior, always so naughty.' She shook her head in a reproving fashion.

'We're rather busy in here, Seb.' Genevieve appeared quite flustered by his joining them.

'All work and no play makes Genny a dull girl.' He helped himself to one of the biscuits from the trolley. 'And has Genny roped you into helping her with her latest charitable efforts, Miss Kitty Underhay?'

'Miss Underhay has offered her assistance, yes. Millicent and Kitty are here to support the theatrical performance for the boys' orphanage.' Genny frowned at him as he took another biscuit.

'It all sounds terribly exciting,' Kitty said.

'Will you be helping?' Mrs Craven asked, looking at Seb.

'Peter and I have been dragooned into performing a small skit or two. Genny has roped everyone in, including her mother. Celeste was a huge star back in the day, don't you know.' He rolled his eyes mockingly. 'Darling Genny was even recruiting at the party the other night.'

Kitty's pulse increased. 'Oh dear, wasn't that the same night that poor girl was murdered? Mrs Craven found the body on the green.' She widened her eyes and waited to see Genny and Seb's responses.

'Oh God, yes, frightful affair. They've arrested the chap from next door. One doesn't expect one's neighbour to be a murderer. Seemed to be a nice bloke, too.' Seb brushed some biscuit crumbs from his trouser leg. Mrs Craven glanced at Kitty.

'Someone told me she was one of the party guests? She came with another girl, I believe?' Kitty took a sip of her almost cold tea. She tried to keep her tone gossipy and mildly interested.

Genny frowned and pushed her black-framed spectacles back onto the bridge of her nose. 'Was she? There were so many people here.'

'Good Lord, who knows? There were so many people milling around. Peter had invited just about everyone and then I think they had invited even more people.' Seb's posture shifted slightly, and Kitty sensed he was more alert to her questions, although he was trying to be nonchalant.

She frowned. 'Oh, perhaps I'm mistaken; I'd heard that she was a friend of Peter's.'

Genny paled and gave an audible gasp. Seb, too, appeared rattled by her statement.

'Peter knows lots of people, he's a popular kind of chap, but I don't know if that particular girl was at the party or a friend of his. We both had quite a lot of champagne that night. That police inspector fellow has been here and questioned everyone.' Seb leaned forward a little in his seat.

'She was involved in the scavenger hunt, I believe, so she must have been at the party.' Mrs Craven set down her cup. 'I also heard that Captain Bryant is to be released from custody soon. It seems he wasn't involved with the murder after all.'

Kitty blinked at Mrs Craven's cool demeanour. She hadn't heard anything about Matt being released, although she certainly hoped it was true and not just a bluff to get more information from Seb and Genny.

'My brother certainly does have a great many friends, and everyone certainly did have rather a lot of champagne.' Genny's tone was disapproving.

'Yes, the whole thing was a bit of a blur.' Seb leaned back again as if pleased to grasp at Genny's explanation. 'One talks to so many people at those kinds of things.'

'Scavenger hunts are such fun, aren't they? What a good idea for a party! Was that Peter's suggestion?' Kitty asked.

'Yes, it was you and Peter, wasn't it, Seb? You'd been to several in London.' Genny looked at Seb.

'We thought it might prove amusing. Bit of a lark for everyone. Then that girl ends up dead, whoever she was.'

'Let us hope they catch her murderer soon. I'm sure I shan't feel safe, knowing a killer is on the loose,' Mrs Craven said.

'I agree. Let's have no more talk of something so horrid.' Genny gave a shudder and with that, the conversation was returned to the charity performance at the Pavilion theatre.

They took their leave of Genny and Seb shortly afterwards and were soon installed in the back of Mr Potter's taxi for the return journey.

'Well, I feel quite exhausted after all of that.' Mrs Craven settled herself and straightened her jacket.

'Was that true, what you said to Seb and Genny? About Matt being released?' Kitty couldn't resist a quick glance at his house as they drove past. A dark blue Bentley, which she presumed must belong to Matt's parents, was parked next to Matt's motorcycle.

Mrs Craven blushed a little. 'I believe he will be released soon. I would not usually wish to lie, but we know that he was not involved with the murder of that girl.'

Kitty suppressed a sigh of disappointment. She had hoped that Mrs Craven might have been privy to new information about the case. 'It was a pity the other family members weren't present at the house.'

'Well, you will have plenty of opportunity to discover more when you assist Genny on Sunday at the fundraising tea. I shall confirm it with her. They will all be there for that.' Mrs Craven looked out of the car window at the passing scenery as they headed towards Kingswear, a satisfied smile playing around her lips. 'You cannot expect me to do everything for you, Kitty, if you wish to help Captain Bryant. My influence only goes so far.'

Kitty opened her mouth to respond but promptly closed it again with a snap. There was no point in making her relationship with Mrs Craven any more awkward than it was already. There was also no point in informing the woman that Sunday was her only day off and that she would be working until late this evening to make up for the time she'd taken off already.

Mr Potter pulled the motor car to a halt outside the hotel, allowing Kitty to alight before continuing on to take Mrs Craven home. She couldn't help but feel weary and more than a little dispirited as she entered the lobby. So far, she had learned little except that she was certain Seb and probably Peter knew something about the murdered woman, and she appeared to have been lumbered with a load of charity work for Genny – charity work which threatened to take up what precious little free time she had. Still, if it meant she could clear Matt's name then it was a sacrifice she was prepared to make.

'Miss Underhay.' A tall, familiar male figure unfolded himself from one of the armchairs in the lobby where he had clearly been waiting for her. 'May I have a word?'

'Inspector Greville, I didn't expect to see you. Come through to the office.' Surprised to see the inspector, she led the way to the small, wood-panelled back office behind the reception desk. 'Can I get you some refreshments?' She busied herself removing her gloves and hat before sitting down behind the desk which filled the one corner of the room.

'No, thank you.' The inspector took his place opposite her.

She was a little astonished at his refusal of food and drinks. The inspector was normally very keen to enjoy hospitality. 'How may I help you?'

He steepled his hands together and surveyed her with a level gaze. 'General Bryant and his solicitor have been to see me. Naturally, Captain Bryant's father is keen to see his son released from custody as soon as possible.'

'As am I, and all his friends.' Kitty wasn't sure where this was leading.

'My dilemma is this. General Bryant has been on the telephone to the chief constable. The chief constable wishes to see results swiftly and Captain Bryant remains the only person besides your maid Alice's cousin Betty who admits to having seen the victim and her companion. To add to the concerns, Captain Bryant's housekeeper has informed my officers that she has witnessed damage to the house in the past which she claims is due to the captain's temper and disturbed mental state.'

Kitty drew in her breath in indignation. 'Poppycock! Matt suffers at times from bad dreams as a result of his war service, that is all. Upsetting a table in one's sleep is a far cry from committing cold-blooded murder.'

The inspector raised an eyebrow at her impassioned outburst but continued calmly, 'I agree. However, there is a great deal of press interest in this case. I think the national press is now reporting upon it. Indeed, General Bryant complained that journalists were gathered outside his house distressing his wife. A young woman is dead and unidentified, and the Davenports are linked to the case. Mr Davenport is also keen that the matter is resolved swiftly. His son, Peter, is to announce his engagement soon I believe, and he does not wish this to overshadow the occasion.'

'What is this to do with me?' Kitty asked.

'You will be pleased to hear that I shall be releasing Captain Bryant. Indeed, I do not think I can detain him any longer without further evidence. Everything I have is circumstantial. However, although his parents are staying at his home and General Bryant has offered to stand surety, I believe it might be better if he were to reside elsewhere for a few days. Until press interest in the case has subsided and we have had the opportunity to gather more evidence or at least make an identification of the girl. There are also some other reasons which I would prefer not to reveal at this point.'

'You wish him to stay here?' Kitty asked. Her mind whirled. She would have loved to know what those other reasons were, but it was clear the inspector was not prepared to elucidate.

Inspector Greville sighed. 'I realise this is a slightly unusual request, but I believe it to be sensible if you and Mrs Treadwell are prepared to offer him a place to stay. I would prefer some distance to be maintained between the Davenports and Captain Bryant.'

'Of course Matt is welcome here. Both I and my grandmother are happy also to stand surety if that is required.' Her spirits rose at the realisation that he would soon be free.

A smile lifted the corners of the inspector's lips. 'Thank you, Miss Underhay. I thought you would agree. I will make the arrangements.'

'Thank you, Inspector. By the way, I visited the Davenport house today with Mrs Craven. On a matter unconnected with the case,' she hurried to say.

'Of course.' His smile grew a shade broader.

'You may wish to question Peter Davenport and his friend Sebastian further. I am quite certain they spoke to that girl at the party and very probably know full well who she is. This must confirm what Betty saw. It worries me that her companion has not come forward.'

The inspector rose and gathered his hat from the desk. 'I will, Miss Underhay. I already had it in mind to do so. I am sure many members of the house party were less than frank with me. Yes, it is most suspicious that we have not yet found the other girl. Thank you for your assistance. You may expect Captain Bryant in a couple of hours' time.' He bowed his head and departed.

CHAPTER FIVE

Matt stared glumly at his sole remaining cigarette. His throat and chest hurt from the amount he had already smoked, and Kitty's peppermints were long gone. His eyes were sore from lack of sleep and he suspected that he looked like hell.

His father and his solicitor had been closeted with Greville for several hours, according to the constable who had brought him a cup of tea. There still seemed to be no move to release him from his incarceration, however.

The sound of keys jangling in the lock roused him from his thoughts and he stowed his cigarette case back in his pocket.

'Good news, Captain Bryant, it seems you are to be released.' The young constable held open the cell door.

Matt breathed a sigh of relief; at last his ordeal was over. He couldn't wait to return to his house, bathe, shave and change clothes.

'This way, sir, Inspector Greville needs to see you.'

He followed the policeman along the white-walled corridor and up a small flight of stairs. The inspector was seated behind his desk in the small, untidy office where he'd first been questioned.

'Captain Bryant, please take a seat. I'm sure you are most relieved to be released from custody.' The inspector smiled thinly beneath his moustache. 'I apologise that it has taken so long to secure conditions which permit your freedom.'

'Conditions?' Matt was confused. Either he was free to go, or he wasn't. What was going on? Surely Greville didn't think there was a case against him still?

'I hope you will agree to co-operate with the proposals. It will only be for a very short time, I'm sure. It will offer you a degree of protection from the intense press interest in this case, amongst other things.'

Matt stared at the inspector. His head ached and he wanted to go home, get outside and breathe fresh air. 'What is it?'

'I'm prepared to release you into Miss Underhay's care providing you reside at the Dolphin Hotel in Dartmouth until I can absolutely exonerate you from any connection with this case. I would like you to refrain from returning to your home, contacting any of the Davenport household or visiting the area near your home at least for the next few days.'

Matt couldn't believe what he was hearing. 'Refrain from returning home? But my parents are at my house.' He wanted to thump the desk and shout his indignation in Greville's face. It was completely ridiculous.

'I am not for a moment suggesting you do not see your parents during their stay. I am suggesting, however, that your meetings should take place away from your home for the next few days. This is for your protection, I assure you.' His gaze met Matt's.

'Fine, anything. I just want to get out of here.' He scrubbed at his face with his hands.

'Thank you.' The inspector slid some papers towards him across the desk. 'Please sign here and you may go. There is a car outside, and Miss Underhay is expecting you at the hotel.'

Matt shook his head in disbelief but picked up the fountain pen to scrawl his signature across the release papers. He was too exhausted to put up a fight. He wondered that his father had agreed to such a condition, but right now he simply wanted to get out.

Kitty had the room prepared on the top floor of the hotel where Matt had stayed previously when he had been taking charge of the hotel's security. It was a few doors away from her own room and one of the few that were available at this point in the season. Guests were not allowed on that floor and usually the room was used for staff or storage.

Her grandmother had been amenable to Matt staying and had telephoned Patience to have some of Matt's belongings packed up and sent to the hotel. Kitty had heard Matt's father bellowing in the background while her grandmother had been speaking to Patience and she guessed he was unhappy with Matt coming to the Dolphin.

She busied herself about the lobby while she waited for Matt to arrive. She dreaded to think how he had managed to cope with confinement in that small cell. The lobby door was pushed open once more and Matt stepped inside.

His appearance shocked her. His eyes were red-rimmed and bloodshot; a five o'clock shadow darkened his jaw. His clothes were crumpled, and she could sense his weariness even from the other side of the room. She hurried over to him.

'Matt, I'm so glad you're here. I've put your things in the room you had before.'

'Thank you.'

'Come on up.' She walked with him to the elevator and opened the brass cage doors so they could enter. A few minutes later they were on the top floor landing.

'Can I get you something sent up to eat or drink?' Kitty asked as she unlocked the door to his room.

'I just want to bathe, shave, change and sleep.' His voice was dull and monotone.

Kitty handed him the key. 'There are clean towels ready for you in the bathroom and your things are all waiting for you. Grams telephoned your mother and had them sent over.'

He nodded. 'Thank you.' He gave her a small smile as her gaze met his.

Impulsively, she reached up and kissed his cheek. His skin felt rough and stubbly against her lips. 'Go and have a bath and a rest. If you want anything just call down for room service.'

He nodded. 'Kitty, take the key back. Come back later and lock me in.'

He pressed the key back into the palm of her hand and went inside his room, closing the door behind him.

Kitty stayed where she was for a moment, not sure what to do next. She had expected him to be tired, to be stressed... angry, even. She hadn't expected this defeated side of Matt. He had asked her to lock him in his room once before when he had thought trauma might trigger the horrific nightmares that still haunted him from his time in the Great War. Her fingers tightened around the key, pressing the metal into the flesh of her palm and in that instant, she decided she hated Matt's housekeeper and the aspersions she cast on Matt's character.

Aware that she was loitering, she hurried towards her own room to change, ready to supervise her staff in the ballroom for the evening's entertainment later. She selected a navy satin evening dress with a dipped back and chiffon trim. She put the key to Matt's room inside her small beaded evening purse.

Once dressed, she hastened to her grandmother's salon to take a light supper before making her way to the ballroom.

'How is Matthew?' her grandmother asked as she slipped into her seat.

'I don't know. In a bad way, I think. I've never seen him like this before.' Kitty drew a white linen napkin across her lap as her grandmother served them each a cheese omelette from the silver salver the waiter had left in the salon. She thought it best not to mention Matt's request that she lock him in his room.

'Hmm, did you manage to learn much at the Davenports?'

'I think Peter Davenport and his friend, Sebastian, know more than they have said so far about the woman who was killed. It was obvious from what Seb said that he was lying, and they knew her and her friend.' Kitty cut a piece of her omelette and speared it with her fork.

'Millicent said you were intending to assist Miss Davenport on Sunday at her fundraising tea?'

'Mrs Craven placed me in an impossible position. I had no choice. At least I should be able to meet the rest of the family and their guests, so I suppose it will be helpful in that respect. Although I would hope Inspector Greville will be able to identify the woman soon. Someone must know who she is, and why has her friend not come forward?'

Her grandmother, resplendent in a dark blue velvet gown, patted the corners of her lips with a napkin. 'Perhaps the information Betty provided may be helpful to the inspector. He must have a good reason for keeping Matthew away from his home.'

Kitty frowned. 'I thought that too. The reasons he gave seemed a little weak, but he wouldn't enlighten me any further.'

'Perhaps Matthew may have some ideas himself when he's rested and recovered from his ordeal.' Her grandmother took a sip of water.

'I hope so, this seems to have really affected him.' Kitty was concerned. The Matt who had arrived at the Dolphin was not the confident Matt she knew. She placed her knife and fork down neatly on her plate. 'I'd better go to the ballroom. I'm still not sure about the new barman.'

'No dessert?' her grandmother asked.

'Not tonight.' Her appetite seemed to have vanished. She kissed her grandmother's delicately powdered cheek and set off towards the hotel ballroom.

The Dolphin had a year-round entertainment programme to boost their revenue, attracting guests to the hotel and drawing in local residents for an evening of dancing with drinks and supper. The tourist season started before Easter and had been launched earlier in the year by Miss Vivien Delaware, an American jazz singer.

The current entertainment was being provided by the house band and a local male vocalist who always guaranteed a full house. The sound of voices mixed with trumpet and piano reached her as she drew nearer to the double oak doors of the ballroom.

Mickey, the hotel maintenance man and general helper, was attired in evening wear and stood at the entrance to check people in and out.

'Evening, Miss Kitty.'

'Good evening, Mickey, is everything all right?'

'Yes, miss, nice crowd in tonight.'

She lowered her voice and checked no one was in earshot. 'Captain Bryant is staying with us for a short time. He's occupying the room he had before. I wondered if you could ensure he is not disturbed. He's been through quite a traumatic time.'

'Of course, Miss Kitty. It'll be my pleasure.' He opened the door to the ballroom for her and she stepped through into a wall of sound and people.

Men in evening suits mingled with ladies dressed in smart evening gowns. The air was fuzzy with cigarette smoke which tickled at her nostrils. She slipped through the crowd, smiling and greeting people she recognised as guests or from the town.

Kitty checked the staff circulating the room from a discreet position amongst the fan palms at the side of the stage. The dance floor was full, and everyone seemed to be enjoying the musical entertainment. She stationed herself so she had a view of the new barman. She had suspicions that he was either pocketing some of the takings or incorrectly charging for drinks and she was determined to establish the truth.

She watched for a few minutes before her view was obscured by the crush of people moving around the room. Absorbed in what she was doing, she barely registered that she was being hailed.

'Miss Underhay, we meet again. May I present Peter Davenport, Miss Kitty Underhay.' Sebastian, elegantly attired in immaculate evening wear, had appeared before her. He was accompanied by a good-looking, fair-haired young man, similarly attired.

'I'm delighted to meet you, Mr Davenport. I didn't know you would be coming here tonight.'

'Please, call me Peter. Mother suggested I entertain Saira; apparently I have been an inattentive host, so we've come as a party with some friends,' Peter explained. He had a half-filled glass of champagne in his hand and Kitty suspected he may have already imbibed quite a bit, judging from the flush on his cheeks.

A pretty dark-haired girl in a slightly old-fashioned forest-green gown came to join them, accompanied by a slender, blonde-haired woman wearing a sparkling diamond necklace and a slightly older man with greying temples.

'Miss Kitty Underhay, may I present Miss Tilly Tilney and her husband, Laurence, and Miss Saira Conners.' Seb made a mock bow.

Tilly gave a tinkling little laugh.

'You may recognise Tilly, of course, from her work on stage and screen,' Peter slurred slightly. Saira frowned and looked uncomfortable.

'It's lovely to meet you all. I hope you're enjoying the entertainment,' Kitty said.

'Fabulous, dear girl. We're having a splendid time. Quite a change for Saira though, isn't it, poppet? She's been used to a much quieter life in India and Switzerland.' Peter took a swig of champagne.

Saira shuffled her feet and looked uncomfortable. 'We only arrived in England a few weeks ago. Everything is quite different here.' She blushed as she spoke, and Kitty felt a little sorry for her. She seemed very out of place next to the glamorous Tilneys and the worldly-wise Seb and Peter.

'Oh yes, poor you. It must all seem very strange,' Kitty said with a kind smile.

'Quite the shock, what with a murder on the doorstep and everything.' Tilly Tilney had a faint American accent.

'Most unpleasant, not what one expects in a quiet English seaside resort,' Laurence Tilney agreed. He had a pleasant, baritone voice.

'Let's hope the police catch the murderer soon,' Kitty said.

Seb shot her a glance. 'I heard they let the neighbour chappie go.'

Kitty gave a small shrug. 'That's what I heard too.' She didn't know why but she intended to stay on her guard around the Davenport group. They definitely knew more about the murder than they were prepared to say, and she didn't trust them. There was no way she would let them know that Matt was actually staying at the hotel.

Peter gave his now-empty glass to a passing waitress and took hold of Saira's hand. 'Enough gloom and doom, darling. Let's dance.' Before the girl could protest, he'd whisked her away into the crowd.

Laurence and Tilly joined them, leaving Kitty alone with Seb. 'Can I persuade you to dance, Miss Underhay?' He gave another mock bow and offered her his hand.

'I am working tonight, but I suppose one dance won't hurt.' She accepted his invitation. She didn't really want to dance with him but thought it politic to keep on the good side of the party if she were to uncover more information about the party and the murder.

Seb was a good dancer but she couldn't help thinking about the last dance she'd had with Matt, a few months ago. It had felt so right to be connected like that, as he'd held her in his arms. Seb steered her expertly past Saira and Peter.

'They make a good-looking couple, don't they?' Kitty observed.

'Peter's darling mother certainly thinks so. She's attempting a match. Poor Saira is pretty enough but dull as ditchwater. Her father is all for the engagement. He's been very ill and wants to see her married off respectably and knows Peter's father well from some business dealings years ago.'

Kitty glanced again at Peter and Saira. They certainly didn't appear to be like a couple about to announce their engagement. Seb's tone had been odd, too. Sneering? She couldn't quite define what it was.

'I assume then this is not a love match? What's in it for Peter?' Kitty asked. She decided to be blunt, matching Seb's tone.

His laugh was harsh in her ear. 'Money, of course. Saira's old man is loaded and according to him, Saira's mother was a bona fide Indian princess. It'll keep his old man sweet too. Mr Davenport is angling for a title so wants his children to ooze respectability.'

Seb's voice vibrated with bitterness, an interesting fact which Kitty stored away to consider later. For now though, she decided to change the subject. 'The Tilneys seem very glamorous.'

'Oh Hollywood, darling. He's producing her latest film and is busy toting around for backers. Her last one was a bit of a failure. Between you, me and the garden wall, so to speak, she's getting a shade long in the tooth to play ingénues.'

The Tilneys swept past, drawing a host of admiring looks from other dancers. A moment later the music ended, and the dancers applauded as the band took a brief break.

'Thank you for the dance.' Kitty extricated herself from Sebastian. He'd certainly provided her with a lot of food for thought.

'The pleasure was all mine,' he smiled at her as she slipped away into the crowd.

CHAPTER SIX

For a split second before he opened his eyes, Matt couldn't remember where he was. The scrape of the key in the lock sent him sitting bolt upright. Light spilled into the darkened room through a crack in unfamiliar rose-patterned curtains. Matt sucked in a breath as recognition dawned. He was at the Dolphin, in the room he'd occupied a few months earlier when he'd been employed by Kitty's grandmother to manage the hotel's security.

There was a light tap on his door. 'Matt?'

He recognised Kitty's voice. Glancing around the room, he was relieved to see no signs of disturbance. He slid out of bed and tugged on his plaid dressing gown before opening the door.

Kitty was the other side. She was dressed for work in a cheerful cherry-patterned frock. A small wooden trolley set with tea things stood next to her.

'I thought you might like something to eat.'

'Thank you.' He was embarrassingly aware of how dishevelled he must look next to the immaculate and perky Kitty. 'What time is it?' He hadn't looked at his watch when he'd woken.

'Eleven o'clock. I'm on my break so I thought I ought to come and check if you were all right.' Colour flared in Kitty's cheeks as she stumbled to a halt.

'Yes, thank you. Um, I'll take the trolley then.' The atmosphere between them felt awkward in a way it never had before. Matt took hold of the trolley handle.

'Of course. I had better get back to work. Will you join me for lunch later? One o'clock?' Kitty stepped back. 'I can fill you in on what I've discovered so far.'

'I'll come to the office.'

She nodded and turned away.

Matt trundled the trolley inside his room and closed the door. A silver cloche covered a plate next to the small metal teapot and china cup. He lifted it up to discover a plate of hot buttered toast and a glass dish of strawberry jam.

The smell reminded him of how hungry he was. Taking a seat on the small chenille-covered armchair near the window he settled down to eat. As he caught a glimpse of his reflection in the dressing table mirror, he grimaced.

It was a wonder that Kitty hadn't fled in horror when he opened the door. Matt rubbed his hand across the layer of stubble covering his chin and sighed. Thanks to Kitty's thoughtfulness, though, after two cups of tea and a few slices of toast, he began to feel better. At least now he was free he could start to clear his name.

At one o'clock, Matt presented himself, clean-shaven and suited, at the door of the small wood-panelled office behind the reception desk. A surly looking middle-aged man in a shabby jacket crashed past him and rushed out of the lobby.

Kitty was seated behind her polished oak desk looking slightly shaken.

'Are you all right, old girl? What happened?' He couldn't help himself. The protective streak which always seemed to appear whenever he was near Kitty had come to the fore again.

'I had to dismiss one of the barmen. I caught him stealing from the till last night.' She sighed. 'It's never a pleasant task.' She replaced the lid on her fountain pen and placed it down in the gilt pen tray next to her blotter before closing the ledger that lay open in front of her. 'Grams is dining with Mrs Craven and the gals. I believe your mother is with them, so I've arranged for us to dine privately in Gram's suite so we may talk freely before they arrive back here.'

Matt's eyebrows raised slightly when Kitty said his mother was dining out with Kitty's grandmother and her friends. He had been half expecting his parents to appear at any moment now his liberty had been restored. 'Thank you.'

As Kitty rose, he caught a faint trace of her soft rose perfume and was instantly reminded of the gardens at her aunt and uncle's home, Enderley Hall. He and Kitty had grown quite close during their time there before they had argued. He had even begun to think… but he shook the thought out of his mind.

'Come on then, or lunch will be cold.' She smiled at him and led the way through the lobby. They walked side by side together up the broad oak staircase to the first floor and Kitty's grandmother's suite.

The table in the bay window had been set ready with a white linen cloth and cutlery while a trolley, similar to the one which had transported his breakfast, stood to the side.

'Take a seat, I'll be mother,' Kitty said and pulled the trolley closer to the table.

He followed her instructions and sat down as she lifted the silver cloches and placed a laden plate in front of him. 'Fish, fresh this morning.' She placed a similar plate at her own setting before taking her place opposite him.

She drew a napkin across her lap, smoothing out the folds of the linen over her knees. 'How are you?'

He copied her action. 'Better today, especially now I've had some sleep.' The delicious smell of the grilled hake made him realise he was still hungry despite the toast he'd eaten earlier. The police had done their best to provide meals, but he had been unable to eat while incarcerated in the cell. The small breaks under escort to stretch his legs in the yard had been most welcome.

Kitty filled her glass with water from the decanter on the table and held it over his glass. He nodded agreement and she poured some for him. She filled him in on all she'd discovered so far while they ate. She was interested to judge from his reactions if he found some of the information she'd gathered as interesting as she did.

'Well done, you've been busy.' He placed his knife and fork down on the empty plate. His gaze met hers and the corners of her mouth quirked upwards in a wry smile.

'Not bad for a woman?' There was a provocative note in her voice.

He raised both hands in a gesture of defeat. 'I've never doubted your ability, Kitty.' That was true; he knew her to be very capable. He had come to realise that her words at Enderley had held a ring of truth. She had made a valid point that she had as much right as he to determine what might or might not be dangerous. He would not have spoken to another man as he had spoken to Kitty that night. She had been right to challenge him, but he still couldn't help feeling protective towards her.

'And you accept that I am quite capable of making rational decisions and of judging risks?' She lifted her chin as she posed the question, referring unmistakably to the hot words which had passed between them.

'If you will accept that I may not always feel happy about your decisions?'

'I suspect we may still argue about this at times,' she mused.

'So long as we agree to not allow the quarrel to be as prolonged as this last one. I have missed… our conversations.' He had missed *her*.

'So, we're a team again?' she asked. 'Equal partners?'

Relief flooded through him and the heavy weight that had been oppressing him ever since he'd left Enderley lifted. 'Yes, we're definitely a team.'

Kitty's smile broadened and she extended her hand for him to shake. A small frisson of electricity passed through him at her touch.

'You do realise that Mrs Craven has lumbered me with assisting Genny Davenport in her charitable endeavours in return for ferreting out information to help you? You owe me, Matthew Bryant.'

'If Mrs C is involved, then I probably do.' He realised he still had hold of her hand and released her as a delicate pink blush coloured her cheeks. She picked up her water glass.

'To Bryant and Underhay.'

He grinned and chinked his glass against hers. 'Then we'd better make a plan.'

The telephone rang in the suite and Kitty placed her glass down on the table and went to answer the call.

'Yes, I see, Constable, and he didn't say what the developments were?' She glanced at Matt as she listened to whoever was on the other end of the line.

His attention had been caught by the word 'constable' and he strained to try and hear the other side of the conversation.

'Oh, yes, of course, thank you.' She replaced the receiver back in its cradle.

'Inspector Greville is on his way here. Apparently, there has been a development in the case, and he wishes to speak to us.'

The meal Matt had just eaten roiled in his stomach. He had no desire to be returned to the cells. 'Did he say what kind of development?'

Kitty shook her head. 'No, it was a constable telephoning. The inspector has already left the station.'

Kitty telephoned reception and arranged for the remnants of their meal to be collected whilst they awaited the arrival of Inspector Greville. Matt paced about the room, only stopping to gaze out of the bay window at the river scene below every few minutes.

'Perhaps he has made an arrest, or found the other girl. It might not be anything to do with you at all,' she suggested.

'Perhaps.' Matt stared out of the window once more.

She jumped up from her seat on the armchair near the fireplace and crossed the room to stand next to him. 'It will be all right; the inspector will exonerate you soon, I'm certain of it.' She placed her hand on his arm, feeling the muscle bunch beneath the sleeve of his jacket.

'I can't go back to that cell, Kitty.' His voice was low, so she barely caught the words.

'I'm sure that isn't why the inspector is coming. He would hardly have sent word ahead if he planned to arrest you. I'm sure he knows as well as I do that this dreadful affair is nothing to do with you.'

'Then he has a dashed funny way of showing it.' The muscle in his jaw jumped.

A knock sounded on the door to the suite. Kitty gave Matt's arm a warning squeeze then went to admit the inspector.

'Miss Underhay, Captain Bryant.' Greville removed his hat and inclined his head politely as Kitty stood aside to allow him into the suite as the maid who had guided him upstairs scuttled back to her duties.

'Please come in.'

The inspector took a seat on the chair that Kitty had just vacated. She perched herself on the sofa and waited for Matt to come and join her.

'I trust you are somewhat recovered?' The inspector looked at Matt.

'Yes, sir.'

'No doubt you are both wondering why I'm here?' Greville surveyed them.

'Have you made an arrest?' Kitty asked, her tone sharp with anxiety.

The inspector sighed. 'Not yet. However, we have discovered the identity of the victim.'

'Who was she?' Matt asked.

'An aspiring young actress, Marguerite Bright, known as Pearl or Pearly. She appeared in some magazines advertising cold cream, I believe, and had a few small parts in various revues. Her landlady came forward a few hours ago. She was concerned that she hadn't seen the young lady and she was behind with her rent. She recognised her from the description circulating in the press.'

Matt let out a low whistle. 'An actress. Have you spoken to the Davenports again, sir?'

'I shall be interviewing some of the Davenports and their house party again when I leave here. They are aware that I wish to question them further so I hope the wait may have loosened their tongues. I am certain, after speaking to that girl, Betty, you sent to me, that the younger members of the group may have some information.'

'Do you know who her companion was, Inspector?' Kitty asked.

The inspector shook his head. 'Not yet. I anticipate that I may be further forward with the affair when I have conducted more interviews. The landlady implied that Miss Bright was friendly with another of her lodgers. However, we have been unable to confirm this at present. I take it you maintain that the young lady was definitely not known to you, Captain Bryant?'

'No, not at all. The night she came to my door was the one and only time I ever saw her. My social circle does not include the theatrical world.' Matt's tone was belligerent.

'Her landlady had asked Miss Bright about the outstanding rent a few days before her death. Miss Bright had laughed and told her not to worry, she was expecting a sum of money any day and would pay her debt then. She also said she anticipated moving to a nicer lodging. The landlady was not impressed at the aspersion cast upon her home. You said in your statement that the young ladies appeared to be in high spirits?'

'She expected money from somewhere?' Kitty mused.

'Or someone? I suppose that would account for them seeming so pleased with themselves,' Matt said.

'It is possible, I suppose, that something may have happened to the other girl… or even that she might be the murderer? There could have been a falling out between the two girls,' replied Kitty.

'We are keeping all the possibilities in mind,' the inspector assured her.

'Thank you for keeping us informed of your progress.' Kitty's heart lifted. It sounded as if there was finally some kind of breakthrough which could lead suspicion away from Matt. 'Oh, what a dreadful hostess I am, I didn't offer you any tea.'

'That's quite all right, Miss Underhay. Mrs Greville has begun to make pointed remarks about the fit of my suits of late.' The inspector ran his hand regretfully over his stomach and Kitty bit back a smile. 'I trust that you will of course return the favour, should either of you uncover information which may be useful to this inquiry?' The assumed blandness of his expression didn't quite conceal his expectation that they would no doubt continue with their own investigations.

'I can assure you, Inspector, that I have a vested interest in ensuring that whoever murdered Miss Bright is captured and my name is cleared,' Matt said.

The inspector rose and collected his hat from the table. 'I would appreciate you remaining here at the hotel for a little longer, Captain Bryant, while I continue with my enquiries. The press are laying siege to both yours and the Davenports' homes at present. Mr Davenport is most unhappy with the situation.'

Matt rose and shook hands with Greville. 'I understand, Inspector, and thank you again for updating us.'

'Miss Underhay.'

Matt showed the inspector out while Kitty remained on the sofa, processing the new information.

'Well, what do you make of that?' The question burst from her lips as soon as Matt returned to the sofa.

'If she was an actress then it certainly explains a link to the Davenports.'

'I knew they were hiding something. Oh, I would love to be a fly on the wall for those interviews the inspector is holding.'

'Perhaps you'll discover more on Sunday when you assist Miss Davenport with her charity event,' Matt suggested, and she caught a glimpse of the dimple flashing in his cheek as he teased her.

'Beast.' She playfully smacked his arm. His gaze met hers and something in his expression stilled her breath.

'Kitty…' Whatever he was about to say was lost as the door to the suite opened and her grandmother bustled in, accompanied by Matt's mother who was clad entirely in black, as if she had attended a funeral.

'Ah, Matthew, Kitty, I thought we would find you both here.' Her grandmother drew off her cream gloves and placed them in her matching leather bag.

'Mother.' Matt stood and embraced his mother.

'Oh, Matthew, thank goodness you're all right! I've been in such a worry. Your father will be here shortly to see you and to take me back to your house. I've only just got everything straight again. The police searched it, you know. I really don't see why you can't return to your own home now. It's quite ridiculous,' Patience wittered as Matt released her.

'The inspector has explained some of his reasons, Mother. It's best if I stay out of the picture whilst he completes his enquiries.' Matt patted his mother on her arms.

Patience took a seat on the sofa and pulled off her gloves while Kitty's grandmother called reception for coffee.

'Well, it's all wrong. It makes you appear in the wrong. There are newspapermen everywhere. Your father is livid. He's had words with the chief constable again this morning about it.'

Mrs Treadwell replaced the receiver and came to sit with her friend. 'Really, Patience, the inspector has to do his job how he sees fit.'

Matt strode about the room. 'Inspector Greville has only just left. They have identified the girl who was killed.'

'An aspiring actress, a Miss Marguerite Bright – Pearl Bright was her acting name,' Kitty added. Hearing that the police had searched Matt's house whilst he had been held at the police station made her feel queasy. It brought home once more the danger that Matt had been in.

'So, it's very likely that the Davenports would know her then, and her friend,' Mrs Treadwell observed.

'Or she wished to get to know them. The Tilneys are staying with the Davenports and he is a film producer. I met them last night in the ballroom. He is supposed to be touting for backing and possibly casting for a new moving picture.' Kitty looked at Matt.

'And what of her companion? Has the inspector found the other girl?' Kitty's grandmother asked.

'Not yet, although he may have a lead.' Matt had paused in front of the window again. 'At least he has made some progress.'

Alice arrived with the refreshments and Matt's father. The maid parked the trolley next to Mrs Treadwell and flashed a small smile at Kitty before retreating.

'Well, Matthew? What is happening with the case?' Matt's father removed his hat and nodded a greeting to Kitty and her grandmother before shaking hands with his son.

'Sit down, dear, coffee has just arrived.' Patience waved at her husband to take a seat.

Matt quickly updated his father on all they had learned so far. Mrs Treadwell poured the coffee into delicate china cups and Kitty handed them out to their guests whilst Matt talked.

'About time that Greville fellow did something. Heaven knows why the chief constable thinks so much of the man. Indolent blighter, if you ask me,' Matt's father huffed over the brim of his cup.

Matt cut his eyes at Kitty. 'These things take time, Father. The inspector is very thorough. I understand there is a lot of press interest in this case which is both a hindrance and a help.'

'Poppycock, the whole blasted business! It'll probably turn out to be the girl's boyfriend or something.' Matt's father continued to grumble whilst Patience made soothing noises of agreement. 'The sooner you can return home and go about your business, the better.'

By the time Matt's parents left, Kitty's head ached and Matt's face was white and pinched with exhaustion.

'I need to finish the staff rotas.' Kitty began to collect the dirty cups ready to place them back on the trolley.

'I'll do that. Why don't you and Matthew go and take the air for a while? It would do you both good.' Her grandmother removed the cups from Kitty's hands.

Kitty glanced at Matt; he certainly looked as if he were in need of a break. 'If you're sure you can spare me? I had to dismiss Crowson, the new barman, so his shifts need to be covered.'

'I can see to the staffing. Go, both of you, while the sun is still shining.'

CHAPTER SEVEN

The late afternoon air was fresh and cool after the warmth of her grandmother's salon and Kitty snuggled into her smart scarlet jacket.

'I feel a little like a naughty child dismissed outside to play by the grown-ups,' Matt commented as he strolled along the embankment beside her, her hand resting on his arm.

She was relieved to see the breeze from the river had restored some colour to his cheeks. 'Do you think your parents will stay for long, now you have been released?' She tried to keep her tone neutral.

The corner of his mouth quirked, and the dimple flashed in his cheek. 'I expect they will stay until my father has decided that I have been completely exonerated and the murderer is under lock and key.'

They paused by the railing to look out across the water towards the small town of Kingswear on the opposite bank. The leaves on the trees were already beginning to be tipped with gold, a sign that autumn was fast approaching. The ducklings that paddled so furiously at the river margin were almost as large as their parents and now moved independently through the reeds.

'Then we need to set to work.' Kitty peeped across at Matt.

'I wonder what Inspector Greville will discover at the Davenports' today?' Matt asked.

'I shall try to find out what I can when I go there on Sunday. I haven't yet met Mr and Mrs Davenport, so that may prove interesting,' Kitty mused.

'It's so frustrating that I can't be there. Greville is adamant that I have to stand back until he can completely clear me of any involvement.'

Kitty felt the muscle of his arm tighten under her touch. 'I know it's annoying but hopefully it's not for much longer. In the meantime, I shall do my best to be your eyes and ears.'

He covered her hand with his fingers. 'You are a good friend, Kitty.'

While his words cheered her, she couldn't help wondering if that was all she was to him. Sometimes she thought there might be something more lying unspoken between them – at least for a time at Enderley she had thought so, maybe even hoped so. They walked on along the embankment, past the Boat Float, the small marina separated by a road bridge from the river. The upper and lower ferries that transported passengers and vehicles across the river were busy as it was the end of the working day. By contrast, the pavement where they were walking was quiet.

As if by common consent, they turned around when they reached the far ferry station and set off back towards the Dolphin. Matt was quiet and Kitty respected his need to be silent. The cool air was helping her headache and she felt better than when they had set off.

'I am very grateful to your grandmother for allowing me to stay here,' Matt said, as they approached the creaking overhead painted hotel sign.

'My grandmother and her friends are very happy to help. You helped me, Mrs Craven and the Dolphin a few months ago and you came to my aid at Enderley Hall. We… we all owe you a great deal.' Colour mounted in her cheeks as she spoke, heating her face.

The wind gave a sudden gust, sending a skitter of leaves swirling around their feet and making the painted dolphin above their heads sway. 'Autumn is on its way already it seems, so much for the summer. Let's get inside.' Kitty didn't wait for Matt's reply, choosing instead to head into the shelter of the oak-panelled lobby.

'Miss Kitty, you have a letter here for you. Come from America,' the receptionist called out to her as she entered.

Her heart leapt; it had to be from her father. 'Thank you.' She collected the envelope and recognised her father's copperplate lettering. Her aunt had given her some information whilst she had been staying at Enderley about her mother's disappearance back in the summer of 1916 when Kitty had been a small child. The mystery remained unsolved but she had passed this on to her father in the hope that it might trigger a memory for him that could open a new line of enquiry.

'A letter from Edgar?' Matt asked.

'Yes, I wonder if he's answered my question about Mother.'

The lobby was empty of guests, so she and Matt took a seat at the small corner table near the elevator. Kitty tugged off her gloves and ripped open the envelope.

'Where is your father now?' Matt asked.

Kitty smoothed out the letter. 'He is still in New York.' She scanned the letter quickly, frowning a little as she did so.

'Is everything all right?'

She nodded. 'Yes. He says he is well and is settled at present in the city.' She continued to read. 'Oh, he has answered my question about Mother. You remember how Aunt Hortense said that when my mother left Enderley Hall she had given her directions for an acquaintance of my father's in Exeter and she wondered if she may have been headed there?'

Matt nodded. 'Yes, your aunt couldn't be certain of the name. Dawson, or Dawkins?'

'Well, it was quite a while ago now. Father is certain that it would have been a chap he used to knock about with. He says, "*I think my sister may be recalling Jack Dawkins, a fellow I used to do a little business with from time to time. We were close in our youth and he knew your mother. I have not heard from him for many years. Indeed, my dear, as he was a little older than me, he may not even still be alive. He had a curio shop in Exeter where he would also accept pawned* articles. *It was not in the respectable part of the city so do not go alone if you intend to try there.*" He goes on to give the address.' Kitty glanced up from her scrutiny of the letter to study Matt's reaction.

He leaned forward in his seat, a gleam of interest in his dark blue eyes. 'I could follow it up for you. Greville wants me out of the way for a while, so I could go to Exeter on your behalf and see what I can uncover. It would keep me busy.'

She read the letter quickly once more as she considered Matt's offer. It made sense that he could go and make enquiries. He had time on his hands at present, whereas she was fully committed, both with the hotel and Genevieve's charity events.

'I suppose you could at least see if this shop is still there and if Mr Dawkins is still around. I'm assuming that if he was an associate of my father, he may not be very respectable either.' Her father was by his own admission a complete rogue.

'It would occupy my time usefully until I am able to start rebuilding my business and reputation in Torquay,' Matt said. He certainly looked brighter now he had the prospect of a mystery to solve and something to do.

Kitty would have liked to have gone to Exeter herself, but common sense told her that it was sensible that Matt should go while she continued to investigate what the Davenports knew about the murder. It might also keep him out of harm's way until the real killer was caught. 'Very well. It sounds as if we have an agreement.'

Mrs Treadwell was still in the small office behind reception when Kitty peeped in. 'Are you feeling better, darling?' her grandmother asked.

'Much better, thank you. I've had a letter from father.'

Mrs Treadwell raised a perfectly arched eyebrow. 'So that reprobate has actually kept a promise?'

'Grams.' Kitty laughed and crossed to where her grandmother was seated at the desk to embrace her.

'And what is he up to now?'

'He is well and settled in New York at present. He has given the name and address of the man in Exeter that Aunt Hortense remembers mentioning to mother before she disappeared.'

Her grandmother gave a disapproving sniff. 'And I daresay any acquaintance of your father's is unlikely to be respectable.'

'I am afraid you are probably right, but it has to be worth investigating. Matt has offered to go to Exeter to make some enquiries on my behalf.'

'So long as you do not set too great a store on this expedition, Kitty. It has been seventeen years and others have tried and failed to find any trace of your mother.' Her grandmother's eyes held the sheen of unshed tears.

Kitty swallowed hard. 'I know, Grams, but I have to at least try.'

Her grandmother dabbed at the corners of her eyes with a lace-trimmed handkerchief. 'Very well. I'm glad Matthew is going in your place. I am aware that your father visited some low places in London, and I expect this place in Exeter to be of the same ilk.'

'It may not even still exist, and this Jack Dawkins may be dead or gone,' Kitty said with a sigh. She knew the chances of learning anything new about her mother's disappearance were slim but even so, it was still exciting.

Matt set off on the train for Exeter the following morning. His motorcycle was still at his house and he had not yet had the opportunity to have it brought to him at the hotel. He had breakfasted with Kitty before leaving and she had entrusted a small photograph of her mother to his care. He knew she had wanted to accompany him, but it was the main change-over day for the larger groups of guests at the hotel and she would be busy all day. She also had Genevieve Davenport's charity event to prepare for.

It felt good to be escaping from Dartmouth and Torquay and to have a purpose again. It was immensely frustrating not to be allowed to investigate Pearl's murder but at least he could try and help Kitty discover if her mother had gone to Exeter after leaving Enderley. The private detective agencies her grandmother had employed in the past had recorded reports of sightings of her but there had never been proof.

The train chugged into Exeter St David's station and Matt disembarked amid clouds of steam, into the hustle and bustle on the platform. The morning was grey with an end-of-summer nip already in the air. He adjusted the collar of his coat and consulted the note he'd made of the address.

He had a rough idea of the direction. He'd consulted Mickey, the hotel maintenance man whose wife was originally from Exeter, who had told him which way to go. As he walked, Matt soon found himself heading through narrow streets away from the town centre into the less salubrious part of the city.

Here, the buildings were closer together and the shops, such as they were, consisted of pawn shops, tiny tobacconists and some tired-looking general shops with dirty windows. A couple of scrawny stray dogs sniffed at something malodorous in the gutter.

It began to rain, soft drizzle soaking into the shoulders of his coat. Matt straightened his hat and studied the signs above the shops. Despite the apparent emptiness of the street, he could feel the gaze of unseen observers burning into his shoulder blades as he made his way to Jacky Daw's Emporium.

The sign over the door had once been navy blue with gold lettering. Now the paint was peeling, and the letters were weathered and faded with age. The window was grimy, like the others in the street. A few pieces of cheap china gimcrack ornaments were displayed on a wooden unit lined with faded, curling sheets of paper. Rainwater trickled from a broken downspout next to the door.

Matt sucked in a breath and pushed the door open. It took a few seconds for his eyes to adjust to the gloom that enveloped him inside the shop. Somewhere in the murky depth behind the counter a bell tinkled, announcing his arrival.

The shop interior was as depressing as the exterior. There appeared to be little on sale and what remained seemed to have been there for a long time. The air smelt of camphor, damp and stale tobacco.

Somewhere in the shadows behind the counter a raspy cough preceded the shuffling of feet.

'We're shut.' A man appeared from the darkness, skeletally thin, with sparse white hair spread thinly across his scalp. His face had so little flesh, it was as if a skeleton had come to life.

'I'm looking for Jack Dawkins,' Matt said.

The sunken face looked him up and down. 'Who wants him?'

'I was sent by Edgar Underhay's daughter, Kitty.'

The man gave a harsh cackle of laughter which disintegrated into a cough that wracked his skinny chest, leaving him gasping for air. He leaned forward on the counter and recovered his breath. 'Edgar's girl, eh? Been a long time since I heard his name mentioned. How old is his girl now?'

'Twenty-three.' Matt watched as the man sank down onto a rickety wooden chair behind the counter.

'Twenty-three. Well, well.' He spoke softly as if talking more to himself than to Matt.

Matt decided to take a direct approach. 'Miss Underhay's mother disappeared in June 1916. She was last seen at Enderley Hall, where she visited her sister-in-law. Lady Medford gave Mrs Underhay your name.'

'Did she now?'

The air inside the shop seemed to shift and the small hairs on the back of Matt's neck prickled. When Jack didn't appear to be about to volunteer any more information, he pressed on. 'It was a long time ago, but she believed she was coming here. To see you.'

'Elowed,' Dawkins breathed her name. 'Smart as a whip and pretty as paint. Too good for Eddie Underhay.' For a moment he appeared lost in the past.

'Did Elowed come here, that summer? To ask about Edgar?' Matt asked.

The man's rheumy eyes grew gimlet sharp. 'Why now? Why is Eddie's daughter asking now?'

'She and her grandmother have been looking for answers for the last seventeen years.' He wondered what the old man knew.

Dawkins shuffled to his feet. 'Then they are wasting their time. Let the dead rest in peace.'

Matt drew in a breath. 'Is she dead?'

The old man started retreating back into the shadows. 'I can't help you. Best you leave now.' A door banged and Matt heard the unmistakeable sound of a bolt being shot. He would get nothing more from Jack Dawkins today. Indeed, from Dawkins' skeletal appearance he judged that the man might not have many days on this earth left.

CHAPTER EIGHT

Matt arrived back in the lobby just as Kitty was directing the last of a large party towards their rooms. He caught her eye as she instructed the youthful porter about the luggage before ordering tea and scones for the party in the small salon.

She took the opportunity to order tea for herself and Matt at the same time, to be brought to the small office behind the reception desk as soon as someone was free to take over reception.

'How did it go? Did you find him?' she asked once the guests were gone and they were free to escape into the office.

Matt hung his damp coat and hat on the carved coat stand before taking a seat on the opposite side of Kitty's desk.

'Yes, I found him.' He described his visit to Jack Dawkins' emporium while Kitty poured the tea from an elegant silver teapot.

Her heart thumped as he told her about the shop and the mysterious and frail Mr Dawkins. 'So, he believes my mother is dead?'

Despite having assured both Matt and her grandmother that she would not get her hopes up for discovering new information about her mother's disappearance, she had still nurtured the faint belief that they might learn something.

'His manner was very strange but judging from his appearance I would say he was a very sick man.' Matt took a sip of tea, the hot drink reviving his spirits after the long, damp journey.

'He gave no indication about why he thought my mother was dead?' Kitty asked.

'No, he seemed perturbed that you were asking questions now after all this time. But he wouldn't say if your mother had come to see him or not.'

She refilled his cup as soon as he set it back on its saucer. 'Is it worth trying him again? Should I accompany you?'

'Truthfully, I doubt if he would see us. You could perhaps try writing to him. I don't know if he was afraid or protecting someone or simply genuinely believed your mother was dead.' He seemed to sense her disappointment. 'I'm sorry, old girl, I'd hoped for better news for you.'

'It was to be expected, I suppose.' She forced a smile and tried to rally her spirits. 'I appreciate you trying.'

Mrs Craven arrived in Mr Potter's taxicab on the Sunday, shortly before luncheon, to whisk Kitty to the Davenport house. Kitty had shared the disappointing news from Exeter with her grandmother over breakfast on Saturday morning. Grams had been unsurprised, but Kitty knew the outcome had still saddened her. Even after all this time, it was impossible not to have a tiny spark of hope.

Mrs Craven was dressed in her church-going finest with a very fetching and elaborate hat in pale blue. Kitty by contrast felt somewhat under-dressed in her pale green two-piece and plain straw hat as she clambered in beside the former mayoress. Matt had already left the Dolphin to meet his parents for lunch in Torquay, promising to meet her back at the hotel later to see what she had learned.

Mrs Craven spent the journey across the river and through the countryside to the Davenports' lecturing Kitty on what her roles and responsibilities would be during the course of the afternoon. Kitty hoped they would include getting something to eat. Despite a good breakfast she was already hungry and didn't think the apple she had secreted in her bag would sustain her for long.

The same maid who had received them previously opened the door and showed them through to a bright sunroom at the back of the house. Large glass French doors stood open onto a broad flagstone terrace set with tables and chairs. Uniformed maids scurried back and forth carrying floral arrangements and trays of china. Genevieve presided in the midst of the chaos, her spectacles crooked on her face and her hair heaped untidily on the top of her head.

'Oh, I'm so glad you are here. There is so much to do,' she wailed as she caught sight of them.

Mrs Craven's eyebrows lifted, and it wasn't long until she had taken over. She relegated Kitty to the tombola stall with Genny whilst she organised the maids and positioned the raffle prizes.

'I really am terribly grateful to you for helping with all of this,' Genny said as they stuck numbers on packets of bath salts and folded tickets for the drum. 'I'm usually much more on top of things but it's been so difficult lately.'

'Oh dear, whatever has been the matter?' Kitty asked as she popped another batch of tickets inside the gaily painted wooden drum and stirred them up with her hand.

Genny sighed. 'Well, that police inspector has been hanging around wanting to talk to everyone again. It seems the poor girl that was killed was an actress of some sort. He interviewed us all again. I couldn't tell them anything though and Father and Mother were both very upset. Mother suffers with her nerves, you know.'

'How dreadful. And did anyone know her? The girl?' Kitty did her best to sound casual and disinterested.

Genny's fingers stilled for a moment from folding tickets. 'Peter and Seb knew her slightly I think, and Dickie – that's BeBe's husband – said she was one of those girls who are always hanging around. Laurence Tilney said he thought she may have approached him about a film role, but he wasn't certain.'

Kitty added another batch to the drum. 'Poor you, and with all this to organise too,' she sympathised. Kitty suspected that the girl didn't often have someone to unburden herself to.

'Mother took to her bed with her nerves; she's very highly strung. I had to try and entertain Saira and her father, the colonel, and he is quite unwell also so we had to have the doctor out. Peter and Seb disappeared as usual. Father was ranting and raving. I'm sure you'll have heard, he has been nominated for a knighthood, so he wants this matter tidied up as soon as possible. He has to be seen as squeaky clean if he is to get the nod. The police were checking all the cars for some reason and the whole house was in disarray.' Unshed tears shone in Genny's eyes.

'That's awful, so you've had no one to help you out until we came today.'

Genny blinked hard behind her glasses. 'Saira isn't interested in my charity work. Well, why would she be? She has enough to worry about with caring for her father. Mother does what she can but of course, with her problems she can't do much. Seb and Peter are of no use at all. Larry and Tilly are guests and Father is a busy man. BeBe and Dickie are going to entertain everyone this afternoon, so that at least is something.' She sniffed and dropped the last of her folded tickets into the container.

'That will be nice.' Kitty's tummy growled as she spoke, and she hoped her hostess hadn't heard.

Genny took off her glasses and polished the lenses with a clean cotton handkerchief from her pocket. 'BeBe is a frightfully good singer. Seb says she could be the next Josephine Baker. He would know of course, as he helps Peter write and organise all the shows for our London halls.'

'Gosh, it will be fun to hear her then. I take it you're expecting a good turnout this afternoon?' Kitty asked as Mrs Craven bustled past, barking directions at a wide-eyed servant girl.

'Oh yes, just about anyone who is anyone in Torquay. Daddy knows lots of people and everyone seems keen to support the orphanage, and the amateur dramatics society has a good following here. The Orphanage Christmas Fund is such a good cause.' Genny replaced her glasses and blinked at Kitty, before peering at her rather masculine leather strapped wristwatch. 'We should go and get some lunch. There are some cold cuts in the dining room with salad. The kitchen is busy preparing the things for tea, so Mother judged it best if we all had something light.'

'Super, thank you.' Kitty followed Genny, and after washing her hands in the luxuriously appointed cloakroom with its sparkling pale green tiles and gold-framed mirror, she rejoined her hostess in the dining room.

Mrs Craven was already seated next to a thin woman in a well-cut navy silk blouse. 'We were just about to send someone to collect you girls,' the woman said. 'Honestly, Genny, you should keep a better track of the time.'

'Sorry, Mother.' Genny motioned to Kitty to take a seat and introduced her to Mrs Davenport.

'It's very good of you to offer to help out today, Miss Underhay. Millicent tells me you are going to assist with the theatre gala too?' Mrs Davenport motioned to one of the maids to begin serving the salads and cold meats.

'Yes, it all sounds very exciting, and for a good cause,' Kitty said and earned an approving smile from Mrs Craven.

'Where's Daddy? I thought he would be here for lunch?' Genny asked.

'Oh, he's busy with Saira's father. They've gone to the club as the dear colonel felt a little better. The others have all gone for a boat trip I think. They should be back in time for the tea.' Mrs Davenport beamed as the maid stepped forward with a bottle of white wine.

'Mother, perhaps some water?' Genny suggested as the maid filled her mother's glass.

'Darling, really, a little drink now will settle my nerves wonderfully. You know I find these big social events rather stressful.' Mrs Davenport smiled at her daughter and Kitty could see that Peter did indeed favour his mother in looks.

Celeste Davenport was a handsome woman with fine eyes and an aquiline nose. Her short, wavy hair was immaculately dressed. In her youth she must have been quite stunning. However, Kitty could see faint lines beneath her foundation and a faint tinge of yellow in the whites of her eyes.

'One glass, mother.' Genny glared at the maid who removed the wine bottle once she'd offered it to Kitty and Mrs Craven.

'Genevieve was just telling me how awful this murder enquiry was for you all. We saw all the journalists hanging around at the top of the road.' Kitty took a tentative sip of wine and felt quite decadent.

'Oh, my dear, it's played havoc with my nerves. I'm quite delicate, always have been ever since I was a child. The artistic temperament, you know.' Celeste's hand trembled as she too picked up her wine glass to drink. 'I can't believe the inspector has released that man from next door. It's absolutely shocking. His parents are at the house now I understand, and they seem very respectable.'

Kitty's hackles rose but she managed to sound calm and unaffected. 'I heard Captain Bryant had been completely exonerated so I suppose the inspector would have to release him. He could hardly keep an innocent man locked up.'

'I told you Captain Bryant had nothing to do with it, Mother. He has always been very pleasant and polite to me.' Genny glared at her mother and Kitty warmed to her new friend. She also wondered why Matt hadn't mentioned his acquaintance with Genny.

'Really, Genny, a man only has to smile at you, and you would think well of them. I find it very troubling. And he hasn't returned home. A sign of guilt, I would have thought. To strangle the girl at the golf club too of all places,' Mrs Davenport said.

'I know. I found the girl,' Mrs Craven said sharply.

Celeste Davenport smiled gently. 'Oh, my dear, do forgive me, I'd quite forgotten. It must have been a dreadful shock. I don't play there myself.' She drained her crystal wine glass and looked hopefully around her for the maid.

Genny's colour rose in her cheeks and she gave her mother what Kitty considered to be a warning glance.

'I keep telling Genny she should take up golf or do some sort of physical exercise. There are some marvellous classes these days. They can do wonders for a girl's figure,' Celeste continued, ignoring her daughter's distressed expression as she signalled to the maid to refill her glass.

'I'm far too busy for that nonsense, Mother.'

Mrs Craven glanced at Kitty.

'Such a shame Peter couldn't join us for lunch. He'll be here later of course with Saira. Such a delightful girl, very pretty, her mother was a princess.' Celeste Davenport smiled at them. 'Confidentially of course, I'm hoping she'll soon be my daughter-in-law.'

Kitty caught Genny rolling her eyes at this pronouncement.

'How lovely, weddings are such fun,' Mrs Craven said.

'Of course, it would be better if that friend of his wasn't always hanging around,' Celeste mused.

'Sebastian?' Kitty asked as she placed her knife and fork down on her empty plate.

'The dear boy is an old chum of Peter's and of course he can be most amusing, but when one is courting, a third person playing gooseberry is not what is required.' Celeste took another drink from her wine glass and stared defiantly at Genny.

The maid discreetly removed the empty plates and replaced them with Eton mess in delicate glass bowls.

'I heard Peter and Sebastian knew the murdered girl and her friend,' Kitty said.

Celeste paused fractionally as she lifted her spoon and eyed Kitty distastefully. 'One knows lots of people in the theatre. Often one doesn't remember names or anything unless they have been part of one's company. I myself have worked with all the stars. I'm quite sure Peter didn't know her well at all. One has a lot of hangers-on and my darling Peter is such a good-looking boy. Perhaps Sebastian knew her.'

'The murdered girl, Pearl Bright, was an actress, they're saying.' Mrs Craven applied herself to her dessert.

'I don't recall hearing the name. Perhaps the Tilneys would know her better, then. Larry is casting for his new film and has been trying out lots of young actors and actresses for various minor parts. Tilly is to star, of course. Such a dear thing, I've given her lots of tips, one likes to be helpful.'

Genny glanced at her watch. 'Oh dear, everyone will be arriving soon. We really do need to press on.'

'Of course, Genny dear, run along and play with your boxes. I shall arrange coffee in the garden room for you all. I'm sure it's going to be a splendid affair. The mayor of Torquay is coming, Millicent. I'm sure you know him.' Celeste continued to talk to Mrs Craven as Kitty followed Genny's lead and slipped away back to the garden room.

'Please don't mind Mother,' Genny said as they began to tidy away the debris from the morning. 'She often can sound… well, a bit cutting, but it's just her nerves.'

Or the drink, Kitty thought, but she smiled cheerfully at her friend. 'Not at all, she seems perfectly lovely.'

CHAPTER NINE

To Kitty's frustration, Mrs Craven didn't reappear to assist them. She only emerged once the rest of the setting up was completed and Genny had gone to change her clothes ready to greet their guests. She made a brief tour of inspection before vanishing once more.

Since the promised coffee had also not materialised, Kitty inveigled a maid to supply her with a cup of tea. She had just tucked herself away with it in a discreet corner when she heard approaching voices.

Aware that she was not readily visible behind a display of raffle prizes and a dark green velvet curtain, Kitty shrank back a little further out of sight and shamelessly listened. Since she didn't know anyone here, she doubted she'd suffer the eavesdropper's proverbial fate.

'I told the inspector chappie I barely knew the wretched girl. What else could I say?'

Kitty recognised Peter's voice.

'I told him the same thing,' Sebastian said. So, she was right, they did know the girls. 'What about the other one? Her friend?'

'Salome? Yes, I've received a note asking me to meet her. Have you had one too?' Peter sounded anxious.

'No, are you planning to go?' Seb asked.

'We don't have a choice, do we? We don't know if she has anything.'

'She hasn't gone to the police. Hold your nerve, Peterkins, we can sort this out.'

Much to her annoyance, the two men moved farther away, and Kitty was unable to hear any more. At least she now had a name for Pearl's friend, though. She smiled to herself and finished her drink.

As soon as she judged the coast to be clear, Kitty hurried to the cloakroom to freshen up once more in readiness for the arrival of the Davenports' invited guests. She could hear music coming from the grand piano in the drawing room and guessed that Dickie and BeBe had arrived for their set.

Sebastian was in the hall when she came out. Dressed in the latest style in a striped blazer with a royal blue cravat, he looked quite dashing. After what she had just heard however, Kitty was on her guard.

'Kitty, darling, Genny said you were helping her today like the little angel of mercy that you are. How perfectly lovely to see you. Peter has just gone to the harbour on "Mummy's orders" to retrieve Saira and the Tilneys from their boat trip. Are you all set to prize the guineas from the pockets of Torquay society?' He kissed her cheek in greeting and gave an outrageous wink. The scent of his pomade tickled her nose.

'I was under the impression that you had all gone on the boat trip?' Kitty said as they strolled back towards the drawing room. She was curious to know where Peter and Seb had been all morning, as they hadn't been with the others.

'Peter gets horribly seasick unless the sea is positively like a mill pond, poor lamb. But Larry and Tilly were frightfully keen to visit Goodrington to see a seaplane land. They are supposed to have one landing there on the beach today, and Saira went with them. They were going to luncheon at a hotel there. I knew if we hung around here Genny would have us winding wool or doing something else that was deathly boring, so Peter and I nipped off to Totnes for a spell.' He made a mock grimace of horror.

Kitty couldn't help but laugh at him; Sebastian was so refreshingly unrepentant. 'Well, you succeeded in avoiding the work,' she agreed.

A man in his early thirties, who Kitty assumed must be Dickie, was seated at the piano. Next to him was a petite black woman in a crimson frock. Startlingly attractive, she had close-cropped hair and dark, expressive eyes. Kitty assumed she must be BeBe.

'Darlings.' Sebastian advanced on both of them, kissing BeBe and pumping Dickie's hand in greeting. 'Kitty, may I introduce BeBe and Dickie Deville. Dickie is the most marvellous pianist and composer and BeBe a *chanteuse* unparalleled.'

BeBe rolled her eyes at Seb's nonsense. 'Pleased to meet you, Kitty.'

'Likewise,' Dickie added.

'Kitty owns the Dolphin Hotel in Dartmouth. She has the most divine singers and entertainers to play to the masses in her ballroom.'

'Good to know,' BeBe said. 'I don't believe we have ever played there.'

Kitty smiled, she couldn't help but warm to this woman. 'Perhaps we can fix that sometime. I'm looking forward to hearing you sing today. A friend told me you gave a wonderful performance here the night that actress was murdered,' Kitty said.

'That was quite the party on Monday, wasn't it, Seb? The police still haven't caught the murderer yet though, and that gives me the creeps.' BeBe gave an exaggerated shudder.

'Did you know the girl who was killed? Pearl Bright, was it? I heard she knew quite a lot of people in the theatre and stage world.' Kitty couldn't resist fishing a little further and was rewarded by a discomfited expression flashing across Seb's handsome face.

'It didn't dawn on me at the time, but when I heard her name I remembered she and her friend applying for some parts in various shows locally,' Dickie said.

'I believe the police are keen to find her friend. It's odd she hasn't come forward with all the press attention, don't you think? I don't suppose you can recall her name?'

BeBe shrugged. 'Something biblical. I don't remember what exactly.' She shuddered again. 'I swear someone is walking over my grave with all this talk of death.'

'Enough gloominess, my angels. Nearly showtime!' Seb smirked at Dickie and Kitty sensed he was eager to end the discourse. She also knew that he knew Salome's name.

'Trust you to appear now the work has all been done.' Genny had entered the room unnoticed and stood glowering at Sebastian. She had changed into an unflattering lime green summer frock which seemed to fit in all the wrong places.

'Genny, darling, I swear I shall make it all up to you this afternoon by wooing your visitors and making them part with oodles of cash for your orphans.' Sebastian flashed her a winning smile, making Genny soften and blush to the roots of her hair.

The drawing room door opened once more and Peter, Saira and the Tilneys appeared. Saira trailed dutifully in Peter's wake while Larry, dressed in similar fashion to Peter and Sebastian, wore his wife draped possessively on his arm. Tilly was wearing the extravagant diamond ring that Betty had remarked on and an elegant, expensively cut day dress in pale blue.

'Darlings, have you had a wonderful time? Were there seaplanes on the sands?' Seb asked.

'Only one plane, Seb. Quite extraordinary, I think you would have enjoyed it. We did have a lovely lunch at a hotel in Goodrington and a most delightful boat trip. Saira spotted a dolphin through Larry's bins. You and Peter should have come,' Tilly said, smiling playfully at Seb.

'No, thank you. I am not meant to be a seafarer,' Peter declared. 'Dickie, let's have some music, I can hear the hordes approaching.'

Dickie duly obliged and began to play as the first of the guests entered the room. Mrs Craven reappeared and commandeered Kitty to sell raffle tickets whilst Genny took care of the tombola.

'I must go and greet the mayor and mayoress with Mr and Mrs Davenport. Have you managed to discover anything to aid Captain Bryant's case?' Mrs Craven leaned her head close to Kitty's.

'I believe so.'

'Good. Now, please make sure you put the names on the backs of the tickets.' Her orders given, Mrs Craven bustled away.

The next hour went quickly and Kitty was kept busy on her stall. Over the noise of chatter and the tinkling of china cups on saucers she could make out the piano music emanating from the drawing room. She hoped she would be able to hear BeBe sing, especially after Betty's description of the party. Although she suspected it would be a somewhat different performance for Genny's audience. More importantly, she also wanted to find an opportunity to talk to Saira and the Tilneys about the murder.

As if on cue, her stall emptied of customers and Saira appeared, bearing a cup of tea in an elegant china cup. 'Mrs Craven asked me to bring you this. She said you would need a break.'

Kitty accepted the drink gratefully. 'Thank you, that was very kind of her. It's been frightfully busy.'

'I know. I think BeBe is about to sing, so most of the guests have gone to the drawing room to hear her.' She glanced towards the drawing room as she spoke.

'Are you going in to listen?' Kitty asked, smiling as Saira flopped down on a nearby wooden-backed chair.

'No, I saw her at the party, and I feel quite exhausted after this morning's excursion. I can watch your stall if you would like to go though,' Saira offered. She looked tired, with shadows beneath her large dark eyes.

Kitty glanced around and saw the room was pretty much deserted apart from Genny, furiously counting change on the tombola stand at the far end of the room while the maids cleared the tea things. 'I would have thought you would be with Peter, watching BeBe.' Kitty sat down on the vacant seat next to Saira, keeping her tone gossipy as if inviting confidences. 'I do hope I am not speaking out of turn, but Mrs Davenport has intimated that congratulations may soon be in order.'

To her surprise Saira's eyes filled with tears, dampening the long black lashes.

'Oh, I'm sorry. Have I offended you?' Kitty was alarmed at the distress evident in the girl's face as she battled to regain her composure.

'No, it's fine. I'm sorry.' Saira pulled a handkerchief from her bag and blew her nose. 'It's just—' She stopped abruptly as if unsure if she should continue. Kitty waited patiently to see what else she might say, a sympathetic expression on her face.

'My father is elderly, frail and somewhat old-fashioned. You are aware that my mother was Indian?'

Kitty nodded.

'My father wishes to see me married and accepted in society here in England. Not everyone is accepting of people of mixed race. He and Mr Davenport are old acquaintances from their boyhood days and in business. A marriage between Peter and I would suit them both. It would give me security and Peter respectability as a married man.'

'But?' asked Kitty, her tone gentle.

'Perhaps it's rather foolish but… I'd always hoped to marry for love.' She glanced at Kitty.

'That doesn't seem unreasonable to me. I take it then that is not the case with you and Peter?'

Saira gave a short, bitter-sounding laugh. 'Peter is not in love with me. I don't think he is even remotely interested in me, or any woman for that matter.' Colour tinged her cheeks.

Kitty frowned, shocked by the scandalous boldness of Saira's statement. 'Then, excuse me for asking, but why not tell your father that this match isn't going to happen?'

'My father is an ill man. I have no other family. He worries that I will be alone and friendless with no roots, either here or back in India. I have money and he fears that it places me at risk of an unwise match.' She laughed bitterly.

'And Peter? Why does Mrs Davenport promote the match if, as you say, Peter does not seem interested?'

Saira sighed. 'I believe she wants to see him settled. She feels his lifestyle is somewhat wild and a wife and family would settle him down. There have been rumours about his proclivities. Perhaps a respectable English girl would not accept him. And my money would of course be welcome.'

'Whatever will you do? It sounds so difficult,' Kitty asked. She could see Saira's problem and she felt sorry for the girl. She would have some difficulty obtaining work if she wasn't trained for anything and her heritage might tell against her if she was unmarried. If her inheritance was large, then fortune-hunters would be hammering at her door.

'I don't know. You won't say anything to Genny or anyone, will you?' A look of alarm spread across Saira's face as if she had suddenly become aware that she had been indiscreet.

'No, of course not. I hope you find a solution that will bring you happiness.' Kitty gave her a reassuring smile.

She left Saira to watch the stall for a few minutes while she slipped into the drawing room to listen to BeBe and Dickie. Dickie was clearly a talented musician. She had heard enough pianists over the years at the Dolphin to recognise real talent when she heard it. She was surprised she hadn't heard them before as they were local, but performers moved around so much and they may have been working in London.

The drawing room was full of people so at first, she was unable to see much as there were several tall people blocking her view. After a minute, however, a gap opened up and she was able to see

BeBe. Animated and beautiful in her dashing scarlet dress, she had a good singing voice. It seemed she was not about to reprise the performance that Betty had described. Clearly this afternoon's audience were of a somewhat different nature.

Laurence and Tilly Tilney were at the front of the crowd, Tilly looking every inch the star in her diamonds. Peter and Seb were standing close together at the side of the room, deep in hushed conversation as if conferring about something. Mrs Craven was with a man Kitty assumed must be Mr Davenport, as well as Saira's father and the mayor and his wife. Mr Davenport was resplendent in a rather flashy suit and a red carnation in his lapel. She wondered where Mrs Davenport had gone.

Kitty watched for a few minutes more then made her way back through the hall towards the garden room. Saira had disappeared and Genny was in her place, totting up Kitty's takings.

'I do hope it's all correct.' Kitty smiled at Genny.

'We've done rather well. Plenty of donations and tickets sold for the charity gala at the Pavilion theatre. The orphanage will be thrilled. It will help enormously with some repairs to the building and giving the boys some Christmas treats. It was such a good idea of the local am-dram group to hold a charity gala.'

'I'm sure they'll be very grateful. You've done a wonderful job. Your expertise and connections must be invaluable to them,' Kitty said.

Genny's plain face coloured with pleasure at Kitty's praise. 'I always feel that if one is in a privileged position one should try to aid those less fortunate. Father has always encouraged my little efforts, and of course it helps him too.' The sound of applause reached them from the other room.

'I think Dickie and BeBe have finished,' Kitty said.

'Time for the last push then, before everyone goes home or Mother starts to ply them all with cocktails.' Genny muttered the last part of her statement as she scuttled back across the room to her stall.

Sure enough, people began to filter back into the garden room. Genny ended her tombola and returned to Kitty, ready to draw the tickets for the raffle prizes.

Kitty stepped away from the stall as Genny asked Mrs Craven to make the draw and announce the winners. She found herself next to Dickie, who had abandoned his piano to join the crowd in the garden room.

'Is BeBe not joining us?' she asked.

'Powdering her nose,' Dickie said. He gave Kitty a quizzical glance. 'Say, are you the girl who helped catch that murderer in Dartmouth a few months ago?'

Colour heated her cheeks. 'Guilty.'

'So you and Captain Bryant, the fellow they arrested, are friends?' Dickie asked, his gaze narrowing as he studied her response.

'Yes.' She saw no point in denying the truth.

'I take it you have a personal interest in this latest murder, then?'

Kitty let out a sharp laugh. 'Oh I'm not investigating, I assure you. But Matt has been dragged into this case by pure chance and I will help him if I can. He went to the police and offered to help with the case by telling them what he knew. Mrs Craven found the poor girl's body on the golf course. I don't understand why no one admitted knowing the girl or her friend when the police first interviewed everyone.' She looked directly at Dickie and he shifted uncomfortably under her gaze.

'The Davenports can make or break you in the business. For myself, it wouldn't be so bad but for BeBe... they could finish her. It seemed wise to go with the flow, if you get my meaning. They were anxious to avoid bad publicity and tales of a wild party wouldn't help Mr Davenport's bid for a knighthood.'

'Even if keeping quiet was at the expense of an innocent man being incarcerated and possibly charged with a murder he didn't commit?' Kitty snapped.

A dull flush rose in Dickie's face. 'No one knew that would happen. I guess we all thought Salome would come forward or someone would identify Pearl more quickly.'

'So, you know Salome? Pearl's friend? Where is she?' Kitty pounced on the admission, her pulse racing with excitement.

'I've seen her a few times at various auditions. Pearl was a local girl, from near Brixham I believe, but Salome is from the north – Leeds or Liverpool, or somewhere. Perhaps she has returned there and doesn't know the police are searching for her. Peter and Seb know her too and she was all excited at the party about auditioning for Larry Tilney's new film.'

'Have you spoken to Inspector Greville about this?' Kitty asked.

'No. A constable took a brief statement from BeBe and me after Pearl's murder, but I haven't heard anything from the police since.' Dickie looked around as if afraid someone might overhear their conversation, but they had spoken in low voices and everyone was focused on the prize draw.

'You need to tell the police what you know. This Salome may be in danger herself, or could even be the murderer,' Kitty said.

He shuffled his feet. 'I can't afford to upset the Davenports.'

'The inspector can be very discreet.' Kitty wanted to shake him. He had to tell the police what he knew.

Dickie sighed. 'Very well.'

Kitty released a breath. 'Thank you. It's very odd that Pearl's friend has not come forward.' She hoped nothing bad had happened to the other girl, but Peter had mentioned receiving a note from her. It was very strange.

'Yes, unless she is afraid of something or someone. Or like I said, she may have gone back up north. Perhaps she knows the killer's identity.'

A shiver ran down Kitty's spine. 'Maybe. Surely all the more reason for you to go to the police.'

Mrs Craven drew the final ticket and the crowd erupted into a round of applause as the last of the prizes was claimed. Dickie seized the opportunity to slip away as people began to disperse. Kitty felt quite exhausted now from the business of the day and the tension of trying to probe the Davenports and their friends. At least she had some new information for Matt and Inspector Greville.

CHAPTER TEN

Matt waited in the lobby of the Dolphin for Kitty's return. Lunch with his parents at the Grand Hotel in Torquay had been a tedious affair. His mother had constantly wittered on about how unfair it all was, and his father had been as irascible and unreasonable as ever. Several times he had been forced to bite his tongue when his father had made disparaging remarks about his life.

He wondered how Kitty had got on at the Davenport house. She was usually adept at persuading people to confide in her. Even so, he wished he could have been there with her to make the Davenports spill the beans about what they knew of Pearl and her companion. For he was absolutely certain they had a lot more information to give.

He amused himself by watching the guests check in and out at the reception desk in between flicking through the pages of the Sunday paper. The murder had now moved to page five and only merited a few lines, to the effect that the police were still looking for Miss Bright's friend.

Alice, the young maid who had accompanied Kitty to Enderley Hall earlier in the summer, served him with a tray of coffee.

'Thank you, Alice.'

'That's all right, sir. I reckon as Miss Kitty won't be much longer now. Mrs Craven don't care to be out of an evening. She likes her supper at home these days unless 'tis a big dinner affair.' The girl glanced at the wall clock behind the reception desk. It was already approaching six.

Alice was proved to be correct when the lobby door opened a few minutes later and Kitty appeared. She looked pale and exhausted and he instantly felt guilty that she had sacrificed her day off to try to help his cause.

He put aside his paper and jumped up to greet her. 'Come and sit down, tell me how you got on.'

The lobby was quite deserted now as the guests had gone upstairs to change for dinner. Kitty allowed him to lead her to the cosy corner table where she dropped down onto one of the over-stuffed dark green leather seats with a deep sigh.

'Oh, I am all in. I have such a lot to tell you though.' She filled him in on everything she had learned that afternoon, including Saira's bombshell revelation about Peter.

'We need to speak to Inspector Greville, to give him the name of this girl.' Matt's spirits rose. At last, this was the breakthrough he had been hoping for. This Salome woman should be able to exonerate him completely by backing up his version of events.

'Already done. Mrs Craven instructed Mr Potter to call in at the police station in Torquay before we returned. The inspector was out so I left a note for his attention with all the information.' She leaned back in her seat and smiled at him.

'You've done well, old girl.' She had, too. 'I wonder what else was in Salome's note to Peter, and why she wrote to him. Peculiar, don't you think?'

'Extremely,' Kitty agreed. 'Still, at least now there is something to get our teeth into. I wonder if Inspector Greville has turned up any leads? Genny said the police had checked all their cars although I fear that will be in vain as the chauffeur had cleaned them all before the police arrived. Apparently Mr Davenport dislikes a dirty car.'

'Interesting. Probably to see if there was any sign of one of them being used to move Pearl's body to the golf club. Shame they had been cleaned.'

Kitty looked smug, 'I told the inspector that you couldn't have moved Pearl's body on your motorbike.'

Matt grinned at her. 'Thank you for your support, Miss Underhay.'

'My pleasure, Captain Bryant.' Her smile widened and his pulse speeded. 'How was your lunch with your parents?'

He blew out a sigh. 'The same as usual. I love them both dearly but the sooner this case is solved and they can return home, the better it will be for all of us.'

She collected up her bag. 'I had better go and dress for dinner, Grams will be expecting me. Are you joining us this evening?'

'No, your grandmother has invited me, but I think I need some time to sort my thoughts out.'

'Shall I see you tomorrow?' she asked as she stood ready to ascend the stairs, a little disappointed that he would not be dining with them.

'Breakfast at eight?' he asked, standing himself.

'I'll meet you in the dining room.'

Impulsively, he bent his head and kissed her cheek, her skin soft beneath his lips. 'Till tomorrow.'

A pretty pink flush brightened her face and she hurried away up the stairs past the first hotel guests heading for the dining room. Matt watched her go, the faint rose scent of her perfume lingering in his senses.

His mother had tried probing him about Kitty and his feelings for her during lunch. He knew Patience hoped he would remarry and perhaps start a family again. Twelve months ago, he would have said that was impossible. Despite the passage of time, the deaths of his wife and daughter during the war were still raw to him and he had not yet fully worked his way through his grief at their loss.

His father had made his thoughts on the matter clear years ago. He had never approved of Edith, partly because she had been a few years older than Matt, and socially, she was from a different background. His father's opinion of Kitty over lunch however was that she was 'a very modern young woman'. Matt's lips twitched into a smile. The general hadn't intended it as a compliment.

Kitty was seated at a quiet, discreet table in the dining room the next morning. She refused to admit to herself that she had taken extra care with her hair and chosen a blue sprigged pattern dress that Alice had once assured her brought out the colour of her eyes.

Her pulse fluttered as Matt entered the dining room and made his way past the white linen-covered tables to where she was seated. Several guests were already taking breakfast and the delicious aroma of bacon mingled with the scent of coffee and toast.

'Good morning.' She smiled at Matt as he slid onto the vacant seat opposite her own.

He smiled back at her, the dimple flashing in his right cheek. 'You seem very cheerful this morning.'

'I am. I feel more positive about clearing your name after yesterday.' She gave a discreet signal to one of the passing waiters and a silver toast rack piled with hot toast was deposited before them, along with a matching teapot and milk jug. Two plates of egg and bacon also appeared a few minutes later.

'How do you feel today?' she asked.

'Good. I went for a stroll along the embankment last night and ran into Mickey.'

'I take it you ventured to a public house then?' She poured them both a cup of tea.

He laughed. 'I promise I just had a couple of pints with Mickey at The Ship.'

A noise near the entrance snagged her attention and she turned her head to see Inspector Greville being directed to their table. She nudged Matt under the table with her foot.

'Inspector, good morning, please take a seat.' She indicated to the waiter to bring another cup and fresh tea and toast.

Inspector Greville took a seat. His expression was grave and Kitty's previous good humour seeped away. 'Miss Underhay, Captain Bryant.' He nodded to both of them before continuing, 'Thank you for your information yesterday, Miss Underhay.'

'Did it help? Have you found her? This Salome girl?' Kitty asked. The inspector must have some news for them to bring him to the Dolphin so early.

The inspector took a sip of tea and surveyed them both. 'We have located Miss Salome Donohue.'

'That's good news, isn't it?' Matt eyed the policeman.

'May I ask your whereabouts yesterday, Captain Bryant?'

Kitty saw Matt stiffen, his spine straightening.

'I had lunch with my parents in Torquay, returned to the Dolphin, saw Kitty, then walked along the embankment where I bumped into Mickey, the hotel maintenance man. We then went to a nearby public house where I spent a couple of hours before returning with him to the hotel.'

Inspector Greville nodded and produced his notebook, making indecipherable squiggles in it.

'What's happened?' Kitty asked. She regretted eating the bacon and eggs as her stomach had started to churn.

The inspector sighed. 'When I said Miss Donohue had been found, that was not, strictly speaking, true. We have her address and have visited her rooms but the lady herself appears to have disappeared.'

'Disappeared?' Kitty echoed.

'Her landlady has not seen her since the day before yesterday when they had a disagreement over the rent. Miss Donohue owes money for the last two weeks' board and lodgings. She told her landlady not to worry, that she was expecting a large sum of money in the next few days. She then planned to pay her bill and move to a better establishment. Her landlady was not pleased.' Inspector Greville helped himself to a piece of toast and spread it generously with butter while Kitty and Matt took in the new information.

'Isn't that the same tale as her friend Pearl?' Kitty asked.

'Yes, it is the same lodging house. The landlady only takes theatricals so she tends to give them some slack when it comes to the rent and turns a blind eye to the comings and goings as they keep odd hours. All a bit odd but the woman is a former actress herself. She says she knew they were friends, but Miss Donohue had denied being the girl we were looking for when the woman questioned her about it. By the time my men arrived, Miss Donohue had done a bunk.' The inspector crunched his toast.

'How very vexing!' Kitty exclaimed indignantly.

'The landlady didn't believe her though and thought her manner a little odd. When it became obvious the girl had taken some of her stuff and vanished, she came forward. Beats me why she didn't tell us all this when my constable went there earlier last week.' Inspector Greville eyed the remaining slices of toast longingly.

'You now fear something may have happened to her?' Matt asked.

'Precisely. Odd that only some of her things were gone. I had to ascertain your whereabouts yesterday in line with other members of the Davenport party. Mr Peter Davenport and his friend were quite perturbed late last night at the police station, when questioned about Miss Donohue.' The inspector patted his mouth with a napkin, brushing crumbs from his moustache.

'What did Seb and Peter say? Did they talk about the letter from Salome?' Kitty noticed the pile of toast in front of the inspector had considerably diminished in such a short space of time.

Inspector Greville opened his pocketbook and took out a folded piece of cheap, lined paper from the back of the book. He passed it across to Matt. Kitty leaned forward in her seat as Matt moved the note around so they could both read it.

Dear Peter,

I'm sure you will be surprised to hear from me in this fashion, but I think we need to meet soon as there are outstanding financial matters to discuss since Pearl's death. I suggest we arrange a meeting next week. I will call you with the details.

Sincerely, Salome

'Brief and to the point. Did Peter disclose why he thought Salome wished to meet him?' Matt asked.

The inspector popped the last morsel of toast from his plate into his mouth and stared sadly at the rack for a moment before answering. 'He claims it's about a show he's putting on in London. Salome wants a part.'

Kitty's brow rose in disbelief. 'I don't think he was telling the truth.' She recalled the conversation she had overheard between Peter and Seb. 'Did Sebastian confirm this nonsense?'

'He admitted that Peter had shown him the letter and they had discussed it.'

Matt frowned. 'Did anyone else know of this letter?'

The inspector drained his teacup. 'Peter says not.'

'The question is, where is Salome now? Do you think Dickie is right, and she has gone north?' Kitty looked at Matt.

His brow furrowed. 'She could be in hiding, if she knows who killed Pearl or thinks she knows.'

'Why not simply come forward to the police?' Kitty asked.

Inspector Greville patted his mouth with his napkin once more. 'If the money she mentioned to her landlady is the result of blackmail, as I suspect it may be, then she may well wish to lie low until she has collected some cash. It may be that she and her friend, Pearl, were in this together.'

'Does that mean she thinks Peter is the murderer, if she sent him a letter?' Kitty looked at the inspector.

'Possibly, but we can't rule out that she may also be sending those letters to a number of people hoping that one of them hits the jackpot. That would account for the ambiguous brevity of the note and is a line of enquiry we are following. Or, Peter was the original target of Pearl's blackmail.'

Matt's frown deepened. 'That's a dangerous game to play. Presumably however, Peter must be concerned about something, judging by his discussion with Seb.'

'And what Saira said about his mother wishing to secure his respectability. She mentioned his… ahh… proclivities.' Kitty blushed.

The inspector heaved a sigh. 'Those two are certainly hiding something. I dare say it will all come out in the wash. I've enough on my hands with the murder case without worrying about their other possible illegal activities right now. I have my men out looking for Miss Donohue. Should either of you come across any new information, please let me know straight away.'

'Of course, Inspector,' Kitty agreed.

Inspector Greville rose to take his leave. 'I am hopeful we will have news of the lady soon. I have contacted my colleagues in the north. In the meantime, Captain Bryant, I would appreciate you continuing to remain here at the Dolphin.' His expression was grave as he shook Matt's hand.

'Will it be for much longer?'

The inspector's expression remained serious. 'I do have my reasons for the request.'

'Very well, I understand, sir.' Matt retook his own seat once the inspector had gone.

'Well, that was a surprise,' Kitty said.

The dining room was full now and the noise levels had risen as her guests chattered to one another over their breakfasts. She could tell from Matt's expression that he was thinking through the information the inspector had given them.

'Shall we take a turn outside before I start work?' she suggested. His demeanour troubled her, and she sensed he needed to be in the open air. She placed her hand on his arm, the grey wool of his jacket soft beneath her fingers.

He moved his free hand to cover hers and gave her fingers a gentle squeeze. 'Thank you.'

A frisson of electricity ran through her as his gaze met hers. 'Um, I'll just get my jacket.'

He met her in the lobby a few minutes later, after she had hurried to her room to collect her jacket and a rather darling felt hat that matched her dress. She was rewarded by a flash of a smile when she stepped down the polished oak staircase and walked to join him.

'After you, Miss Underhay.' He stood aside to allow her to walk out onto the street ahead of him, catching up to her side when they were on the pavement next to the river.

'Are you all right?' she asked as they stopped by the railings to look across the river. On the opposite bank, the leaves on the trees were already starting to change colour from their bright summer green to paler, softer, yellowy tones.

Matt leaned his elbows on the railing. 'It's so frustrating, Kitty. I want to get out there talking to the Davenports. I want to rattle them a little to find out what they know. I want my name cleared and my life back. I want to know what the inspector's reasons are for keeping me away. There are still a lot of things we don't know and that bothers me.'

Kitty covered his hand with hers, the intensity in his tone stirring so many emotions inside her. 'I know. The inspector is doing his best though and it surely won't be long now before he makes an arrest. I'm sure we'll know everything soon. Once they find this Salome and discover what she knows, that must move things forward.'

He glanced at her, his eyes bright blue in the late summer light. 'Salome may be able to indicate a motive for Pearl's murder. That's what's been puzzling me. Pearl wasn't molested in any way, and there's been no mention of a boyfriend for either girl so I don't think it was a crime of passion. Blackmail certainly provides a motive. She must have been killed elsewhere and her body dumped on the golf course or why else would there have been tyre tracks. No one saw – or will admit to seeing – her or Salome after they left my house, yet at some point they must have become separated.'

She gave his hand a squeeze. 'I'm seeing Genny again on Thursday. We're meeting at the Pavilion theatre in Torquay. She wants to show me the backstage area so I can take on some of the tasks for her for this charity performance. I believe the others will be there too, having a first rehearsal.'

'I know you'll find out all you can. I just hate feeling so useless in the process, sitting around here, twiddling my thumbs.' His gaze locked with hers.

'Inspector Greville will exonerate you soon, I know he will, and then you'll be free to work on the case openly and rebuild your business and reputation.'

CHAPTER ELEVEN

Matt left her at the lobby in the hotel. He intended to try and make himself useful assisting Mickey for a few hours. Kitty headed for her small office behind the reception desk.

'The post has come, Miss Kitty. I've put the letters ready for you on your desk.' Mary, the receptionist, smiled at her as Kitty walked around to open her office door.

'Thank you.' She smiled back, approving the girl's neat navy uniform dress with smart white collar.

She hung her hat and coat on the cane stand in the corner of the office and settled behind the small mahogany desk. The mail was placed in a tidy pile in the centre of her clean ivory blotter. Kitty selected her paperknife from the brass pen tray and started to deal with her post.

The first few she opened were circulars that she tossed into the wastepaper basket. One was a booking request which she set to the side. The next envelope made her pause. It bore an Exeter postmark and the address was written in an unfamiliar spidery copperplate script. It was addressed to her personally as 'Miss Kitty Underhay care of the Dolphin Hotel'. She slit the envelope open and shook out the contents.

At first she struggled to read the letter, the writing was so shaky in places and littered with blots.

Dear Miss Underhay,

I fear that by the time this missive reaches you I shall be no more. I hope you will overlook any brevity in this note and my poor penmanship. The disease which has ravaged my body these last few years is finally claiming me entirely. I was surprised when your agent called at my premises enquiring after your mother, Elowed.

I knew your father, Edgar, very well when we were young men, and we transacted some business together. Hearing your mother's name after all these years was something of a shock to me. It has been a long time now since anyone spoke of her.

I wish I were well enough to see you. To see if you are like her. I remember well the last time I set eyes on her. She came to see me, as your agent asked, in June 1916. She had received my name from your aunt and thought I might be able to give her your father's whereabouts. She believed he had left America and might have gone to Ireland.

I hope I do not cause you distress if I tell you that your father was being sought by many people at that time. When he left England, he left many unpaid debts behind him.

Your mother called at my shop and I was unable to tell her anything. I had not heard from your father since he had fled to America to avoid enlisting. I was exempt from joining up due to a heart murmur, caused by rheumatic fever as a child. My health has never been very good.

She left my business with, I believe, the intention of returning to Dartmouth, but I have since come to believe she was prevented from doing so.

Kitty broke off from reading; her hand shook as she fumbled for a handkerchief. 'Oh, my poor mother.' She blew her nose and steadied herself to read on.

I received a note, pushed under the door of my shop a day after your mother visited. It was unsigned but warned me to say nothing about her visit and to forget I had ever seen her. I do not know who sent it but there were many people around the city at that time that it was not wise to cross. Several other businesses near mine had suffered mysterious robberies and fires. There was a sense of lawlessness with so many men gone to fight.

I have no proof, but I have always supposed that someone may have followed your mother that day. For what purpose, I do not know. I read in the newspapers later that she was missing, and I assumed she must have met her end at the hands of whoever warned me not to speak out. It has lain on my conscience for many years that I have never come forward. Especially when I learned from the papers that she had a child.

May God forgive me, I never thought that you might still be seeking answers. Now I am about to leave this earth and move beyond the reach of mortal man I wanted to finally clear my soul of this burden.

Miss Underhay, have a care, old sins cast long shadows. I beg of you, let the dead rest in peace.

Sincerely,
Jack Dawkins Esq.

Kitty laid the letter aside with a trembling hand. Tears coursed freely down her face unchecked as she tried to process the contents of Jack Dawkins' letter. She dabbed her cheeks fiercely with her handkerchief. What had she uncovered?

Once she had regained her composure, she read the letter once more, noticing the scratches and marks. A letter from a dying man. She set it down once more. The letter was dated the same day Matt had visited the shop. Jack Dawkins must have written it after Matt had gone.

Her mind whirled. What should she do? What about her grandmother? Should she be told? She had to go and find Matt. She refolded the letter, slipping it back inside the envelope, and headed out of the office and along the corridor to the staff area hoping to find Mickey and Matt.

Matt could see something had happened as soon as he saw Kitty hurrying along the hotel corridor towards him. Her pale expression and pink eyes told him something was badly wrong.

'Kitty?' He left Mickey to continue fixing the squeaky door to the kitchen and went to meet her. 'What's wrong? What's happened?'

She waved a small white envelope at him. 'I just opened this, in the post. From Mr Dawkins. Oh Matt, I need you to read it.'

He placed his arm around her, shocked by her shaken tone and appearance. 'Chin up, old girl. Come on, let's go somewhere quiet and we can look at it together.'

He felt her relax under his touch, her shoulders dropping as she permitted him to guide her gently back along the corridor to her office. Once safely inside, he steered her to her seat and closed the door.

'Here.' He took the stopper from the small cut-glass decanter of brandy that stood on a narrow side table and poured a shot into a glass. Matt placed it in front of her. 'Take a sip, whatever is in that letter has shocked you deeply.' He took a seat opposite her.

She pulled a face and he thought she was about to refuse. However, she picked up the glass and took a sip, grimacing at the fiery taste of the liquor as she sipped. To his relief, colour started to return to her pale cheeks.

He took the letter from the envelope and read through the contents. Kitty was silent as he studied Jack Dawkins' note.

When he had finished, he placed the letter down with care in front of Kitty.

She pushed the brandy glass away and turned her attention back to the letter. 'What do you make of it all?'

'My impression of Dawkins when I saw him was that he was an extremely ill man. After my visit he must have realised that time was running out for him and he wanted to clear his conscience of something that has troubled him for a long time. It does, however, raise more questions than it answers.'

Her expression was troubled. 'Why would anyone have been following my mother? How would they know she would be there and what did they think she had that they could have wanted?' She bit her lower lip as she puzzled over the conundrum.

Matt considered her question. 'There is the valuable ruby, of course, that we discovered she had been keeping, but that seems unlikely, as no one knew of its existence until a few months ago when your father returned. No, I think it more likely that your mother may have stumbled upon something that she shouldn't have. But we don't know what, dammit.'

'The wrong place at the wrong time, you mean?' Kitty asked.

'Exactly.' He was pleased to see her complexion was slowly regaining its usual rosy hue.

'Poor Mr Dawkins. Can we discover if he is still alive, do you think? Perhaps there is something we can do for him?'

'You have a kind heart, Kitty.' He smiled at her. 'I will try to find out, but do not be too hopeful,' he cautioned.

'I know. It's all so terribly complicated, isn't it? I shall have to tell Grams what we have learned, and then I shall need to write to my father.'

Matt nodded. 'Yes, he may have some ideas perhaps about anything going on at the time which may have placed your mother in jeopardy, and of course you will have to inform him about his friend.'

'It's Grams I'm worried about. This will bring it all back again.' Her fingers brushed the corner of the letter.

Matt's heart twinged. He rose from his chair and came around the desk to place his arm around Kitty's narrow shoulders. He released a slow breath as she leaned her head against his shoulder.

'She has you to support her. It will be all right.'

Kitty raised her head and her gaze locked with his. Something shifted imperceptibly in the air and his pulse kicked up a notch. Time seemed suspended until a commotion outside in the lobby broke the spell between them.

'What on earth?' Kitty jumped up from her seat as the office door opened and Mrs Craven, resplendent in tweed with a fox fur collar, swept into the office with the receptionist hot on her patent heels.

'I'm terribly sorry, Miss Kitty. I did explain to Mrs Craven as you were busy.' The young receptionist wrung her hands.

'It's quite all right, Mary,' Kitty reassured the girl as Matt collected up Jack Dawkins' letter from the desk and tucked it into the inside pocket of his jacket.

Mrs Craven pursed her lips and gave the discarded brandy glass a disparaging glare as the girl returned to her station at the reception desk, closing the office door behind her. Matt moved to offer her his recently vacated seat. Mrs Craven inclined her head in acceptance and sat down, carefully placing her large, cream leather handbag neatly on her lap.

'Good morning, Mrs Craven, to what do we owe the pleasure of this visit?' Matt asked. Kitty had resumed her seat behind the desk.

'Good morning. I tried to speak to that policeman, Inspector Greville, this morning about the progress of our case and I was informed by the sergeant that he was on his way here. I had some business in town so I thought I would call in for a progress report before I returned home.' Mrs Craven looked at each of them in turn and Matt bit the inside of his cheek in an attempt not to smile at Kitty's bemused expression.

'The inspector called here about an hour or so ago as we were finishing breakfast. It seems that Miss Donohue, the friend of the murdered girl, has disappeared from her lodging house.' Matt perched on the corner of the desk.

'I see. I presume you have insisted he use all available manpower to find this young woman?' Mrs Craven fixed him with a steely glare.

'I'm not sure it works quite like that, Mrs Craven. However, I'm sure the inspector is working hard to locate her,' Kitty said.

'Humph.' Mrs Craven summed up her feelings with a single sound.

'You seem to be taking a keen interest in this case, Mrs Craven,' Matt observed in a mild tone.

'Well of course I am. To murder that young woman and to deliberately leave her body on the golf course, knowing that Tuesday is ladies' day at the club… Why, it is a deliberate affront, designed to insult the members of the club and I assure you, Captain Bryant, as captain of the ladies' team I take it most seriously. Then, to try and besmirch your name also. It's quite insupportable.' Mrs Craven practically bristled with indignation. 'Therefore, I am determined to lend you my support to solve this case.'

'That is very generous of you,' Matt jumped in to reply before Kitty could speak as he anticipated that her reply might not be as polite.

Mrs Craven immediately appeared mollified. 'Kitty's grand-mother is most distressed by this whole affair and naturally, as her friend, I offered to supervise Kitty as she is inexperienced in these matters.'

Matt shot Kitty a warning glance as her mouth dropped open in indignation.

'I gather that the chief suspects in the case are still the Davenports and their guests. Personally, I can't say that surprises me. I mean, Genny is probably the best of them, if only she would try and make something of herself. Stanley Davenport is full of his own self-importance. Celeste is a dipsomaniac. Peter is a very silly boy, always hanging around with that feckless friend of his. Then there is the colonel and his daughter. They have been recently living in Switzerland, I believe, and as for those film people and that jazz singer and her husband, well…' Mrs Craven ran out of air and looked expectantly at Matt.

'Thank you, a most valuable insight into the house party,' he said.

'I pride myself on being an excellent judge of character.'

Matt thought Kitty was about to explode. Even the tips of her ears had pinked at this outrageously immodest statement.

'Did you learn anything from Mr and Mrs Davenport or the colonel on Sunday to aid the investigation?' Matt asked.

Mrs Craven adjusted the fox fur collar on her jacket and settled herself more comfortably on the chair. 'Well, Celeste was her usual self, totally vague about everything and of course after the wine at lunchtime she was even more nonsensical. She was quite determined that you should be the villain. She said strangulation was a male thing and a girl couldn't have done it. I soon put her straight and said the girl's friend might be the culprit. Stanley Davenport was as pompous as ever, bragging to the colonel, who is an old chum of his, about how well his theatres are doing in London.' She paused for breath and gave a ladylike cough to clear her throat. 'My, it's a little dry in here.'

Kitty took the hint. 'I'll call for some tea.' She rolled her eyes at Matt when she was certain Mrs Craven's attention was elsewhere and slipped past him to make the request to the receptionist, before retaking her seat.

'Do please continue, Mrs Craven,' Matt said, once Kitty was sitting down.

'I knew I had to get any questions in before the mayor arrived, so I mentioned that Peter had apparently known the dead girl,

Pearl. Stanley was immediately all bluster and denial. I must say, he too tried to blacken your name. No doubt he had been listening to his wife.'

'I hope you put him straight, too? I must thank you for all the work you've been doing on behalf of my good name.' Matt smiled.

There was a discreet tap on the office door and a small gilt and onyx topped tea trolley was wheeled inside with a merry jingle of china teacups and silver spoons. Kitty set out the cups and served tea under the watchful gaze of Mrs Craven.

Once Mrs Craven had taken a restorative sip, she continued with her tale. 'Naturally, I quizzed Stanley on why he should suspect you and of course he could give no good reason other than that you had admitted seeing the girls and it was your bootlace. I remarked that you would have found it difficult to place the girl's body on the course as you have a motorcycle and the police had discovered car tracks on the green—'

'Which is what I said to Inspector Greville,' Kitty interjected.

Mrs Craven raised an eyebrow at Kitty's interruption and resumed her narrative. 'Stanley, of course, continued to bluster but the colonel remarked that Stanley had been complaining only that morning that someone had removed the travel rug from the back seat of his car. Now I had intended to tell the inspector that piece of information, but it completely slipped my mind till now. But what do you make of that? That could be a clue.' She sat back in her chair and smirked triumphantly at Kitty before taking another sip of her tea.

'Or the chauffeur or one of the family may have moved it for perfectly innocent reasons. After all, Pearl wasn't found lying on a picnic rug,' Kitty said.

Matt intervened quickly before the relationship between Mrs Craven and Kitty soured completely. They needed Mrs Craven onside so that Kitty could continue investigating the Davenport connection. 'I think both of you have made excellent points. Someone could have used the blanket to move Pearl, or of course it could be a coincidence. It's worth informing Inspector Greville either way though so he is aware.'

Mrs Craven finished her tea and replaced the cup neatly back on its saucer. 'Well, I must be off; I have a luncheon date. Kitty, I understand you are assisting Genny at the Pavilion theatre on Thursday?'

'Yes, I am to look after props, prompting and some other small tasks for the charity performance. Genny wants me to familiarise myself with the running order and my duties ahead of the show.'

'I expect to be kept informed of any developments.' Mrs Craven gathered her bag and rose from her seat to take her leave.

'You may be certain of it, and thank you for your help.' Matt opened the door for her and saw her out. He watched her cross the lobby and depart before returning to Kitty's office. He had barely closed the door before Kitty exploded. 'Oh honestly, that woman! Since when did it become "our" case? And she needs to "supervise" me?'

She gave a great huff of indignation as she tidied the cups back onto the trolley. Her cheeks were now a healthy rosy pink and the spark was back in her blue-grey eyes. Matt grinned; the shock of Jack Dawkins' missive had been swept away entirely by Mrs Craven's unexpected call.

'Oh, do stop looking so pleased with yourself,' Kitty snapped as she caught sight of his expression. 'Some of us have a business to run.'

'Then I shall leave you to get on. I'll go and make those enquiries at Exeter for you and meet you later for dinner.'

A shadow crossed her face at the reminder of Jack Dawkins and before he had time to think Matt took Kitty gently by the shoulders. 'Chin up, best get back to your books.' He bent his head and kissed her swiftly on the lips. He had a brief second to register the tender yielding of her mouth against his and the startled expression on her face before he released her and disappeared out of the office with a cheery wave of his hand.

CHAPTER TWELVE

Kitty sat back down with a bump as the office door closed behind Matt. Her fingers strayed to her mouth and she touched her lips. They still seemed to hold the slight impression of his kiss. Her pulse was rapid as she stared at the blank polished oak panels of the closed door. It really was turning out to be the most extraordinary day.

Kitty worked through lunch, sending to the kitchen for sandwiches which she ate at her desk as she tried to make up for the time lost recently. Images of her mother kept floating into her mind, making it difficult to concentrate on sorting the invoices and filling in the accounts.

She wondered if Matt had made any headway with his enquiries about Jack Dawkins and if Inspector Greville had located Salome. Eventually, she replaced the lid on her fountain pen and placed it down in the pen tray. Her head, neck and shoulders ached, and the office had grown darker whilst she'd been working, relying as it did from borrowed light through a small stained-glass porthole window.

There was a tap at the door and Alice popped her head in. 'Miss Kitty, I didn't know as you was still in here. It's going dark, shall I put the lights on?' She suited the action to her words and Kitty blinked as the wall lights came on, filling the room with soft yellow light.

'I had just finished, Alice. I need to go and change ready for supper.'

The maid bustled into the room and started to collect the debris from Kitty's lunch. 'You look tired, miss.'

'It's been a busy day.' Kitty bit back a yawn.

Alice picked up the crockery. 'Maybe get yourself an early night with some cocoa.'

Kitty smiled. 'Maybe. How is your cousin, Betty?'

Alice pursed her lips. 'Got a proper bob on herself she has. That film producer chap, Mr Tilney, told her she'd got a good profile for the pictures and it's gone right to her head.'

'Oh dear.' Kitty had to hide a smile, aware of how much Alice loved the pictures and would love to have been told the same.

Alice sniffed as she whisked crumbs from the desk with her cloth. 'Been hanging about with these actors and actresses, giving herself airs and graces. Thinks she's a film star already. Always been one for trying to make herself important, our Betty. She said that she saw somebody yesterday that was the spit of that murdered girl's friend. Said she was at one of them lodging houses the theatre folk stop at.'

Kitty sat up straight. 'Alice, the police are looking everywhere for that girl. Is Betty sure it was her?'

Alice appeared taken aback at the eagerness in Kitty's tone. 'That's the thing, miss. Our Betty reckons as this girl had changed her hair and she couldn't be absolutely certain it was her.'

'Do you know where she saw her?'

'You can ask her, miss. I go off duty in ten minutes and she's waiting for me in the lobby on account of how it's started raining and she hasn't brought her brolly with her.' Alice gave a scornful tut at this last part of her statement.

Kitty jumped up from her chair and headed out into the lobby with an astonished Alice trailing in her wake. Betty was at the far end of the room leafing through a pamphlet from the information rack. She was dressed in what Kitty judged to be her best coat and hat as if she had been for an appointment somewhere.

When she saw Kitty coming towards her, Betty immediately flushed and started to look flustered. 'I were just waiting on our

Alice, Miss Underhay. Tes raining heavens hard.' She gesticulated with the leaflet towards the window.

'That's quite all right, Betty. Alice just told me you thought you saw a woman similar to the one the police are searching for, Pearl Bright's friend.'

A cunning light came into Betty's eyes. 'I reckon it was likely to be her, except she'd changed her hair and she was acting a bit shifty, like she didn't want to be seen.'

'And this was yesterday?' Kitty persisted.

'Might have been,' Betty muttered.

'You best tell Miss Kitty what you told me and none of your nonsense or your ma will hear of it.' Alice confronted her cousin, her hands on her narrow hips and a fierce expression on her face.

'Keep your stupid frilly cap on.'

Kitty raised an eyebrow and Betty subsided. 'Sorry, begging your pardon, miss. Yes, yesterday afternoon. She had a little bag with her.' She glared at Alice.

'Where was this?'

Betty pouted but gave the address. It was a part of Torquay that Kitty was not very familiar with. She knew however that there were lots of cheap lodgings and workers' cottages in that area.

'Why did you not come forward with this information before?' Kitty asked.

'I only got a glimpse, like, and it might not have been her and then what?'

Alice tossed her head and glared at her cousin. 'Honestly, our Betty.'

'I'll pass this on to the inspector. Alice, you'd better hurry along since Betty is waiting for you.' Kitty nodded to Alice. 'Thank you, Betty.' She left the cousins quietly bickering together and hurried back to her office to call the inspector.

The inspector had already left for the day, so she left her message with the desk sergeant. She had just replaced the handset when

Matt popped his head through the open doorway. 'Are you still working, Kitty? Your grandmother will be expecting us shortly.'

Kitty quickly told him the information she'd gained from Betty.

'I know that area quite well. It has a mix of housing. Much of it is respectable, but some parts are not so nice.' Matt frowned.

'Inspector Greville has left for the day. The desk sergeant said they would go there tomorrow as soon as they had the resources to send someone.'

The creases on Matt's forehead deepened. 'That may be too late. You say Betty was a little doubtful if it was Salome she saw?'

'She said she thought her hair was changed but she was confident enough to boast to Alice about seeing her.' Kitty shrugged. 'I think Betty probably did recognise her, but she was too busy about her own business to go to the police.'

'I'm sure you're right. The question is, what do we do now?'

'Matt…' Kitty said his name warningly. She recognised the note in his voice. 'You must not get involved. Leave this to Greville and his men.'

'Suppose she's gone by tomorrow though? If we find Salome it would be a real chance to clear my name.'

'Matt, we can't go in there muddying the waters, however hard it may be. If you go storming in there, you could be accused of pressurising a witness.' She rose from her seat and placed a hand on his arm. 'Come, Grams is expecting us for dinner. A few hours won't make much difference. The inspector will be on the case first thing in the morning.'

The hard muscle tone of his arm relaxed as he considered what she'd said. 'Very well. We need to talk to your grandmother about Mr Dawkins and his letter and I'll tell you both what I've learned this afternoon.'

From the sombre tone of his voice she assumed the news about Jack Dawkins was not good. 'We'd better hurry. Grams hates unpunctuality.'

*

Kitty changed quickly into a dark red satin evening gown with chiffon cap sleeves and a low back. After dinner she intended to walk around the ballroom greeting her guests and checking up on her staff. The recent problem of the dishonest barman still weighed on her, and she knew she had to stay on top of her business.

Matt was already in her grandmother's suite when she entered. Dressed in a smart black evening suit with wide lapels, he stood at the side of the marble fireplace, sipping one of her grandmother's pre-dinner aperitifs.

'Kitty, just in time.' Her grandmother presented her with a glass of sherry and sat back down on the sofa, smoothing out the skirts of her dark green chiffon gown as she did so. 'Matthew has forewarned me that you have learned new information about your mother.'

Kitty perched on the opposite end of the sofa and took a sip of sherry. She was not looking forward to sharing Jack Dawkins' letter with her grandmother. She knew she would be as shocked and upset as Kitty herself had been when she had first read it.

'I received a letter today, from Father's friend in Exeter. The contents may be distressing.' Kitty looked at Matt. He produced the note from the inside pocket of his jacket and handed it to her grandmother.

'Pass me my glasses, Kitty,' she commanded.

Kitty picked up the glasses case from the top of the small mahogany writing bureau and passed them to her grandmother. For a few minutes the only sound in the room was the ticking of the wooden casement clock on the mantelpiece as she studied the contents of the letter.

Kitty's heart squeezed as her grandmother produced a lace-edged handkerchief and dabbed at her eyes. 'It affected me terribly when I first read it.'

Her grandmother blew her nose discreetly. 'Yes, it is hard to read but it is a step closer to the truth. I do not want to go to my grave not knowing what happened to Elowed, however awful the story might be.'

A knock sounded at the door of the suite and a uniformed waiter pushed in the dinner trolley. He set the trolley near the table, which had already been laid for dinner with crisp white linen and crystal glassware. He placed a china soup tureen and ladle into the centre of the table.

'Thank you, we will serve the rest ourselves,' Kitty said, dismissing him.

They took their places and Kitty served the delicate clear broth into the white porcelain dishes. Matt passed around a small basket of fresh bread rolls. Kitty was relieved to see colour returning to her grandmother's complexion. On reading the letter she had become quite pale.

'I have made enquiries at Exeter about Mr Dawkins,' Matt said, looking at her grandmother. 'Sadly, he passed away in the early hours of yesterday morning.'

The news, whilst not unexpected, was still distressing to Kitty. Jack Dawkins' death closed another door on the mystery of what had happened to her mother. She also found it infinitely sad that he had seemed such a lonely soul. 'The poor man,' she murmured.

'I spoke to a Father Lamb. He was Mr Dawkins' parish priest and was with him until the end. The funeral will be on Friday at the Sacred Heart church in Exeter. He indicated that he did not expect there to be anyone in attendance. Mr Dawkins has no family.' Matt's voice was sombre.

'That is a terrible thing. We must attend, Matt. This man was once my father's friend and I am sure if he were here he would go, so the least I can do is go in his place.' Kitty looked at her grandmother.

Mrs Treadwell touched her napkin to the corners of her mouth. 'I am inclined to agree with you, Kitty. This man should have come forward sooner, but I can understand why that may not have been possible back then. God knows, your father has many faults, but I do believe he would not wish Jack Dawkins' death to go unmarked.' She rose and cleared their empty soup bowls before lifting the silver cloches to reveal plates of roast mutton with vegetables. She served them to Kitty and Matt as Kitty assisted by placing a gravy jug and tureen of boiled potatoes in the centre of the table.

Once everyone was seated again, Kitty's grandmother resumed the conversation. 'Will you escort Kitty to this man's funeral, if you please?' She looked at Matt.

'Of course. And it's possible that Mr Dawkins may have said something to this Father Lamb which could be useful. Obviously if it was during confession then the Father would be bound by a vow of confidentiality.'

Kitty's grandmother considered. 'Yes, of course. Thank you.'

'Alice's cousin Betty believes she saw Salome Donohue, the murdered girl's friend, at a theatrical boarding house in Torquay yesterday.' Kitty helped herself to another potato from the serving dish.

'Really? Is the inspector aware of this?' Kitty's grandmother asked.

'I spoke to the desk sergeant earlier this evening,' Kitty said.

Mrs Treadwell looked at Matt. 'No doubt you would like to visit and make enquiries yourself, Matthew?'

Matt swallowed the meat he was eating. 'I'm worried that by morning this girl may have moved on, assuming Betty is right and it is her. She is evading the police for some reason. It could be that she is hiding from the person she believes is the murderer, or she may even be the murderer.'

'The note that Peter Davenport received could have been an attempt at blackmail, perhaps because of his partialities or something scandalous to do with that,' Kitty suggested.

Mrs Treadwell appeared unsurprised by this revelation.

'The inspector suggested she may have sent several of those notes. From what she told her landlady, she was clearly expecting a payout from somewhere or somebody. Much as Pearl was, also,' Matt added.

'Let us hope the police find her tomorrow then,' Mrs Treadwell remarked as she placed her cutlery neatly on her empty plate. 'You will heed the inspector's request to stay away, I hope, Matthew?' She fixed him with a steely look.

'I have already said the same thing, Grams,' Kitty said. 'It is very frustrating, but our hands are tied for now. It's important that Matt is completely exonerated from anything to do with Pearl's murder.'

'The sooner that happens, the better.' Matt also placed his cutlery on his plate.

Kitty rose and cleared the empty plates and the rest of the crockery, placing them back on the trolley before setting a small glass bowl of sherry trifle each in front of her grandmother and Matt. She put the final one on her own place setting and took her seat again.

'Your parents are very anxious that this should be resolved soon too,' Mrs Treadwell remarked as she dug into her trifle.

Matt sighed. 'Yes, my father is most concerned that it may affect my business if it drags on and I am inclined to agree with him on that score. I have already had one client cancel a job and have had to delay others.'

'Once you have been cleared then I'm sure you will have no trouble bouncing back. If we can help catch the murderer that would be even better,' Kitty mused.

'But not until you have been cleared,' her grandmother gave Matt another severe look. 'Your mother seems happy that you have settled down, at least.'

Kitty was not deceived by her grandmother's innocent expression and the sly peep she sent her way as she spoke.

'So she keeps telling me,' Matt agreed.

Kitty's cheeks heated at the glance he gave her, reminding her of the kiss they had shared only that morning. It had not been unwelcome, but it had been unsettling and she couldn't tell from his demeanour towards her now how Matt felt about it. She hoped they would be able to solve Pearl's murder and clear Matt soon. The weeks they had spent without speaking after the argument had been hard enough. If his business failed and he were forced to move away, she didn't want to consider what that would be like, especially now they seemed to be connecting on a deeper level.

CHAPTER THIRTEEN

Kitty was hard at work in her office the following day when Matt appeared in the doorway.

'Good morning, has there been any news from the police?' Kitty asked.

'No, nothing yet. I came to ask a favour, and before you say yes or no, I must tell you that I have your grandmother's permission.'

Kitty put down her pen, her interest piqued. 'What is the favour?' Experience told her that her grandmother was up to something.

'I need to check on the office in Torquay, see if there is any post and so on. Do you fancy a trip out and a spot of lunch?' Matt grinned at her. 'Too much work makes Kitty a dull girl, after all. Your grandmother has said she will hold the fort here this afternoon for you.'

'And we are only going for lunch and to collect the post from your office?' she asked.

'On my honour.' His grin widened. 'It's a lovely day out there, the sun is shining, and I'll give you a slap-up lunch at Bobby's café by the waterfront.'

She looked at the pile of paperwork she still had to complete. 'We are not going to look for Salome Donohue?'

'Kitty Underhay, you wound me, such a suspicious mind.' He attempted to look hurt by her remark.

'You are such a fraud.' Kitty laughed. 'I am never going to get this lot done.'

'But you will come out to play?' Matt laughed back at her.

'I suppose I'd better. Someone has to keep you out of trouble.' She shook her head in mock despair.

'I'll organise a taxi, meet you in the lobby in ten minutes.'

The door closed and he disappeared, leaving Kitty wondering quite what she'd agreed to and if she should bring up yesterday's kiss.

She ran upstairs and donned her favourite dark-red coat and a smart new grey hat with a red trim. Matt was ready and waiting for her in the lobby when she arrived back downstairs.

Mr Potter's taxi was already outside the hotel. Kitty cracked open the windows in the back of the taxi and snuggled into her coat. The sun might be shining but there was already an autumnal nip in the air. The warmth of summer was vanishing with each passing day. She knew too that the claustrophobia which had dogged Matt since his time in the trenches made the enclosed space inside a car intolerable for him unless there was fresh air.

She was conscious of his closeness to her on the rear seat of the car, the scent of the soap he used and the faint outdoor woody smell of smoke that clung to his overcoat. Mr Potter's casual conversation regarding the weather and the prospects of the various football teams served as a welcome distraction.

The sparkling blue waters of the bay spread out before them as they drove down the hill towards Torquay. Kitty resisted the urge to look towards the Davenports' house and Matt's home.

'I'm looking forward to visiting your office,' Kitty observed. She knew he rented a small workspace above some shops in Fore Street but had never had occasion to call upon him there.

'It's not very exciting, I'm afraid, and if Inspector Greville doesn't solve this case soon I may not require it for much longer.' He kept his tone light but her familiarity with his body language told her he was concerned.

Mr Potter drove them past the Pavilion theatre and the ornamental gardens which bordered the seafront, before turning inland into Fore Street.

'Just here will be splendid, Mr Potter.' Matt signalled for the car to stop.

He assisted Kitty from the taxi, and she looked around her with interest. They had alighted near the narrower part of the street where the road started to curve uphill slightly once more. There was a doorway between a gentlemen's tailoring establishment and a bootmakers. On the wall were a series of polished brass doorbells with discreet white cards. Next to the one advertising the manufacture of teeth she saw Torbay Private Investigative Services.

'Let us see what awaits in the office.' Matt led the way through the smart black painted door and up a short flight of stone stairs to a landing area. The teeth manufacturers were situated opposite Matt's office. There wasn't much of note about the plain wooden door, but Kitty averted her eyes nevertheless. He produced the key from his coat pocket and unlocked the door. A small pile of post lay on the mat just inside.

Matt stooped to scoop up the mail and then gestured to Kitty to follow him into his workplace. The room was slightly chilly from lack of use. There was a small black fireplace set into one wall with kindling laid ready in the grate. A wooden filing cabinet stood in the corner topped by a somewhat depressed-looking aspidistra plant in a brass pot. Matt's desk was of a functional light oak and a clean blotter and brass pen tray lay atop, not dissimilar to her own. Placed next to it was a leather-cased clock and a letter rack to match the pen tray.

A dark-green leather upholstered desk chair was behind the desk and two wooden seats, for clients' use, she assumed, in front. A tea tray with a kettle, cups and biscuit barrel stood on a small wooden side table.

The walls were painted cream and devoid of any artwork. The only other item in the office was the black telephone, which was also on the desk.

'Take a seat, Kitty. It won't take me long to look at these and then we can go for lunch.' Matt picked up a gilt letter opener and began to open his post. Kitty amused herself by wandering over to the office window to admire the view of the street.

From her vantage point she could see the cars below trickling along in and out of town. A horse-drawn cart was delivering to a shop further along and shoppers strolled past, women with baskets and packages, some with small children clutching at their mother's hands. Gentlemen in trilby hats or caps walked briskly about their business.

'This is a fine outlook. I often wish my office had a window with a view but then I suppose I should spend all my time daydreaming out of it,' Kitty said. As she turned around to face Matt, the telephone on the desk rang out, startling them both.

'Torbay Private Investigative Services,' Matt spoke into the handset.

Kitty perched herself on one of the wooden chairs.

'Yes, Inspector, Kitty is with me now. Of course.' Matt glanced at her. 'Yes, I know the street. We can be there in about fifteen minutes.' His face asked a question of Kitty and she nodded her acquiescence, guessing the inspector wanted them to meet him somewhere.

Matt replaced the handset. 'Inspector Greville has located Salome Donohue. A letter in her belongings has confirmed her identity.'

A chill settled on Kitty at the sombre note in his voice. 'What has happened?'

He thrust his hands into the pockets of his overcoat and appeared to be gathering his thoughts before answering her question. 'She is dead. The landlady found her this morning drowned in her bath. Apparently, water began to permeate through the ceiling into the parlour. The landlady couldn't open the door although she could hear running water. One of Greville's men obligingly showed up at just the right moment and broke open the door.'

'Suicide? Accident?' Kitty asked, the horror of the event seeping into her as she asked the question. 'Oh, it's too awful.'

'Dr Carter is on his way there now and the inspector has requested we meet him at the address.'

'Then we had better set off.' She gathered her handbag and tidied her chair back into its place. She couldn't help but feel somewhat anxious about what the inspector might want or what they would discover when they saw him.

Matt locked the door behind them, and they set off, walking away from the busy shopping area towards the cottages and houses in the narrower side streets. He offered her his arm and she was glad of his support as they headed upwards into the steep roads.

They walked steadily for some ten minutes or so until they entered a small side road. The houses appeared shabby but respectable. A small group of people were gathered outside a house at the far end and a black car stood at the kerb.

'I see Doctor Carter has arrived. That's his Humber, if I'm not mistaken.' Matt urged her forward and they increased their pace.

Inspector Greville was deep in conversation with a tall thin woman clad in an all-enveloping floral pinafore apron when they arrived. Doctor Carter was nowhere in sight.

Kitty peered at the lodging house. It was a skinny, three-storey building in the centre of a terrace of similar houses. Whitewashed on the outside and with the front step freshly scrubbed, it appeared clean and respectable. A uniformed constable stood guard at the open front door and Kitty suppressed a shiver, imagining the scene inside.

The inspector completed his conversation and crossed the pavement to greet them. 'Miss Underhay, Captain Bryant, thank you both for coming, I thought you would appreciate the latest information and it saves me a trip across the river as you are already in Torquay. I called the hotel and Mrs Treadwell kindly gave me your office number.' He addressed the last part of his remark to Matt.

'Mrs Jacobs, the landlady, said Miss Donohue requested a room for a couple of nights. The majority of her tenants are theatricals or commercial travellers, so she didn't find it odd that Salome had very little luggage. There are people booking in and out all the time, many of them just for a night or so. She called herself "Sally Soames" in the visitor's ledger and paid her rent up front, so Mrs Jacobs did not ask too many questions.'

'Did Mrs Jacobs say if Salome had any visitors or if she seemed to know anyone else staying at the house?' Matt asked.

The inspector consulted his notebook. 'She doesn't take much notice of the comings and goings, so didn't spot anything out of the ordinary.'

'Was anyone else in the house when Mrs Jacobs noticed the water coming through the ceiling?' Kitty asked.

'Everyone was out, surprisingly enough. Usually there are tenants about at that time of day but not this morning, it seems. Mrs Jacobs says she heard the front door bang shut about fifteen minutes or half an hour before she noticed the water and she assumes that was when the last occupant went out. She shouted for help when she couldn't open the bathroom door and there was no one around. The constable happened along, following on the information you left for me last night, and helped break down the door to discover Miss Donohue.' The inspector closed his notebook.

'The poor, silly girl. Why ever didn't she come forward to the police?' Kitty asked. The inspector's matter-of-fact description of events had made her feel quite queasy.

'We have assumed then that this was not some tragic accident, or even suicide?' Matt asked.

Inspector Greville sighed. 'We'll have to see what Carter thinks about it all, but I am inclined to believe this was murder. There was no suicide note and Mrs Jacobs said Sally Soames appeared positively jubilant when she paid the money for her lodgings. "Smug", was how she described her.'

'Greville! And Captain Bryant with the lovely Miss Underhay. We must all stop meeting like this.' Doctor Carter's jovial tones made them turn towards the open front door of the lodging house.

'Indeed.' Matt's tone was dry, but he smiled a welcome as the doctor came to join them. Doctor Carter always reminded Kitty of a middle-aged cherub, with his innocent eyes twinkling behind his glasses. He was always unfailingly cheerful despite the nature of his work. He was also passionate about motor cars and speed and Kitty and Matt had previously experienced some hair-raising rides as the good doctor's passengers.

Today he had his usual cheery expression and carried his familiar dark brown leather medical bag.

'Well?' Inspector Greville asked his colleague.

'I'm sending a bottle and some glasses to the laboratory for tests. It looks to me though as if the lady had taken something in her champagne. This could have made her sleepy and unlikely to resist if held under the bath water.'

'Hmm, yes, there were no signs of a struggle that we could see but I did notice the champagne and the glasses. We have checked for fingerprints. It looked as if she'd been having a bit of a celebratory drink with someone – bit early, but that's actors for you. She was a fit, young lady. If there are no bruises or bumps then it would seem a possibility that she was drugged first.' Inspector Greville scratched his temple with the end of his pencil, knocking his hat slightly skew-whiff.

'I'll know more after I've run some toxicology tests and completed the post-mortem.' The doctor beamed cheerily at them. 'So I'd better run along and make a start.'

Kitty tightened her grip on Matt's arm as two men emerged from the house carrying a covered stretcher between them which they loaded carefully into the back of an anonymous grey van.

'Do you still have the Sunbeam motorcycle?' the doctor asked Matt as he prepared to climb into the driver's seat of his Humber.

'Yes, it's going well, thank you.'

Memories of her own journey riding pillion on the back of Matt's motorcycle at Enderley Hall rushed back into Kitty's mind.

'Splendid, I'm thinking of changing the Humber for something a bit nippier.'

'They do seem to be making the new cars faster,' Matt agreed.

Doctor Carter closed the car door, gave a pip of the car horn and a cheery wave and departed along the road in a cloud of dust.

'Of course, you realise I have to formally note where you were at the time of Miss Donohue's death?' Inspector Greville looked at Matt.

'We were together at the hotel this morning and travelled to Torquay in Mr Potter's taxi. We went straight to Matt's office which is where we were when you telephoned,' Kitty said.

'Thank you, Miss Underhay. It's not that I doubt the veracity of either of you, but the chief constable likes things done properly. As he has been constantly reminding me.'

Her cheeks pinked a little as she knew her tone had been slightly sharp when she had answered his question.

'Of course. We understand, Inspector.' Matt's hand covered hers, and he gave her fingers a gentle warning squeeze.

'Certainly,' Kitty agreed.

'Would it be possible for us to see Miss Donohue's room and the bathroom now the area has been cleared? Kitty's insight proved useful before, at Enderley,' Matt asked.

Inspector Greville eyed them both levelly. 'Very well, just for a few minutes.' He nodded to the constable at the door to allow them inside.

Kitty's heart raced as she followed Matt into the parquet tiled hallway and up the wooden staircase to the first floor. Salome's room was neat and tidy. The single bed, covered by a dark green satin eiderdown, was against the cream painted wall. A small bedside locker stood on the other side. Round ring marks on the wooden surface indicated where the champagne bottle and glasses must have been placed.

A small battered carpet bag lay open on the floor, the meagre contents spilling out: a clean, peach-coloured slip, some undergarments and some rolled up stockings. Kitty opened the light wood wardrobe to reveal a skirt, blouse and jacket hung neatly next to a gaberdine raincoat. A pair of high-heeled patent black court shoes stood below.

On the tiny dressing table, a small array of cosmetics and a hairbrush lay in front of the mirror. Kitty frowned.

'What is it?' Matt asked.

'I wonder if the police have removed her handbag.'

Matt joined her in looking around the room. 'I don't see it. Her hat is here, and her gloves. Let's have a quick look in the bathroom and then we'll check with the inspector.'

The bathroom was directly opposite Salome's bedroom and was clearly intended to be shared by the occupants of that floor. Two other doors led off the small landing, both closed tightly, and a narrower flight of stairs continued to the top floor. Kitty suppressed a shudder at the puddles of water still evident on the linoleum of the bathroom and landing.

A pink satin wrapper – presumably Salome's – hung from a hook on the back of the bathroom door, along with her matching negligee. The green-tiled room housed a large claw-footed bath, a lavatory and a sink with a mirror-doored cabinet. Pink house slippers lay discarded where their owner had kicked them off before entering her final bath.

Kitty didn't linger in the bathroom. The sight of the wrapper and slippers made her feel queasy, thinking of Salome's demise. Matt appeared to sense her unease.

'Come on, old thing, let's go and find Inspector Greville.'

He led the way back downstairs and outside into the fresh air. The inspector was deep in conversation with a round-faced young man in his mid-thirties.

After a few minutes, the policeman came to join them. 'That gentleman was the last of the boarders to leave this morning. He claims he saw a thin man in an ill-fitting suit, cloth cap and a muffler hanging around near the house as he left.'

'Not much to go on then, sir. Did he see Salome at all?' Matt said thoughtfully.

'No, he didn't see Miss Donohue or hear any noise from her room. He was in a hurry to get to the dentist; he had an appointment for a bad tooth and was a little late.' The inspector sighed and eyed them both keenly. 'Any insights from viewing the room?'

'I wondered if you had removed Salome's handbag?' Kitty asked.

Inspector Greville's brow furrowed. 'Not as far as I'm aware. There was only the carpet bag containing her belongings.'

'But surely she would have had a handbag containing her purse?' Kitty queried.

The inspector strode away to speak to Mrs Jacobs, the landlady, who was now busy talking to the boarder with the bad tooth. Within a few seconds he was back. 'Yes, black patent leather to match her shoes. Mrs Jacobs remembers it from when she took out her purse to pay for her room. You say it's missing?'

'Yes, sir. Kitty noticed it was gone when we looked inside the wardrobe.' Matt glanced at Kitty.

'Well spotted, Miss Underhay. I'll get my men to start searching the house and the nearby streets. Someone has removed it and I'd like to know why.'

CHAPTER FOURTEEN

Matt's mind worked overtime as he escorted Kitty away from the lodging house and back in the direction of the town centre.

'Are you all right?' he asked as they crossed a road and strolled towards the harbour and seafront. Kitty had been unusually silent during their walk.

'Yes, I suppose it was upsetting seeing those few bits and pieces of Salome's, knowing she'd never use them again. It made everything more real and personal somehow.' She shivered, and Matt moved to place his arm around her, offering her support.

'We're nearly at the café, a cup of tea and some hot food will make you feel better.' Perhaps he should have tried to insist Kitty stay outside the lodgings. Not that she would have taken any notice and they wouldn't have spotted that Salome's handbag was missing without her.

Ahead of them, the sun glistened on the sea and the boats moved up and down on their anchors in the harbour. The Pavilion theatre gleamed white in the sunshine and the last of the summer bedding plants gave a splash of colour around the centrepiece fountain on the promenade.

Bobby's café was quietening down as they entered, the main lunchtime rush dispersing as they secured a table near the window with a view of the sea. Kitty sat down with a sigh of relief and drew off her white gloves, placing them in her handbag for safekeeping.

Matt placed an order for a pot of tea for two from one of the waitresses while they decided what to eat. Kitty looked around the café with interest. Potted plants were arranged in large china pots and art prints of stylish women decorated the walls. The café hummed with the chatter of diners and the tang of vinegar and chips was in the air.

'I don't think I've been in here before.'

'I sometimes take my lunch here if I'm working in the town.' Matt passed over the menu.

Kitty opened the red leatherette menu and studied the list of dishes inside. 'What do you recommend?'

'Fish, chips and bread and butter?' Matt suggested as the waitress returned with a tray of tea. The girl set the teapot, milk jug, cups and the sugar bowl in front of them before taking out her waiting pad from the pocket of her starched white apron.

'Fish and chips it is, then.' Kitty closed her menu.

'Make that two,' Matt said. The waitress collected the menus, smiled and hurried away with their orders.

'Shall I pour?' Kitty asked, picking up the teapot. He watched as she placed the small metal tea strainer over his cup and expertly poured the tea before adding the milk.

'Thank you.'

She picked up her cup, cradling it in her hands before taking a sip. 'Oh, that's better.'

Her obvious enjoyment of a simple cup of tea made his own smile grow wider. 'It was a tough morning.'

Kitty replaced her cup back on its saucer. 'So, penny for your thoughts? Do you think Salome was murdered? The inspector seemed to feel it likely and if so, is her murder connected with that note she sent to Peter? Did she know who the murderer was? Or was she trying to get money from several people? It rules her out as a suspect in Pearl's murder, I suppose.'

'I am inclined to believe she may have sent those notes to several people, as the inspector suggested. I wonder if he will find anyone else admitting to having received one. One of them could have been Pearl's killer. I think Salome thought she'd taken precautions to keep herself safe and those precautions failed.' He toyed with his teaspoon.

'Who else could she have tried?' Kitty asked.

'It all keeps falling back to the Davenports' house party. What's troubling me is, why was Pearl killed? If Salome was killed because she was trying to blackmail a killer, then why was Pearl murdered? What did she know or see that placed her in danger?'

She appeared to consider his question. 'Hmm, I see what you mean. Salome must have been comfortable enough in her killer's company to drink champagne in her nightwear and then go and run a bath.'

'A woman, then? Or a lover?'

The waitress returned with their order, bringing the conversation to a temporary halt as she slid full plates of delicious-smelling crispy battered fish and golden chips in front of them.

Once she'd gone and Kitty had drawn a napkin across her lap, she resumed their conversation. 'At least the inspector appears to be able to exonerate you now. I presume that must be one of the reasons he requested us to go there this morning.'

'True, no one pointed at me and said, "It was him!"' Matt gave an imitation of a radio drama act.

'Let's consider our suspects.' She picked up the small glass salt cellar and sprinkled her chips.

'Very well. Peter Davenport and his friend, Sebastian. Peter had received a note from Salome and Seb was aware of this.' He added salt and vinegar to his own meal, suddenly aware of how hungry he felt.

Kitty tucked into her lunch as she thought about his response. 'True. Then there are the Tilneys. Laurence Tilney's name keeps cropping up, as does the theatre connection. Pearl and Salome were both actresses. I don't know what the Tilneys' motive could have been, unless they were also being blackmailed for something?'

'What about Dickie and BeBe? I got the impression from the information he gave you that he and BeBe knew more than they were prepared to say to the authorities. You had to persuade him to come forward to the police.' He speared a chip with his fork.

'Dickie and BeBe aren't rich, so they would be an unlikely source of money for Pearl and Salome. Saira and her father seem to be on the periphery of things, but they are wealthy so there might be something there. The colonel is too physically frail, though, to have killed the girls. Genny is rather closed off so it's hard to judge if she knows anything or not. She's very focused on all of her charity work. Mrs Davenport dotes on Peter and has little time for Genny, not that that is a motive for Genny to kill Pearl or Salome. No, I don't think it can be Genny.' Her brow furrowed as she pondered their choice of suspects.

'What about Mr and Mrs Davenport? They were quick to point the finger at me,' Matt asked. It seemed they both had been very keen to divert all suspicion away from their household.

'Celeste is very keen for Peter to marry Saira, but she seems to be a slave to the bottle and doesn't interact much with her guests. I can't think how she would have known the dead girls.'

'And you said Saira appears ambivalent about marrying Peter?' Matt asked.

'She says he isn't interested in her. He only seems to pay attention to her at his mother's instigation, which isn't very nice. There is the speculation also around the nature of Peter and Sebastian's friendship.' Kitty blushed.

'Well that could give rise to blackmail, if there was evidence of their relationship.' Matt was not unduly surprised by the idea. Such relationships were more common in the theatre world, or at least, more tolerated, even if still illegal.

Kitty gave a happy sigh as she popped the last morsel of fish into her mouth. 'Oh, that food was delicious.'

He smiled as she dabbed the corners of her mouth with the napkin. 'I'm glad you enjoyed your lunch.'

'I do my best work when I've eaten.' Her eyes twinkled.

He finished his own meal as Kitty topped up their teacups, calling the waitress over for more hot water.

'I wonder what Salome's killer hoped to find in her handbag?' Kitty mused. 'They must have been disturbed or in a hurry or they would have simply searched for whatever it was there and then. I don't think it was simply a robbery.'

'Or perhaps they couldn't find what they wanted but the bag had something else in it? If we think that Pearl and Salome were blackmailing someone, then I suppose they must have had evidence of some sort.' Matt frowned.

'Maybe whatever the murderer is searching for is back at Salome's other lodgings? Where all her belongings are?' Kitty's eyes widened.

'I wonder if her previous landlady has packed up her room?' If the police hadn't already searched Salome's possessions, then they clearly needed to make that a priority. The clue to both murders could lie in Salome's things.

A sharp rapping on the glass window broke into Matt's thoughts. Outside the café, a tall, good-looking man was waving at Kitty. He glanced at her to see her cheeks had turned peony pink. 'It's Sebastian, Peter's friend,' she explained.

She waved back at Sebastian and he promptly took that as an invitation to join them, breezing into the café with a gust of cool sea air. Matt fought down a surge of jealousy as Kitty made the introductions. Seb shook Matt's hand before pulling up a seat to their table.

'Well, lovely Kitty, out and about with Peter's disreputable neighbour. I didn't realise you two were such good chums.' Seb looked at Matt as if trying to provoke a reaction.

'Matt is hardly disreputable,' Kitty replied, refusing to be drawn.

'What a shame, it makes life more interesting.' Seb winked at Kitty, making her laugh. Matt suppressed a growl and realised he was clenching his fists under the table.

'Kitty and I have known each other for a while and the police are satisfied that I had no involvement in Pearl Bright's murder.' He kept his tone level.

'Drat, I rather hoped I'd be able to boast that I knew a murderer. One needs good meaty topics of conversation at the dinner table these days. It would have been quite the social coup.' He pulled out his silver cigarette case and proffered cigarettes to Kitty and Matt. Kitty shook her head and Matt also declined. Seb shrugged, took one out for himself and returned the case to his pocket before lighting up. 'Wait, I seem to remember reading in some rag that you two had caught some murderer a few months ago. Don't tell me you're a female gumshoe, Kitty darling?' His tone was light, but Matt noticed there was a shrewd glint in his eye.

'You really are being too ridiculous, Seb. We're simply out having lunch on my day off. What brings you into Torquay today?' Kitty asked.

Seb glanced about the café and blew out a narrow plume of smoke. 'Rehearsals, darling, at the Pavilion and then Peter wanted to get his hair cut. Apparently, there's a rather good barber not far from the theatre.'

'Did everyone come to town?' Kitty smiled at Seb and Matt's jealousy spiked again, despite the inference at the intimate nature of Peter and Seb's friendship.

'Genny is faffing about rather with the fundraising and she's dragged Saira along. Peter's mother is rehearsing and playing propriety, of course, lest we all get into mischief. Larry and Tilly are rehearsing with Dickie and BeBe and sorting out the running order. Say, aren't you going to be lending a hand too?'

'I'll be there on Thursday. I do have to work at the hotel too, as well you know.'

'You must have been at the theatre quite early?' Matt asked. Any of them could have gone to see Salome and killed her if they were all in the town. At the moment, he wasn't inclined to tell Seb that Salome had been murdered. He wanted to see what the man would say without being on his guard. This was a precious opportunity to quiz a member of the house party.

Seb pulled a face. 'Ugh, tell me about it. Genny is a positive slave driver. We were all up at the crack of dawn lugging costumes and props into the cars. Celeste and Stanley were at the theatre early with Genny. Peter and I pootled along later, and Stanley went back to meet the colonel. Laurence and Tilly were last to arrive, with Saira.'

'I'm looking forward to seeing the rehearsals. It's all terribly exciting. I suppose Dickie and BeBe will be starring?' Kitty asked.

'Oh darling, please, the arguments about who should get star billing have been endless. Tilly feels she should be top as she's a film star, don't you know, and BeBe thinks she's Josephine Baker. Then Celeste used to be a huge music hall star, but she won't reveal her actual act until the night of the show, so poor old Larry Tilney is pulling his hair out. Peter and I are doing song and dance with a spot of comedy, but we are keeping well out of the billing war. There's a local magician and a fire-eater too, plus the am-dram lot, so quite a show.'

'It should raise a lot of money for the orphanage. Genny said ticket sales are going well.' Kitty gave a delicate cough as some smoke drifted her way.

'Sorry, darling.' Seb extinguished the end of his cigarette in the glass ashtray on the table. 'Yes, some of the children are in the show as part of the am-dram act. Well, I'd better push off. Peter will be finished at the barber's and we have to collect Saira and take her out and amuse her. Celeste's orders.' He jumped up and shook hands once more with Matt before kissing Kitty on the cheek as he made his farewells.

'That was interesting,' she remarked as Seb left the café.

'Yes, very.' Matt appeared thoughtful.

'Admit it, you couldn't wait to finally be able to grill one of the Davenports' guests,' Kitty teased.

'He's a rum cove, I swear he was wearing make-up. I suppose most theatrical people do.'

She laughed aloud. 'Yes, from my own limited experience of booking acts for the hotel and when they have stayed, they are a little eccentric, to say the least.' That was something of an under-statement. Her grandmother had been forced to have very stern words with some of the acts that had stayed at the hotel.

'I thought it best not to mention Salome's death. Inspector Greville might wish to explore their alibis and it could interfere with the investigation if they were pre-warned.'

'I thought the same thing. I'd love to know if anyone else received a letter from Salome. Laurence Tilney perhaps. I wish Greville would tell us,' Kitty mused. 'She must have written to others besides Peter, and if she didn't, then maybe he's our man.'

Matt signalled the waitress to bring the bill. 'Seb and Peter are very close. It could just as easily be Seb, I suppose, if you are correct about the nature of the secret they wish to hide. It affects them both equally.'

Kitty waited for Matt to pay for their lunch and the waitress to leave the table. 'Yes, he's quite possessive of his friend and always slightly disparaging about Saira. I think Genny has a bit of a secret pash on Seb, too. She's doomed to disappointment, isn't she?' She pulled on her gloves and collected her handbag, checking to make sure she hadn't left anything at the table. 'I'm almost certain that the drawing she didn't want me to see the other day was a sketch of Seb.'

Matt held open the door of the café for Kitty to pass through onto the pavement. 'Really? I rather formed the impression just now that he wasn't too enamoured of her, despite his affection for her brother.'

'She always says quite cutting things about him too but at the same time she constantly looks for him. I really don't think he's interested in her, though. I rather think Saira hit the nail on the head about Peter and Seb.'

They fell into step and crossed the road to walk next to the sea along the promenade towards the theatre and pleasure garden.

'Yes, I'm inclined to think you're right, despite Seb's attentions to you,' Matt said.

Kitty blushed.

Their stroll had taken them around the back of the theatre by this time and closer to the railings overlooking the sea. They paused for a moment to admire the view, staring out at the tide which had begun to creep up the curved red sand beach which lay a few feet below them. A couple of children were busy making sandcastles and a small dog was barking at the waves.

'Poor Genny will indeed be sadly disappointed then, if she hasn't realised.' Matt glanced at Kitty.

She gave a slight shrug. 'There seems little love lost between brother and sister. I don't know if she chooses not to see what is under her nose or if she is very naïve. Peter is clearly the favourite child of the family and poor Genny is left to her charitable works.'

A gull wheeled overhead, screeching into the sea breeze that tugged at Kitty's hat, threatening to tear it loose from her head.

'Come, it's growing cooler and we have still to find a taxi to take us back to Dartmouth, unless you would rather ride the omnibus?' Matt suggested, offering her his arm once more.

She knew Matt would dislike being sandwiched on a crowded bus even more than he liked being closed in the rear of a car. 'Taxi?

I don't mind having the windows down to let the air in.' She smiled at him. A frisson of electricity coursed through her as she accepted his support. She wondered if there might be a repetition of the kiss they had shared previously.

They turned back and started to walk towards the concert hall once more, passing the large ornamental fountain and the flower-beds filled with late summer colour still. Kitty placed her hand on Matt's arm. 'There is Mrs Davenport with Genny now, just leaving the theatre. If we quicken our steps, we might catch them.'

She had spotted Celeste Davenport's tall, elegantly slim figure next to Genny's shorter, dumpier one walking out of the small pale green side door to the Pavilion. She raised her hand and waved to try and catch Genny's attention. Her ploy worked and mother and daughter waited for them to catch up.

'Kitty, and Captain Bryant, how marvellous to see you both,' Genny exclaimed, her cheeks flushing an unbecoming shade of red which clashed with her puce-coloured hat.

Mrs Davenport looked slightly less enthusiastic to greet them, barely shaking Matt's hand but favouring Kitty with a smile.

'We ran into Seb earlier while we were at lunch, and he said you had all been busy rehearsing.' Kitty pretended not to notice Celeste's disinclination to talk to them.

'Yes, there's so much to do still. We would have carried on for longer, but Mother is beginning to get one of her heads and that policeman turned up to talk to Laurence and Tilly, so we thought we might as well go home,' Genny explained breathlessly.

'I don't suppose you saw Peter at all, did you?' Mrs Davenport asked, directing the question more at Kitty than Matt.

'Seb said he had gone to the barber's.' Matt answered the question, forcing Celeste to look at him.

'Oh, I see. He was supposed to call back to the theatre for Saira. As it is, that policeman is busy talking to her as well as Larry and

Tilly. Luckily, they have agreed to bring her back to the house.' Mrs Davenport glanced at her watch. 'Our car is late.'

'Hobbs will be here in a moment, I'm sure, Mother. May we give you both a ride somewhere? Captain Bryant, are you returning home?' Genny asked, a delicate flush tinting her cheeks as she looked at Matt.

'Thank you, that's very kind but I have to see Kitty back to Dartmouth.' As Matt spoke, a large black Bentley pulled up to the kerb.

The driver, a youngish man in a dark green liveried uniform and peaked cap clambered out and came around to open the door for Celeste and Genny.

'I expect I shall see you on Thursday as arranged, Kitty?' Genny asked as her mother entered the car ahead of her.

'I'm looking forward to it,' Kitty assured her.

Genny smiled at them both as the chauffeur closed the door.

'Mrs Davenport was rather frosty, wasn't she? They didn't mention Salome, so Inspector Greville must be playing his cards very close to his chest at the moment,' Matt mused as the Bentley pulled away and Kitty waved farewell to Genny.

'I think Mrs Davenport still believes you are somehow complicit in Pearl's murder.' Kitty slipped her hand into the crook of Matt's arm as they continued on their way back into town and the taxi rank.

'Or she would rather I was the murderer so the spotlight would be lifted from her family and guests,' Matt suggested as he caught the attention of a taxi driver who was standing having a cigarette next to his taxicab.

The man immediately sprang into action, extinguishing his cigarette, straightening his muffler and cloth cap before opening the rear door of the cab for Kitty. She climbed inside, sliding across the leather back seat to make room for Matt.

The driver let them out at Kingswear so they could cross the river as foot passengers. The ferry was fairly quiet, with only a few vehicles and no other travellers. The breeze had stiffened, and Kitty was forced to hold the brim of her hat to keep it in place as the chain ferry groaned and clanked its way over the river. The breeze whipped up wavelets on the river surface and tiny particles of spray damped Kitty's skin.

The frontage of the Dolphin Hotel was easily visible from the ferry, the black and white half-timbered building standing out amongst its Georgian and Victorian neighbours.

Matt extended his hand to assist her to alight from the ferry onto the paved slope of the slipway. The stones were slippery underfoot from the lapping river water and she was glad of his support. The intimate moment they had shared after she'd read Mr Dawkins' letter floated back into her mind. She peeped at Matt and wondered if he felt the connection between them in the same way. The day had not turned out quite as she had anticipated, especially with the discovery of Salome's body. Memories of that scene were enough to drive thoughts of romance from anyone's head.

When Matt released her hand to open the doors to the Dolphin, she felt almost bereft. 'I must tell Grams that I'm back.'

'Excuse me, Captain Bryant, your mother wanted me to tell you that she is in the lounge taking tea.' The receptionist informed them as they approached the desk.

'Duty calls,' Matt smiled.

'Thank you for a lovely lunch.' Kitty smiled back and tried not to stare after him as he walked away towards the guest lounge to find his mother.

'I have your post for you here, Miss Kitty, and your grandmother is in her suite finishing the trade accounts.' The receptionist passed over a slim bundle of mail.

'Thank you, Mary.' Kitty took the letters and walked towards the elevator. She decided to take her outdoor things off in her room and tidy her hair before opening the post and finding her grandmother.

She dropped the bundle of envelopes onto the surface of her small polished wood dresser while she drew off her gloves and removed her hat. She took a seat in front of her dressing table mirror and sighed with despair at her windswept appearance. Once her hair was tidy once more, she collected up her post and began to leaf through the pile.

There were eight items; two were invoices, two were booking requests, two job applications and one letter from a kitchen supplier with a quote for some appliances. The final envelope had a local postmark and the envelope was typewritten.

She slit it open with her little brass paperknife, expecting to find another job application or the invoice from the local florist for the flower display in reception. A piece of white paper folded into quarters tumbled out. She smoothed it out and stifled a gasp as she read the contents.

Instead of the invoice she had expected, a message had been cut out of what appeared to be newspaper print and glued to the paper.

You think he's innocent. He's not. He killed her.

CHAPTER FIFTEEN

Kitty's hands trembled as she scanned the brief note for any kind of clue to who could possibly have sent it. She could only assume the message was aimed at Matt. Someone obviously believed he was a murderer. But who could have sent it? Someone she knew? One of the Davenport party? It could be almost anyone. She would have to show Matt the letter and tell Inspector Greville. How would Matt react? She folded it back up and replaced it inside the envelope.

The note had shaken her. Matt was no murderer, she knew that. She had known he was innocent from the first moment Mrs Craven had told her he had been arrested. Someone believed he was guilty, however. Or did they simply want to believe it because it suited them? Celeste Davenport appeared to believe it. She wondered what those people would think when the news of Salome's murder became public. Would it clear him in their minds, or would they believe he had killed both women?

Her little wooden cuckoo clock sounded the hour and she gathered up the other letters ready to go and see her grandmother. She locked the anonymous letter inside her jewel box. It wasn't something she wanted to share with Grams.

She arrived at her grandmother's suite just as she was closing her ledger. As usual, Mrs Treadwell was immaculately dressed, in a neat navy suit with a pale pink silk blouse. Her pearls were around her throat and her grey hair neatly styled in a bun at the nape of her neck. 'Kitty, darling, have you and Matt had a nice day?'

'A very interesting one. We had a lovely lunch at Bobby's café, but the morning was rather traumatic.' She perched herself on the end of her grandmother's sofa and gave her a carefully edited version of the day's events.

'Oh, my dear, that's dreadful. Has the inspector any idea who the miscreant might be?' her grandmother asked.

'I don't know. At least Matt cannot be a suspect this time as he was here at the hotel and then with me right up until they found the girl's body. This must help his cause.'

'That at least is some comfort. Matt's parents are most anxious that this case is solved soon, and he can return home. If it drags on, then it may also damage his business beyond repair. Patience is fretting that he may have to move elsewhere and start all over again.'

Kitty sighed, and hoped Matt's mother was wrong. 'Matt has gone to the guest lounge to take tea with his mother. She had left a message at the desk.'

Her grandmother quirked an immaculately arched eyebrow. 'Patience arrived earlier. I wanted to finish my work, so I arranged for her to take some refreshment downstairs. I am very fond of Patience, but I must confess, she can be a trifle tiresome.'

'Matt's father is quite fearsome,' Kitty observed with a wry smile.

'Don't tell me you are scared of General Bryant?'

Colour pinked Kitty's cheeks. 'Maybe just a little,' she confessed. She wondered what Matt's father would think of the contents of the note she'd received.

Her grandmother tidied away her work and locked her bureau. 'We had better go and see Patience before Mr Potter arrives to take her back across the river. She may be offended if I don't at least say hello.'

Kitty accompanied her grandmother as they walked together down the beautiful polished oak staircase into the hotel lobby and along the hall to the guest lounge. A small but comfortable room, it had a handsome marble fireplace and dark green velvet drapes. The armchairs and sofas were upholstered in floral chintz and set out in small groups so residents could sit and relax with a newspaper or book. A large wireless radio stood at the side of the room for guests to enjoy.

Mrs Bryant was seated beside the fireplace. A tiered stand containing a selection of dainty cucumber sandwiches and small cakes was in front of her. Kitty could see the green feather in her hat band waving as she talked animatedly to Matt.

He looked up as they entered the room and straightened in his seat. Mrs Bryant looked up and waved at Kitty and her grandmother. Matt stood to greet them.

'Patience, my dear, I'm so sorry not to have been able to join you sooner. I do hope my staff have made you comfortable?' Mrs Treadwell greeted her friend and took a seat next to her.

Matt smiled at Kitty and waited for her to take an armchair before resuming his own seat.

'Oh yes, this is a wonderful treat. Thank you so much. I hope I didn't disturb your work? I was quite bored at the house with Edward busy with his paperwork.' Patience waved her hand vaguely in the direction of the cake stand.

'I expect Father is anxious to return home?' Matt asked.

'Well, we both are, but until this ghastly business is resolved we feel we should stay to support you. I do wish this inspector fellow would make more progress on this case. It's quite absurd that you can't reside in your own home.' Patience huffed and adjusted the mink stole draped about her shoulders.

'Mother, the inspector will solve the case soon, I'm certain. It won't be long before I can return home,' Matt said.

'Inspector Greville is very highly thought of,' Kitty added.

Patience looked at her. 'That may be so, but to suspect Matthew of such a terrible crime is most reprehensible. The damage to his name and reputation, my dear.' She gave a delicate little shudder.

Matt's lips compressed into a thin line and Kitty guessed his mother's conversation before they had joined them had probably been on the same lines of complaint.

'Are you enjoying being in the area?' Kitty's grandmother asked. 'It's been such a long time since you were here last.'

Kitty released a silent sigh of relief at the change of topic. Suitably diverted, the chatter continued in an amicable fashion and she saw the tension gradually seep from Matt's shoulders. She debated if she should tell him about the note she'd received. He was under enormous strain and knowing someone believed him guilty would be most unpleasant.

By the time one of the maids appeared to inform Patience that her taxicab awaited her, Kitty had made up her mind. She would say nothing about the note to Matt for now. Instead, she would go to the police station and give the offending letter to Inspector Greville.

The receptionist signalled her as soon as she entered the lobby. 'Excuse me, Miss Kitty, but you're required on the telephone.'

'Thank you, Mary, I'll take it in the office.' She opened the small back office behind the desk where she conducted most of the hotel business and picked up the handset. Taking a seat, she waited for the call to be transferred.

'Kitty, what is this about the police finding the body of the other girl? This Salome person?' Mrs Craven's crisp tones sounded in her ear.

Kitty stifled a sigh and gave Mrs Craven a brief update, emphasising that Matt had a rock-solid alibi for the time of Salome's death.

'Well, I am most relieved to hear it. Perhaps the inspector will allow him to investigate the case now. It is most important that this person is caught.'

'I have been actively investigating on Matt's behalf and intend to continue.' Kitty was more than a little annoyed by Mrs Craven's implication that only Matt was capable of conducting the investigation. Especially when Mrs Craven had been all too quick to rope her into the enquiry in the first place.

'Celeste answered the telephone when I called to speak to Genevieve. She told me about Salome; apparently the police had been to the theatre and to the house and had questioned everyone. Laurence Tilney, Peter and Sebastian have all had to attend the police station. I can only assume that they consider one of them to be the main suspect. We must redouble our efforts on Thursday when we are at the theatre,' Mrs Craven declared.

Kitty gritted her teeth. Another day with Mrs Craven. 'I fully intend to find out as much as I can.'

'Yes well, I'm sure you'll try, dear. I'll see you on Thursday.'

'Argh, that wretched woman!' Kitty growled as the telephone went dead. She raked a hand through her hair, undoing the work she had put in earlier. Mrs Craven appeared intent on supervising her every move. However, instead of playing Watson to Kitty's Sherlock, it seemed Mrs Craven was intent on playing Sherlock herself.

Kitty was somewhat frustrated that neither she nor Matt heard anything more from Inspector Greville the next day. Matt was commandeered into spending the day with his parents and she had a lot of her own work to catch up on. She determined to take the note to the police station in Torquay on Thursday. Mrs Craven was to meet her at the theatre with the rest of the Davenport house party.

She took the earlier ferry crossing and caught the omnibus to take her into Torquay. Alighting near the harbour, she made her way through the town to the police station. The desk sergeant recognised her from her previous visits.

'May I help you, miss?'

'I need to speak to Inspector Greville if he is available. It's only for a moment.' She didn't want to take up too much of the inspector's time, but hoped she might manage to learn of his progress on the case before she went to the Pavilion.

The desk sergeant nodded and requested she take a seat on one of the simple dark wood chairs which stood against the plain cream wall of the front office. She perched herself down and looked around her with interest at the various posters on the wall for wanted persons while she waited for the sergeant to return.

He re-emerged through the small door behind the counter. 'The inspector can spare you a few minutes, Miss Underhay, if you would like to follow me.' He lifted a hinged area of the counter and Kitty stood and followed him through the dark green painted door. The sergeant led her a short way along the corridor to the small office she had visited before.

Inspector Greville rose to greet her. 'Miss Underhay, please take a seat.' He moved a sheaf of papers from the chair in front of his desk and added them to the precarious pile in his in-tray.

'I hope I am not disturbing you, Inspector. I appreciate that you are a busy man, but I had to bring this to you.' She opened her bag and took out the note she had received on Tuesday.

Inspector Greville's eyebrows rose slightly as he opened the envelope and perused the contents. 'Is Captain Bryant aware that you have received this?' he asked.

Kitty shook her head. 'No, Inspector. I didn't want to tell him. I can't believe that someone would send me such a thing.'

'He may even have received mail like this himself. In fact, I would be surprised if he has not, if they have sent this to you. Hate mail is not uncommon, unfortunately, when a culprit is still at large. People reason there is no smoke without fire. But then if he hasn't, why would someone feel the need to warn you but not send a note to Captain Bryant himself?' The inspector leaned back in his chair and steepled his hands together, surveying Kitty with a narrow gaze.

'I had not considered that.' Kitty frowned. 'It concerned me as I thought it must be from someone who knew we were friends, and therefore someone we knew.'

Inspector Greville's brow furrowed. 'That may be the case, or it may be from someone who is aware that you have been asking questions. Either they are warning you off or it is someone who believes Captain Bryant to be guilty.'

'I have not mentioned this note to anyone. I am expected at the Pavilion theatre shortly to assist Miss Davenport. Mrs Craven is also calling in – she is a member of many charitable boards, as I'm sure you're aware. She mentioned that Celeste Davenport said you had interviewed the members of the house party once more following Salome's death.' She waited for his response and hoped he might share some of what he had learned from those interviews.

'Yes, you probably saw that Miss Donohue's death was indeed murder. The newspapers were full of the story yesterday. As you are aware, Captain Bryant had to be considered as a suspect for Miss Bright's murder.' He held up his hand to stop Kitty from protesting. 'However, he has a solid alibi for the killing of Miss Donohue. I did not realistically believe that he was culpable but like I said before, I have to be seen to be completely impartial. It will not be enough in this case to simply catch the murderer. There will always be those who will say there is no smoke without fire or that Captain Bryant was somehow treated leniently. In order to prevent this and to ensure that when this sorry affair is concluded Matthew is not only cleared but is seen to be completely exonerated, it is vital that he does not become involved in the investigation or become linked to the Davenport family and their guests.'

'You are convinced then, Inspector Greville, that one of the house party is our man?' Kitty's mind raced.

'Laurence Tilney has now also admitted to receiving a note from Salome similar to the one Peter Davenport received. I interviewed several members of the house party here at the station to try to obtain more information. Mrs Tilney has burnt the letter unfortunately; she is, it seems, a very jealous woman. However, it was couched in the same vague terms as the one received by Peter Davenport.'

'Interesting,' Kitty mused. She wondered what secret Laurence Tilney might be hiding from his wife that he did not wish to leak out. 'What did Doctor Carter say about Salome's death? Was there anything to indicate whether we were looking for a man or a woman?' A jealous wife could easily have killed two potential rivals for her husband's affections and for trying to steal her acting glory. Tilly was very much the leading lady.

The inspector appeared to consider his reply before answering. 'In confidence, Miss Underhay, Salome had been given some kind of sedative in the champagne, hence she did not struggle as much as one might have expected when her assailant held her under water in her bath.'

'Then it could be a woman,' Kitty said. Whoever killed Pearl may even have strangled her in the car, then driven her to the golf course and tipped her out. A woman could easily do that.

'Remember, a witness said he thought he saw a skinny man in a suit with a cap and muffler near the house around the time we believe Salome was killed. Another thing, a fisherman, night fishing in the bay at the time Pearl was killed has also come forward to say he saw lights moving on the cliff top corresponding with the position of the eleventh tee at about two in the morning.'

'The car headlights?' Kitty asked.

Inspector Greville nodded. 'Very likely, he noticed them because it was so unusual and he knows there is no road up there, just the dirt track through the wood. If the Davenport's chauffeur hadn't been so thorough cleaning the cars, we may have discovered something.'

'There was a missing blanket,' Kitty said.

To her surprise, the inspector looked a little uncomfortable. 'Again, this is confidential, Miss Underhay, but the blanket was recovered. A sequin on the blanket matched those on the bodice of the victim's dress.'

Kitty frowned. 'Really, where?'

'In an outbuilding at Captain Bryant's house.'

She gasped out loud. 'But that is ridiculous. It must have been planted there.'

'I am inclined to agree, Miss Underhay. Someone wants us to believe Captain Bryant is guilty and is keen to keep him in the frame. Please convince him to remain at the Dolphin for a little longer. I know his parents would like him to return to his home, but I need him to stay away for now, for his own safety. There is still a great deal of public interest in these deaths. I want no hints that the investigation is not being carried out with proper propriety and standards.'

Kitty swallowed. 'I understand.'

'If you or Captain Bryant receive any more of this kind of mail, please ensure it comes to me. Be very careful, Miss Underhay; whoever killed Pearl and Salome is ruthless and I believe would have no compunction about killing again to protect themselves. Be on your guard.' His tone was sombre, and Kitty could tell he was concerned for her well-being.

'I shall be most careful and discreet.' She gathered her bag and gloves, aware she had trespassed on his time for long enough.

'Thank you, Miss Underhay.' The inspector showed her to the outer office.

She smiled at the desk sergeant and stepped out into the street, her mind busy with the new information she had just learned. A quick glance at her wristwatch told her she needed to hurry if she was not to be late meeting Genny at the Pavilion theatre.

The streets were busy as she hurried through the town towards the harbour and pleasure gardens. The chill air of earlier had begun to lift and the sun had pushed its way through the clouds to give some warmth. Ahead of her, the sea sparkled in the sunshine and the boats moored in the harbour made gentle jangling metallic sounds from their masts in the breeze.

The theatre was a white, modern building, trimmed with pale green decorative tile to match the art deco stained-glass windows. The roof was domed and made of glass with bronze figures at various points around the top of the building.

Dickie and BeBe were about to enter the theatre as Kitty arrived, slightly out of breath, at the foot of the shallow flight of steps leading to the front door.

'Well hello, Miss Underhay, has Genny co-opted you for duties here too?' Dickie greeted her cheerfully but BeBe didn't appear so pleased to see her.

'Yes, she said she was struggling with everything that needed to be done so she and Mrs Craven have prevailed on my good nature to come and help out.' Kitty smiled at them both.

'You are not a performer yourself, then?' BeBe asked.

'Heavens no, I would be simply awful. I admire people like yourselves who are so talented. I believe I am here merely to assist with prompts and props.'

BeBe appeared to relax at this announcement and favoured Kitty with a tight-lipped smile. 'Then I'm sure you will be kept very busy, Miss Underhay.'

'Please, call me Kitty,' she said as she followed them inside the theatre and wondered what she had let herself in for.

CHAPTER SIXTEEN

The heels of her patent black T-bar shoes clicked across the marble tiled floor of the lobby. Mrs Craven was already present and waiting for her.

'Kitty, where have you been? I could have asked Mr Potter to collect you; we could have shared a car.' Mrs Craven adjusted her fox fur stole and fixed her with an accusing gaze.

'I'm terribly sorry, I had to run a few errands in town first.' She was relieved to see Genny arrive, panting, into the lobby, as out of breath as if she had sprinted all the way to the theatre.

'Oh, am I late? So sorry, I had to get all the boxes from the car.' Genny had dressed with her usual calamitous style, wearing a floral print dress in an ugly shade of mauve, teamed with a lime green hat.

'Did you need some assistance?' Kitty asked.

'No, it's all fine. Seb and Peter have just arrived and they've taken the boxes to the stage door for me.' Genny beamed. 'Rather lucky, really. Mother has gone with them to make jolly sure they put them in the right dressing rooms.' She glanced at her watch. 'Larry and Tilly will be here shortly, too. Saira offered to lend a hand but she's had to spend some time with her father this morning as he's not feeling too well again.'

'Dickie and BeBe were at the door when I arrived. I don't know if you're expecting anyone else?' Kitty asked.

'Um, no, I don't think so, not for today's run-through. Kitty, would you mind awfully making sure everyone has drinks while I sort out the flyers and ticketing things for Millicent? The kitchen area is backstage, just off from the dressing room corridor. Every-thing you need is in there.' Genny began to peer around her in her familiar vague manner.

'Of course.' Normally Kitty might have been a little put-out at her role as tea girl but it was such an excellent opportunity to snoop about and ask questions, she was actually quite pleased at the suggestion.

She left Genny and Mrs Craven in the foyer and walked through the double light-oak and stained-glass doors into the body of the theatre. The seats were an elegant dark blue crushed velvet to match the curtain across the stage. Huge palms in pots stood at the back of the auditorium beside the white pillars, which rose to the ornate plasterwork on the ceiling. A balcony ran around the space where the upper floor of the stalls was housed.

It was not a large concert hall, but it was very elegant and perfect for the kind of entertainment Genny had planned. Kitty noticed a door near the stage by the area marked out for the orchestra. She pushed through to discover herself in a small side lobby. A flight of carpeted stairs let to the upper stalls, one door led to the outside of the theatre and the other door had to lead to the backstage area.

She went through this door and immediately heard voices coming from the dressing areas which she surmised must be behind the stage.

'Mother, what on earth has Genny put in those blessed boxes? They weigh an absolute ton.' Peter's voice reached her as she peeped though a partly open door and discovered a tiny room, not much larger than a cupboard, which clearly served as a kitchen.

There was a small sink, a tray of cups and saucers, a little spirit stove with a kettle and a bottle of milk standing in a bowl of ice-cold water. A caddy of tea and a bowl of sugar stood on a miniscule worktop.

Kitty stowed her gloves inside her handbag and hung it on the hook at the back of the door. A pale blue pinafore was also on the hook, so she took that and put it on. It was on the large side, but it would serve to protect her dress.

While she busied herself with filling the kettle and lighting the stove, she continued to listen.

'She says she's here to help Genny.' BeBe's voice.

'Well, be careful darling, she was having lunch with that fellow who was arrested for murdering Pearl, and according to the police, that was when Salome was killed.' Seb's voice floated down the corridor.

'I thought he had been cleared by the police.' She thought that was Dickie.

'Well, if he's in the clear then that policeman will be looking for someone else to pin it on.' Seb again.

'Salome's murder was all over the papers. There were reporters waiting outside the house again this morning. Father is simply furious; he was telephoning the chief constable as I left. I half expect the press to turn up here.' She guessed that was Peter's voice.

'Peterkins, all publicity is good publicity,' Seb reproved.

'I wish Father agreed. All he's concerned about is his perishing knighthood.'

'Your father has worked hard for his knighthood. He deserves to be recognised.' Celeste Davenport's tone was sharp.

Kitty decided to make a bit of noise in her little kitchen by clanging the lid of the brown-enamelled tin teapot in the sink. It had the desired effect when Seb pushed open the door and peered at her, his hand placed over his heart in a suitably dramatic fashion.

'Kitty, darling girl, is that tea I see before me?'

'I was just getting everything ready. Genny asked me to make drinks while we waited for the Tilneys to arrive.' She was careful not to give any indication that she had overheard any of the conversation.

Celeste Davenport appeared in the corridor behind Seb. 'I'll have coffee if you're making drinks.' She raised her elegantly arched eyebrows at Kitty's attire.

Seb rolled his eyes and Kitty stifled a giggle. 'Of course, Mrs Davenport.'

She filled the teapot and loaded everything onto the wooden trolley she'd discovered in the curtained recess under the mini sink. Once out in the corridor, she found that Genny had thoughtfully labelled all the dressing rooms so she could see who was where.

Peter, Seb and Dickie were sharing the room nearest to the kitchenette. BeBe was sharing with Celeste although Kitty was amused to see a curtain on a wire divided their room in half. Tilly Tilney had her own room, which someone had labelled with a hand-drawn star.

The other acts had the remaining two dressing rooms. One other small room was hung with rails of costumes and boxes stood on the floor and Kitty guessed this must be the props area. She dispensed tea, biscuits and coffee for Celeste as she made her way along the corridor. She had decided not to ask anything until later in the day, after what she'd overheard. It would be better to keep a low profile for a while. Her grandmother's adage about eavesdroppers not hearing good of themselves made her smile to herself.

Mrs Craven bustled into the doorway of the kitchenette as Kitty washed up the crockery and the artistes headed for the auditorium.

'Well, what have you learned so far?' she asked in a stage whisper which probably reached the lobby.

'Mrs Davenport prefers coffee.' Kitty dried her hands on the linen tea cloth.

'Please don't be facetious, Kitty.' Mrs Craven glared at her.

'I'm sorry, Mrs Craven, but it's important to build up trust in these matters. They are already suspicious of me as they know of my connection to Matt.' Kitty kept her voice low and hoped there was no one around backstage to overhear her.

'Well, I suppose Captain Bryant has given you instructions on how to proceed. Personally, I would be more assertive in the matter.' She adjusted her furs as she spoke. 'Now, I have to deliver some more flyers to various places around the town and I have a meeting to chair for the ladies' guild so I hope you will make some progress in my absence.'

Kitty thought it highly likely she would make considerably more progress without Mrs Craven supervising her every move. 'I'll do my best,' she said.

The older woman looked at her suspiciously, as if she thought Kitty was being sarcastic. Kitty returned her gaze with wide-eyed innocence.

'Very well, I shall call back for you at three-thirty, then you can tell me anything you have discovered on the journey back to Dartmouth.'

Kitty heaved a sigh of relief once she had gone. Her jaw ached from where she had been grinding her teeth and fake smiling. Her chore completed, she ventured back along the corridor to the auditorium to find Genny.

Laurence Tilney was in the orchestra area with his shirt sleeves rolled up. Dickie was at the piano and Tilly was parading about the stage. Seb and Peter were lolling about on the seats next to the orchestra area and a cross-looking BeBe stood smoking a cigarette in a long ebony holder to one side, next to a red fire bucket full of sand. Celeste was nowhere in sight and Kitty wondered if she had accompanied Mrs Craven to the ladies' guild luncheon.

'What's happening?' Kitty murmured to BeBe.

The singer dropped the remains of her cigarette into the fire bucket. 'Tilly is ensuring that all the lighting is set to favour her and her performance. The rest of us get to watch the amazing Tilly show and waste our time.'

'What is she doing exactly?' Kitty asked.

'For the show, you mean?' BeBe shrugged. 'Some piece from Shakespeare and then, "to show her versatility", she sings.'

It was clear from her expression that BeBe didn't rate Tilly as either an actress or a singer.

'I didn't realise Tilly sang,' Kitty remarked.

'She doesn't, darling. It's like a crow squawking.' Seb had come to join them, draping his arms about BeBe and Kitty's shoulders.

Peter yawned, stretched and came over to them. 'Oh, the Tilly show is going on rather.' He exchanged a glance with Seb.

'She is the star, darling,' Seb said, and made a face of mock adoration.

BeBe rolled her eyes.

'I'm stepping out to get some air, this could go on for ages. Is anyone coming?' Peter looked at Seb.

'Right with you, dear boy.'

The two men vanished through the side door, leaving Kitty with BeBe.

'Do you know where Genny has gone? I don't know what jobs she wants me to do next.' Kitty peered around the concert hall.

'She was sending Mrs Davenport and the other woman off in the car on some errand or other. I expect she'll be back in a minute or two.' BeBe sounded disinterested.

'I'm looking forward to your performance.' Kitty wanted to flatter BeBe a little to see if she would be more forthcoming. It wasn't a lie; she had enjoyed what she'd heard and seen of BeBe's act at the Davenports' fundraiser.

The other woman glanced at her as if judging whether her comment was genuine. 'Thank you.'

'Poor Dickie looks bored,' Kitty remarked and wondered how she could turn the conversation towards Salome and Pearl's murders.

'Dickie is a really good musician. He composes a lot of his own stuff, too.' BeBe drew another cigarette from the slim silver case she had in her bag and slotted it into her holder.

'I take it you aren't living locally anymore? I know most of the performers, as I book them for the hotel through a theatrical agency.'

BeBe blew out a thin stream of smoke. 'I'm originally from Plymouth, and Dickie has family here in the Bay, but we're based mainly in London now as there is more work there. We agreed to do this performance for Genny as a favour for the Davenports and it gives Dickie the opportunity to see some of his family.'

'I believe the Davenports own a number of theatrical venues in London?' Kitty asked.

'Yes, London and Brighton, so it pays to keep in with them as it means you get in the shows. They hold a lot of influence.' BeBe winced as Dickie started to play for Tilly and the actress began to sing.

Kitty winced as well as Tilly failed to hit a note and the music was halted while Tilly demanded a different key. 'I suppose that's why those two girls were hanging around at the party then, if they were hoping to get spotted.'

BeBe shrugged. 'Probably, and of course with Larry casting for a new film then everyone wants to be friends with the Tilneys. I suppose they hope some of that stardust will rub off on them.'

'Tilly doesn't look as if she would be very impressed with anyone wanting star status that might take some of her shine,' Kitty suggested.

BeBe snorted. 'Too right; she is very possessive of Larry. There is only one star in that relationship and that is Tilly.'

'Then she might be very jealous of young actresses like Pearl and Salome?'

BeBe extinguished her cigarette and turned to face Kitty. 'Very jealous.'

'Enough to murder them?' Kitty asked.

Tilly hit another duff note and once again the piano music was halted.

BeBe shrugged. 'Maybe.'

CHAPTER SEVENTEEN

Genny emerged from through the main doors leading from the lobby and hurried towards Kitty.

'Miss Underhay, thank you so much for sorting out the refreshments. Shall I take you and show you the prop room and the costumes now?' She consulted the sheet of paper in her hand. 'I have the running order here for the show so you'll need to ensure people have the right items at the correct time.'

Kitty accompanied Genny to the small room she'd found earlier with the costume rails and boxes.

'I really am terribly grateful to you for helping me with all of this.' Genny gave her the list which told her who was to appear when and the items required for each act. 'Everything needs sorting out and labelling ready. I had hoped we'd have a better rehearsal today, but Tilly is such a perfectionist and Larry of course is a professional so one can't hurry them along.'

'It must make things very difficult,' Kitty soothed. 'It must have made things worse having the police taking up so much time with their enquiries.'

Genny blinked behind her glasses. 'Oh dear, yes, that poor girl, Salome. Discovered in her bath I believe. It could have been an accident, I suppose. It's just too horrid, isn't it, to think it could be anything else. Peter and Seb were very upset when that inspector talked to them and Larry became quite angry. They all spent hours at the police station. Poor Father is terribly annoyed about the press people hanging around outside the house and Mother is still saying Captain Bryant must be involved but I think that's a nonsense, don't you?'

Kitty smiled. 'Very much a nonsense. Why does your mother persist in believing he's involved? It must be obvious by now that he isn't.'

Genny frowned and pushed her glasses more firmly into place on the bridge of her nose. 'I don't know. Mother has always had these irrational ideas; she can't help it. She's very highly strung. It's the artistic temperament, Peter is the same way. Luckily, Daddy and I have always been the practical ones in the family.'

'I'm surprised that Larry was angry about being questioned by the police. He didn't really know Pearl or Salome, did he?' Kitty started to open some of the boxes of props and costumes.

'Well, between you and me, I think he knew them rather better than he let on. Darling Tilly is a very jealous woman though and she guards access to Larry.' Genny raised her brows and gave a meaningful nod.

'Oh, you think there was some kind of liaison between the girls and Larry?' Kitty said, careful to hint at surprise at this information.

'At the party,' Genny added. 'I can't say for certain as I wasn't downstairs for long, but I could have sworn he gave Tilly the slip and was off with those girls. I saw them together in the garden.'

Kitty stored that titbit of information away in her memory to share with Matt. It seemed both of the Tilneys might have a motive for getting rid of Salome and Pearl. A slender one, admittedly, but finally she felt as though her investigation was moving forwards.

Genny left Kitty to continue unboxing, sorting and labelling. She hung the costumes on hangers and labelled them accordingly. It looked as if some could use a good pressing and she decided to ask Alice if she would assist her. It would be nice to have Alice with her anyway. When she had stayed at Enderley Hall it had made all the difference, having the young girl with her. Plus, Alice loved a mystery.

Her stomach started to rumble, reminding her that it had been a long time since breakfast. Leaving her task, she went back to the kitchenette and refilled the kettle. She had packed a wax paper parcel of cheese sandwiches and an apple in her bag before leaving the hotel. While she waited for the kettle to boil, the rising sounds of an argument reached her from a nearby dressing room.

She pulled the door open a crack so she could hear more clearly. It sounded as if the voices were coming from Tilly's dressing room. In the distance she could hear Dickie playing BeBe's music.

'For heaven's sake, Tilly, why not simply stick to the Shakespeare?'

Kitty privately agreed with Larry. Tilly would be better if she didn't sing, especially as the running order at present showed her following BeBe, who was a very talented singer.

'Darling, I have to showcase my talent. My audience expects it, especially after the last film. They'll want me to sing.'

Kitty recalled that Tilly's last film had been a musical number.

'You didn't sing though, did you, darling? Your voice was dubbed. It's going to be obvious it wasn't you.' Larry sounded frustrated.

'You said the dubbing was done for purely technical reasons. I'm the star of this little show and don't you forget it. People pay good money to see me, that's why they back your films.' Tilly's voice rose.

'They back my films because they make money. And your films aren't as popular as they were. There are newer, younger girls out there. Fresh faces.' Kitty held her breath as Larry's reply was followed by the banging about of objects.

'Oh, like those two girls that were killed, I suppose. I saw the way you looked at them. Do you think I didn't notice? Ten a penny, two-bit tarts!' Tilly's voice rose to a shriek.

Kitty rescued her kettle from the stove before it could begin to whistle and alert the Tilneys to her presence in the kitchenette.

'I barely spoke to them.'

'I saw you. I saw you go off with them into the garden before the scavenger hunt started. You disgust me.' Tilly's voice rose from a hiss to a shout.

'Keep your voice down. That girl is somewhere about and it's obvious she's snooping.'

Kitty had to strain to hear Larry's response. Her face flamed – so much for priding herself on being discreet with her questioning. She poured herself some tea and tucked into her sandwiches. She had no intention of leaving the kitchenette until the coast was clear.

She heard nothing else from Larry and Tilly, so finished her lunch and cup of tea in peace. Genny had been right about Larry and his contact with the murdered girls. Her next task had to be to try and get more information from Seb and Peter. Larry was obviously wary of her and would be unlikely to volunteer any information. With any luck, Mrs Craven might find out something useful from Celeste during the ladies' luncheon.

Peter and Seb were on stage rehearsing when she went back into the auditorium. BeBe and Dickie had gone, leaving the hall empty except for the lighting technician up in the gallery at the back of the theatre. She took a seat in the stalls in front of the stage to watch them run through their stand-up comedy act. Peter played a working-class quick-witted straight man and Seb was his upper-class, slow-witted friend.

They bowed in her direction as she applauded at the end of their run-through.

'Thank you, thank you, don't applaud, throw money,' Seb called.

'What did you think, Miss Underhay?' Peter asked.

'You are both terribly good. It was very funny.' Kitty smiled at them as they bounded down the steps at the side of the stage to come and join her.

'You really think so?' Peter asked. 'It's been quite a while since we reprised that little turn and we haven't performed the newer material till now.'

'Well, I thought it was super. You and Seb work together very well. Do you perform on stage when you're in London?' Kitty asked.

'Not so much as Petey would like,' Seb answered, giving his friend a glance.

'Father keeps me busy with the business end, profit and loss, booking shows and the like, so I don't get to perform as much as I would wish. He wants me to take over the business so that he can retire.' Peter's expression was downcast.

'That's a shame, you are very talented,' Kitty said. 'Perhaps Larry could cast you in one of his films. You'd make an excellent leading man. As would you, Seb.' She wondered at first if she'd overdone the compliments, but she wanted to get them talking to her and she knew they were on their guard.

'Getting into film is an ambition of ours,' Peter confided.

'Absolutely,' Seb agreed. 'We intend to go out to California with Larry next month and he's going to introduce us to a few people. There may be an agent friend of his coming to see this show.'

'How exciting.' Kitty could see they were both enthusiastic about the idea. 'Are your parents keen on the movies too?' She directed her question to Peter.

He rolled his eyes and immediately looked glum. 'Father is so old-fashioned. It's getting harder to fill the theatres these days; everyone wants to attend the cinemas instead. As for Mother, she resists the idea of my going anywhere or doing anything. She keeps hinting at grandchildren. I think she's given up on Genny ever marrying.'

Seb gave him a sympathetic pat on his back.

'Perhaps that's why she's so keen on you marrying Saira?' Kitty suggested. She couldn't help thinking that Genny would be a better person to run the business than Peter. Then he would be free to act.

'She has this mad idea that I need to settle down, produce heirs, become a businessman.' Peter looked and sounded even more despondent.

'What are your father's views?' Kitty was curious to confirm Peter's possible motive for murdering Pearl and Salome. It seemed to her from Peter and Seb's interactions with each other that Peter was unlikely to be interested in the girls in a sexual way. Everything seemed to confirm Saira's opinion. And if the two had ambitions in the film industry, that left them with a very strong motive for keeping the truth hidden.

'Father thinks I'm wasting my time looking at the movie industry. His world is that of the theatres and music halls. He met Mother when she was appearing on stage. He knows Saira's father from years ago and she seems a nice enough girl.' Peter's voice tailed off and he sighed.

'Kitty!' Mrs Craven's clarion tones called from the doors at the top of the hall.

'I'd better collect my bag and return this lovely apron.' Kitty smiled at Peter and Seb.

Seb winked at her. 'Must you? It's frightfully flattering.'

'Coming,' she called back to Mrs Craven who appeared deep in conversation with Genny.

Kitty slipped back to the kitchenette and returned the borrowed pinafore before collecting her coat, hat and bag from the back of the door. She strolled back through the auditorium to meet Mrs Craven.

'Do come along, Kitty, Mr Potter is waiting for us.'

'Thank you so much for your help, Kitty. I'll telephone you with the schedule once I've finalised what else needs completing before the performance.' Genny consulted her notebook.

'Of course. Shall I ask one of the girls from the hotel to come with me to assist with the costumes? Alice is a dab hand with a hot iron and a needle.'

Genny's eyes lit up. 'Oh, that would be super. The more assistance, the better.'

Mrs Craven looked pointedly at her watch and tapped her toe impatiently. 'Come, Kitty, we really must get going.'

'Of course.' Genny escorted them out of the theatre to where Mr Potter awaited them in his taxicab.

'Now, tell me everything,' Mrs Craven commanded as soon as they were installed in the back of the car and on the road towards Kingswear.

Kitty obliged her and told her what she'd learned from the others. 'And did you learn anything from Mrs Davenport?' she asked.

'Oh, my dear, that woman. At least there was no alcohol served at the luncheon, although I am certain Celeste had a hip flask concealed in her handbag. She is most unhappy that Captain Bryant appears to have an alibi. I think she believed it would remove any scrutiny of her family and friends if someone external was suspected. The press, I gather, are constantly at the gate. It is perhaps as well that Matthew is staying at the Dolphin. Celeste is also not fond of Sebastian's friendship with Peter and believes him to be a bad influence. Which, considering what you have just told me about the nature of their relationship, well...' Mrs Craven paused for breath.

'And yet she is still pushing for an engagement between Peter and Saira?' Kitty asked as the taxi swept down the hill towards the station and jetty for the ferry at Kingswear.

'She seems completely set upon it.'

Kitty raised her eyebrows. 'Yet neither Peter nor Saira are keen.'

'The girl has money and her father is very ill, I believe. As for Peter,' Mrs Craven lowered her voice and glanced towards Mr Potter's back, 'with those nefarious rumours abroad...' Colour mounted in her cheeks.

'I understand your meaning; she believes it will silence them if Peter is a married man?'

Mrs Craven pursed her lips. 'Any evidence of unnatural and illegal practises could end in a prosecution if Peter is not careful.'

'It would explain why Celeste is pushing for an engagement, especially if her husband hopes for a peerage. It could allay some of the talk,' Kitty suggested.

'But how does this connect to the deaths of those two young women?' Mrs Craven asked as the car bumped its way up the ramp onto the ferry for the short river crossing.

'Hmm, both Peter and Seb would be at risk of blackmail from unscrupulous parties if there were any evidence of their relationship. Then a prosecution and the ensuing scandal would be quite awful,' Kitty mused.

Her companion was silent for a moment as the vessel swayed slightly in the current at the centre of the river. 'Yes, that would definitely give them a motive, either as individuals or acting together.'

The ferry bumped to a gentle halt on the Dartmouth bank and the ferrymen lowered the ramp so their car could drive up the slipway and into town. Mr Potter drew the car to a halt outside the Dolphin Hotel.

'You will of course ensure that Captain Bryant is made aware of our discoveries?' Mrs Craven instructed as Mr Potter opened the car door for Kitty to get out.

'Yes, Mrs Craven,' Kitty assured her.

Mrs Craven appeared satisfied with her response and Mr Potter drove off. Kitty heaved a sigh of relief at being finally free of her unwanted fellow sleuth and went inside the hotel.

She was surprised at how exhausted she felt. It wasn't so much the work itself that had been tiring, rather it had been the constant watching, listening and being on her guard that had drained her energy the most.

*

Matt had waited for Kitty in the lobby. He had spent a frustrating day with his parents and was eager to discover if Kitty had managed to gather any new information. The sooner his name was completely clear, and his parents were able to return to their own home, the better it would be for all of them.

He could see from the droop of her shoulders that she was tired. 'Kitty, come and sit down.' He pulled out one of the plush chairs at the table in the far corner of the lobby and Kitty sank down into it with a sigh. Matt walked to the reception desk and requested refreshments.

When he returned to the table, Kitty had removed her hat and had discreetly slipped off her shoes under the table.

'Tea is on the way. I take it you've had a rough day?' He could see there were smudges of fatigue below her eyes.

She smiled. 'You could say that.' She told him all she'd learned at the theatre, carefully leaving out her earlier visit to the police station.

'Well done, old girl.'

Alice appeared bearing a tea tray, which she set down on the table in front of them.

'Just the person. Alice, I have the most enormous favour to ask of you.' Kitty told the maid of her involvement with the charity and the reasons why she'd become involved.

'Oh, I'd be happy to help, Miss Kitty. It'll be exciting, like when we were at your aunt and uncle's house. It was like being in a film, that was.' Alice's thin face flushed.

Matt did his best to appear stern. 'You appreciate it may be dangerous, Alice. Whoever killed those two young women will probably not hesitate to kill again if they feel threatened so you must be careful. You and Kitty.' He glanced at his companion hoping she wouldn't take his warning amiss.

'Oh yes, sir, I understand. I shall be very careful.'

Alice hurried off back to her duties. Matt picked up the teapot and strainer and poured them both tea into the delicate china cups.

'I'm glad Alice has agreed to accompany you to the theatre.' He added milk to the tea.

'I would rather have Alice than the indefatigable Mrs Craven,' Kitty said.

Matt added sugar to his tea and stirred. 'It seems there are plenty of people who may have motives but without any real proof that either Pearl or Salome were posing some kind of threat then it is all supposition.'

Kitty took a sip of her tea. 'I know. Find the evidence and I think we will have our killer.'

'It occurs to me that we still don't know if there was anything in either Pearl or Salome's possessions that could provide a motive for their murders.'

Kitty helped herself to one of the biscuits that had accompanied their tea. 'True. Even if there had been something, the murderer may have already found it and destroyed it.'

Matt frowned. 'If Pearl had something in her possession then whoever killed her for it must not have discovered it, or thought Salome either had it or had knowledge of it.'

Kitty leaned forward in her seat. 'Salome left most of her possessions at her original lodging house so if she did have something, she may have left it there rather than taking it with her. Did the inspector follow it up, do you think?'

He finished his tea and set the cup down. 'May I use your telephone? I'll call Inspector Greville.'

Kitty handed him the key to her office so he could telephone in private. Matt unlocked the door and went to Kitty's desk to make the call and tell the inspector what Kitty had learned and their thoughts on whether there might be something in Pearl or Salome's possessions that a murderer might be searching for.

Inspector Greville listened, making small sounds of encouragement which appeared to denote his interest in the information. 'There was nothing out of the ordinary amongst Miss Bright's possessions that I recall, but Miss Donohue may have been through them before we got there. They were at the same lodging house originally.'

'What has become of Salome's things? Has anyone checked them?' Matt asked.

'I'll dispatch an officer to check with the first landlady and check again to see what is there. Thank you for the information and please pass on my regards to Miss Underhay.'

Matt pictured the inspector's long, thin face smiling under his ragged moustache. 'I will. Hopefully this case will be resolved soon.' Matt set the handset back in its cradle and after locking the office, returned to Kitty.

'What did he say?' she asked as she accepted her office key back from him.

He told her what the inspector had said, and she relaxed back in her seat. 'I had forgotten they were at the same lodging house to begin with. Did the landlady not say anything when the police came about Pearl's death? I would have thought she would have told them that Salome was her friend and was at the same address.'

'It is odd. Of course, with it being a theatrical lodging with people coming and going at unusual hours and times she hadn't made the connection. Pearl could have had other friends besides Salome and there wasn't much of a description circulated initially. I rather think she did mention something about another boarder but clearly no one made the connection at the time, and of course Salome denied it being her when the landlady asked.' He could see Kitty was not wholly satisfied with the explanation.

'Perhaps not,' she conceded, stifling a yawn with the back of her hand.

'You need to get some rest. We have to make a fairly early start tomorrow if we are to get to Exeter in time for Jack Dawkins' funeral.'

'I have arranged for some flowers to be delivered to the undertakers for the coffin. You said Father Lamb mentioned he had no family.'

Matt smiled at her, his heart warmed by her gesture. 'That was kind of you.'

She made a small dismissive shrug with her shoulders. 'It seemed the right thing to do.' She wriggled her feet back into her shoes. 'I'd better go up to bathe and change ready for dinner. No doubt Grams will have had Mrs Craven's version of the day by now and will want to know mine.' She grimaced as she rose.

'I'll see you at breakfast, I promised Mickey a game of billiards at The Ship.' He leaned forward and kissed her cheek, her skin soft and cool on his lips. His pulse quickened as he recalled their more intimate kiss earlier in the week.

Kitty blushed. 'Have fun. I'll see you tomorrow. And I think perhaps we should talk soon, once this is all over.' She collected her things and made her way up the grand staircase, pausing near the top for a quick look back in his direction – an action that lifted his spirits more than he would ever have believed.

CHAPTER EIGHTEEN

The following day dawned bright but blustery. Kitty dressed with care in the formal black dress, coat and hat she kept for sombre occasions. Matt matched her in a formal black suit, dark overcoat and hat.

'I've arranged for Mr Potter to drive us to the church rather than taking the train to Exeter,' Matt said as he opened the door for her as they exited the dining room after breakfast.

'We can hardly arrive on your motorcycle.' Kitty couldn't resist teasing him a little.

'Indeed, we might shock the good father if we did,' he agreed.

She followed him out of the hotel to where Mr Potter stood waiting.

'Mr Potter, we must be your best customers.' Kitty smiled at him as he opened the rear door of the car for her.

'You probably are, Miss Kitty.' He smiled back at her as she slid onto the back seat. Matt took his place beside her, and after a quick glance to see if it was all right with her, he cracked open the window.

'Mr Potter is expanding his business soon,' she said to Matt as the car made its way up the hill at the rear of the town, past the naval college. 'Isn't that right, Mr Potter?' she called.

'Yes, miss.' Mr Potter kept his attention on the road.

'Mr Potter's son, Robert, is joining him in the business. He has managed to acquire Mr Farjeon's old business and will be operating the Daisybelle touring coach for day trips and excursions.'

'That is good news,' Matt agreed.

'Thank you, sir. It'll be good to put that awful business of the spring behind us all,' Mr Potter said.

The murders in the town earlier in the year had meant the end of Mr Farjeon's touring car business as he hadn't had any family to continue the company. It would be nice to have the excursions running again. Kitty shivered as a blast of cold air came through the window and she adjusted the collar of her coat to shield her from the draught.

Matt immediately draped his arm about her shoulders and blocked the cold from reaching her. She snuggled against him.

The journey passed surprisingly swiftly, and they were soon pulling to a halt outside the grey stone exterior of the church of the Sacred Heart. Mr Potter held open the door and Kitty slid out. Matt paid their fare and Kitty looked around for the entrance to the church.

Matt joined her as the wooden planked door of the church with its great ironwork hinges creaked open. Father Lamb turned out to be a tiny, elderly man. His balding head appearing over a slightly overlarge clerical collar reminded Kitty of a benign tortoise.

'Captain Bryant, Miss Underhay.' The priest extended his hand in greeting. 'Welcome to the church of the Sacred Heart. I am sorry that we meet in such sad circumstances.' His eyes appeared kindly but shrewd, twinkling behind the lens of his wire-framed glasses.

'Matt said you were with Mr Dawkins when he passed? I'm glad he was not alone,' Kitty said.

'Yes, I knew Jack Dawkins well. He was a solitary soul.' Father Lamb's face was sombre.

'Is anyone else expected at his funeral, Father?' Matt asked.

The priest shook his head. 'I rather doubt it. Mrs Fisher will be in attendance, of course. She attends on behalf of the parish for all those who have no one to mourn them.'

The wind gusted, creating a swirl of long-dead leaves and dust around their feet.

'Mr Dawkins and my father were good friends in their youth before my father left for America. I felt that I should represent him.' Kitty felt compelled to explain her presence.

Father Lamb nodded. 'Jack mentioned you. He talked about your parents in his last days.'

Kitty was startled. 'Oh?'

The priest smiled gently. 'He talked a lot about your mother at the end. He was rambling, you understand, it was the morphine.'

'He appeared very ill when I saw him at his shop,' Matt said.

'Jack had been suffering from cancer for a long time. It was in his stomach. He came back to the church when he realised his time on Earth was coming to an end. He wished to clear his conscience. He was not always a respectable gentleman.'

'Poor man.' Tears welled in Kitty's eyes.

Father Lamb took her hands in his. 'He is at peace now, my child.'

'May I ask what he said about my mother? She came to see him before she disappeared in 1916 and I have been searching for answers for a very long time. Forgive me, but poor Mr Dawkins was perhaps my final hope.'

The hearse pulled up beside them.

'Come back to the presbytery afterwards for refreshments and I will share what I can with you.' Father Lamb released her and went to receive the coffin to escort Jack Dawkins on his final journey. Matt took her hand in his as they followed the coffin inside the ornate and beautiful interior of the church.

Kitty found the service unaccountably moving, considering she had not known Jack Dawkins during his lifetime. The morning sunlight streamed through the stained-glass windows behind the altar, throwing multicoloured patterns over Father Lamb. The simple sheaf of white lilies she had ordered lay on top of the plain coffin.

Mrs Fisher, a comfortingly substantial middle-aged lady in a worn black coat and hat was on her other side in the pew. The Mass complete, the coffin was taken back out to the hearse and they joined Father Lamb in a separate car for the final part of the ceremony.

The cemetery was not far away and once at the grave side Jack Dawkins was committed to his Maker. Kitty didn't realise she was crying until Matt silently proffered her his handkerchief.

'I'm sorry. It seems foolish to cry over someone I never met.'

Father Lamb, his task completed, joined them. 'It is entirely understandable, my daughter. Now, let us get out of this cold wind and have some coffee.'

The drive back to the presbytery took only a couple of minutes. Father Lamb sent them into the house where his housekeeper seated them in the cosy, cluttered living room and brought through a tray of coffee and home-made scones before returning to the kitchen.

Once the priest had attended to the car driver, he came to join them, sinking into a tired-looking leather armchair with a sigh of relief.

'Ah coffee, excellent. Miss Underhay, may I prevail upon you to pour?' he asked.

Kitty obliged, thankful that she had recovered her composure during the journey. Once they all had coffee and Father Lamb was tucking into a scone laden with home-made strawberry jam, Matt asked the question that was forefront in Kitty's mind.

'Father, you said that Jack Dawkins talked about Kitty's mother, Elowed?'

The priest slowly chewed the last portion of his scone and swallowed before answering the question.

'You both realise of course that I cannot disclose anything that may have been revealed to me in confession?' He surveyed them both closely through his glasses.

'Of course, Father, we understand,' Kitty assured him.

'From what he said, Jack and your father were good friends when they were young men. They had various business dealings together.' The priest paused and looked at Kitty as if unsure of how to phrase the next part of his story.

'I will not be shocked or distressed by anything you might say about my father. He is not the most morally upright man,' she said.

Father Lamb nodded. 'Very well. Many of these business dealings were not strictly within the letter of the law and they kept some unsavoury company at times. Then, it seems, your father met your mother.' He paused once again.

'Grams said they met in London, Mother was at some rally.'

'According to Jack, your mother was evading the police after a suffragist rally near Hyde Park. Your father assisted her escape.'

Matt raised his eyebrows and Kitty smiled ruefully. 'I'm rather afraid that does sound like Mother from the tales Grams has told me.'

'Jack was with your father at the time your parents met. They had been conducting some business together in London. I rather think that your mother made two conquests that day.'

'Jack cared for Elowed?' Matt asked.

Kitty stared at them both in surprise. 'Really? Oh!'

The priest nodded. 'Jack considered Elowed too good for your father. He only saw them a few times after that when it became evident that they were together and were intending to marry. He stayed in touch with your father however, off and on, even after you had been born.'

'Was my father aware of Jack's feelings towards my mother?' Kitty asked. This was all brand-new information for her.

'I don't believe so. Jack never told anyone. He came back to Exeter and opened his shop. Communication with your father faded and he thought that he would never see your mother again.' Father Lamb took a long drink of coffee.

'But then she walked into his shop that June day asking for help to find my father,' Kitty said. This was the crux of the puzzle. What had happened next? Where had her mother gone? She had the brief note from Jack Dawkins, a dying man's message to the daughter of the woman he had loved, but it didn't answer her questions.

'Jack told me much of this story over the final few months of his life. But until the last few days after you had called upon him at the shop, Captain Bryant, he hadn't spoken of Mrs Underhay's disappearance.'

'You think Matt's visit brought it all back?' Kitty asked. She couldn't help but feel a little guilty that her questions may have upset a terminally ill man. She was relieved when Father Lamb shook his head.

'No, my dear. I think it had lain on his conscience for a long time. I believe he merely became more aware of how little time he had left and that Elowed's daughter might need the information he had.'

'Father, we realise that you cannot break the confidence of the confession, but you said that Jack talked about Kitty's mother as he was dying?' Matt looked at the elderly man.

The priest drained the last of his coffee and set his cup down on the saucer. 'You will also recall that I told you that Jack was receiving high doses of morphine. He was in considerable pain. I stayed with him at his request; he was frightened to be alone and he had no family or friends to be there. He would thrash about wildly and babble incoherently before falling back into a fitful sleep. Whenever he awoke there would be a few moments of lucidity and he would talk for a little while until he was exhausted once more.'

'And this was when he mentioned my mother?' Kitty asked.

A shadow passed over Father Lamb's face. 'Yes, my dear. He kept saying, "I should have done something. I should have warned her to leave it alone or gone with her. She didn't know, you see."'

Kitty blinked back the fresh tears that threatened to tumble down her cheeks. 'How very cryptic. You don't know what he meant by that?'

'I was not the priest here at the time your mother disappeared. I arrived in the parish after the war, but it was a time of change – men returning home, families that were missing their men who would never return. In parts of the city there had been a network of criminal activity. Jack Dawkins was on the fringe of this group. Your father had also known these people in the past. I can only assume that Jack noticed something amiss when your mother called at the shop.'

'He wrote to me. Did you know?' Kitty asked.

Father Lamb exhaled. 'He said he would, just before he was confined to bed.'

Matt reached across to her and squeezed her hand. 'Father, did he give any indication at all about where Elowed might have gone after leaving the shop or who these people who might have harmed her might be?'

The priest frowned, his brow furrowing as he thought. 'The criminal element at the time used to gather at the public house at the end of the street. It was called the Glass Bottle then. The landlord at the time is dead now but his son still runs it, I believe. He may be able to help you.' He turned to Kitty. 'It is no place for you, my child. Permit me to make some enquiries on your behalf.'

Kitty sighed. 'Thank you, Father, that would be very kind. I'm glad Mr Dawkins was not alone when he passed.' She gathered her bag ready to leave.

'Yes, thank you, Father.' Matt shook hands with the priest. 'We had better head back to Dartmouth, Kitty.'

'Yes, my grandmother will be waiting for me. I've been missing too much work what with helping Genny with the fundraising concert for the boys' orphanage in Torquay. Do you know the orphanage, Father?'

The priest appeared pleasantly surprised. 'Yes, I know it quite well. They do excellent work, I believe. There is to be a charity performance at the Pavilion near the harbour. My colleague has sent me a ticket. A Miss Davenport has put together the programme, I believe.'

'Yes, Genny Davenport has done a great deal of work. I'm simply giving her a little assistance.' Kitty smiled. 'Perhaps I shall see you on the night of the concert?'

'I shall look forward to that immensely.' He rose and walked with them to the front door. 'If I discover anything or hear anything that may help you, Miss Underhay, I shall be sure to pass it on.'

'Thank you, Father.' Kitty shook his hand.

'God bless you both,' the priest responded.

'He seemed such a nice man.' Kitty fell into step beside Matt as they made their way along the street towards the cathedral and the taxi rank.

'That was quite a revelation about Mr Dawkins' feelings for your mother.' Matt glanced at her.

'Yes, most unexpected. I had hoped there might be more information to go on, but I suppose it is better than nothing.' She gasped as a sudden gust of wind tugged at the brim of her hat, causing her to reach up and tug it down a little more firmly onto her head.

'Would you like me to make enquiries at the Glass Bottle?' he asked.

Kitty's pace slowed. 'I have to find out, Matt. Jack Dawkins was a dying man. There has to be some truth in his ramblings. Let's see what Father Lamb can discover first.'

Matt's gaze locked with hers, causing her pulse to take a quick skip. 'I promise I'll do my best to find some answers. We are closer to solving the mystery of your mother's disappearance than anyone has been since she first vanished.'

Her heart squeezed. 'Yes, that's true.'

Matt hailed a taxi near the cathedral green to take them back to Dartmouth. Neither he nor Kitty fancied taking the train and she was anxious to return to the Dolphin and her work. The funeral had been strangely moving and unsettling. Matt had been unable to return for Edith and Betty's funeral. Instead, his parents had attended and Edith's friends. His father-in-law had passed away shortly after their wedding from an unexpected heart attack.

Seeing Jack Dawkins' plain pine coffin being lowered into the grave today had triggered all the old memories of grief, loss and regret. He glanced at Kitty. Her face was pale beneath the brim of her black funeral hat as she huddled next to him in the back of the car. The air was chill through the partly opened window, helping to keep the feeling of being incarcerated at bay.

'Penny for your thoughts,' she said, taking him by surprise.

'I was thinking about Edith and Betty.' His words slipped out before he had time to think.

Kitty shifted her position to look at him. 'I know Edith was your wife, who was Betty?' Her voice was soft and gentle.

He swallowed hard, conscious that he had never talked to her about his past. 'My baby daughter. She died with Edith.' There, he'd said it.

Kitty gasped, her blue-grey eyes wide. 'Oh, Matt.'

He closed his eyes for a moment, unable to face his own grief reflected afresh in Kitty's face. The warm touch of her gloved hand on his cheek made him reopen them.

'I'm so sorry.' Her words were barely audible, and he saw her lashes were wet. 'I knew you'd lost Edith but not that there had been a child. How old was she?'

'Nine months. Edith wrote she had started to sit up.' He was aware that his words sounded clipped. He had never spoken to anyone in this way about his wife and child since they had been killed. 'They were caught in a raid in London. They never stood a chance; they were in the wrong place at the wrong time.' His voice failed and he fought the hard lump in his throat.

Kitty stroked his cheek, her touch tender. He closed his eyes again, thankful that Kitty understood that he was unable to say anything more. The rest of the journey passed in silence and before long they were descending the hill past the naval college and towards the Dolphin.

CHAPTER NINETEEN

Kitty's grandmother had listened with interest to her account of Jack Dawkins' funeral and agreed that Matt should visit the Glass Bottle to see if he could learn anything more if Father Lamb thought there was anything to be gained by the visit.

She also agreed to release Alice from her duties to accompany Kitty to the Pavilion. Her ready acquiescence betrayed her concerns for Kitty's safety.

'Do take care, my dear. This person is very dangerous and may not like you asking questions. I shall feel better knowing Alice is with you.'

Kitty blushed and hoped her grandmother had not somehow discovered the anonymous note she had given to Inspector Greville.

Alice was ready and waiting for her in the lobby, wearing her best blue coat and hat. Her thin face lit up as Kitty descended the staircase.

'I'm all ready, miss. Packed a few bits in my bag just in case.' Alice patted her large worn tapestry handbag.

'Thank you for doing this, Alice.' Kitty smiled at her.

'That's all right, miss. It's exciting, like the films and if it will help Captain Bryant then I want to help.'

'We have to be careful,' Kitty warned as they left the hotel and walked towards the ferry.

'I know, miss. I'll just listen out really carefully.' Alice fastened the top button of her coat against the chill air coming off the water. 'Brr, it's nippy today, summer is well gone lately.'

They boarded the ferry to cross to Kingswear. The river was choppy with the turn of the tide, the water dull, reflecting the grey sky. Kitty wondered if Inspector Greville had discovered anything of interest amongst Salome or Pearl's belongings. There had been no message from him when they had returned from Exeter. Not that the inspector was obliged to tell them anything.

The bus was already at the stop when they disembarked from the ferry so at least they didn't have to wait in the cold. Kitty insisted on a seat downstairs, much to Alice's chagrin. The bus chugged its way through Kingswear and up the hill past Collaton Fishacre towards Churston.

'Where does the captain live, miss?' Alice asked as they stopped at the halt near Windy Corner.

'Over there, on the seaward side of Lord Churston's estate, near the golf course. The Davenports live in that large white modern house just there.' Kitty nodded her head in the direction of the golf course. Alice peered forward to look through the slightly grimy window of the bus.

'Coo, it's very swish,' the girl remarked, craning her head for a better view as the bus moved off to follow the coast down into Torquay.

Eventually they reached their destination, leaving the bus at the harbour-side stop. The two women crossed the road and walked towards the Pavilion, keeping their heads down against the stiff breeze blowing in from the sea.

'Genny said to enter via the stage door.' Kitty led the way around the side of the building. She rapped smartly on the small green painted door.

'Kitty, darling, oh and another pretty young lady.' Seb opened the door and smirked at Alice, sending the girl's pale face the same shade as her hair.

'Gosh, it's windy out there today.' Kitty ushered Alice inside and closed the door against the breeze.

Peter lounged against the wall; he and Seb had obviously been enjoying a cigarette. The smoke was still in the air and the ubiquitous fire bucket already contained cigarette ends on top of the sand.

'Kitty, so good of you to help out,' Peter greeted her.

'This is Miss Alice Miller. Alice, Mr Peter Davenport and his friend, Sebastian Prior.'

'Charmed, I'm sure.' Peter winked at Alice, making the girl giggle and the colour in her cheeks flame even higher.

'Is Genny here?' Kitty asked.

'Somewhere abouts,' Peter said, shrugging his shoulders in a careless gesture. 'Larry and Tilly are in the auditorium so she may be in there. Tilly was making yet another complaint about something or other.'

Seb rolled his eyes in sympathy at the dire note in Peter's voice.

'Come on, Alice, I'll show you around.' Kitty led Alice through the door into the concert hall.

'Oh, Miss Kitty, it's proper nice. I haven't ever been in here before and I always wondered what it must be like.' Alice stared all around her at the delicate plaster work, elegant potted palms and rich velveteen-covered seats.

Larry and Tilly were on the stage. Tilly was her usual immaculate self, in a chocolate-coloured dress with an ivory collar. Larry appeared harassed and irritated in equal measures as Tilly waved a sheaf of papers at him.

'Cor, miss. Is that Tilly Tilney, the film actress?' Alice asked in an awed whisper, a rapt expression on her face.

Kitty glanced at her companion; she'd forgotten that Alice was likely to be completely star-struck at meeting one of her heroines in real life.

Larry spotted them and abandoned Tilly to bound down the small flight of stairs at the side of the stage. 'Miss Underhay, good morning, are you looking for Genny?'

'Yes, have you seen her?' Kitty asked.

Larry raked his hand through his hair. 'Yes, she's had to go into the town for something. She asked if you and your friend would be good enough to finish preparing the costumes and props. Dress rehearsal in two days and then before you know it it'll be showtime.' He glanced back at his wife. 'If we're ever ready,' he added drily.

'I'm sure it'll be marvellous,' Kitty said. 'Come on Alice, let's go and get started.' She had to tug gently on Alice's coat sleeve to get her attention.

When they returned back to the backstage area, Seb and Peter had disappeared.

'She's so pretty, isn't she? Tilly Tilney? Like an angel, and her clothes is lovely. Famous for her diamonds, she is.' Alice sighed dreamily as Kitty led the way to the prop room.

'I sorted most of the things onto hangers and labelled them last time,' Kitty said. She hoped Alice wouldn't be too disillusioned when she saw and heard Tilly on stage.

'They all wants a good press.' Alice pursed her lips as she scanned the rails with an expert eye. 'I'll get the iron hot.'

'Thank you, Alice. I'll get the kettle on. I expect everyone will want tea,' Kitty said as Alice set down her bag and took off her coat.

'Do you think as Mrs Tilney would give me her autograph?' Alice asked as Kitty prepared to make her way to the kitchenette.

'I don't see why not. Genny mentioned there was to be a signing after the performance but I could ask her now if you like?'

Alice's face lit up. 'Would you, miss? That would be super.'

Kitty left the girl to organise pressing the costumes while she went to light the small spirit stove in the kitchenette. The kettle had started to whistle when she heard someone knocking at the stage door. She lifted the kettle from the heat onto the cast iron trivet and went to see who was outside.

Dickie and BeBe were huddled together beneath a large black umbrella which threatened to blow inside out just as Kitty opened the door to them.

'It's started to rain. It's more like November than September today.' BeBe shivered as she scurried inside. Dickie followed behind her, collapsing the umbrella as he entered.

'I'm just making tea,' Kitty said.

'You're an angel.' Dickie grinned at her as he followed his wife towards the dressing rooms.

Kitty busied herself making refreshments, ready to take them to the artistes. As she worked, she soon heard the rippling sound of piano music and BeBe's lovely voice coming from the stage. She took the first cup to Alice, who was already hard at work.

'Thank you, miss.' Alice had set herself up with all the things she needed and was pressing what seemed to be a man's shirt with a hot, heavy iron.

'Are you all right in here, Alice?' Kitty asked.

'Oh yes, miss. Right as ninepence. A nice change from Mrs Homer keeping her beady eyes on me.' A cloud of steam emanated from the sleeve of the garment as Alice tackled it with a damp cloth and the iron.

Kitty left her to it and trundled her small trolley along the corridor and through the open door in the wings to the auditorium. BeBe had finished her song and Larry was looking at the lighting arrangements as she entered the side of the stage. Dickie accepted a cup of tea with a grateful smile.

'Thank you, Kitty.' He took a sip from the utilitarian crockery cup.

'How is it all going with the rehearsals?' Kitty asked. To her, it seemed jumbled and disorganised. The local acts had yet to come and slot in with the Davenport party's more sophisticated London acts, so she couldn't see how they were timing everything or setting up the stage ready for the performance. If this was an event she was putting on at the Dolphin, she would have demanded much more organisation.

'Not bad. We have a full run-through this afternoon. Larry is keen to get the lighting rig set.' Dickie lowered his voice. 'Tilly is the big problem. She wants it set up specially to flatter her but that doesn't help anyone else and we can't keep moving stuff around.'

'I take it there are minimal sets and props?' Kitty asked. There were costumes backstage but not too many items for the stage.

'Oh absolutely, it's all about performance.'

Kitty carried a cup of tea to Tilly, who was seated in the front row scowling at BeBe as Larry pointed out the marks on the stage.

'Oh, thank you.' She took the cup with a small wrinkle of her nose to indicate her distaste for the chunky cup.

'My companion was so delighted to see you this morning, she's a great admirer of yours,' Kitty said.

Tilly's face immediately brightened, and she sat up straighter in her seat. 'That's terribly sweet.'

'Yes, she's seen all your films. She's very shy though and wondered if you might autograph something for her, her name is Alice?' Kitty asked.

Tilly handed back her cup and delved into her expensive cream leather handbag, retrieving a photograph of herself which she signed with a flourish. 'Anything for my public.'

Kitty took the picture. 'Alice will be thrilled. Thank you, it's very kind of you.'

Tilly gave a small shrug of her shoulders. 'Not at all. I shall be signing programmes after the show in return for donations for Genny's orphans.' Her attention had wandered back to the stage and her husband, who was laughing at something with BeBe.

'How did you and Larry meet?' Kitty asked.

Tilly's gaze rested on her husband. 'He was acting in the same company as me. He was my leading man. He always wanted to be a producer, although he is a marvellous actor.'

'It must be so difficult for you and Larry, being in the limelight all the time?' Kitty murmured gently.

'You have no idea. Silly girls throwing themselves at Larry virtually nonstop trying to get his attention. All they care about is getting a part in one of his films. Flaunting themselves at him. Not a thought that he is a married man. Hussies.' The last word came out as a venomous hiss.

'That must be awful for you. I suppose you mean girls like the ones who were murdered?'

Tilly shot her a sharp glance. 'There were two of them. Hanging around Larry with their inane giggling, making cow eyes and hinting how far they were willing to go to be discovered.'

'It must be difficult for Larry too,' Kitty suggested, gazing at the stage.

'Oh please. He laps it up. All those girls hanging on his every word. *Yes, Mr Tilney; no, Mr Tilney. Do you think the skirt is too short for my role, Mr Tilney?*' Tilly glowered at her unsuspecting husband as he moved across the stage to converse with Dickie. 'You have no idea of the pressures of being a star. Always some girl who is younger and prettier trying to steal your limelight and your husband.' Tilly sounded quite vengeful.

'I'm sure Larry is devoted to you,' Kitty soothed. It certainly sounded as if Tilly would have no scruples about dealing with any woman who posed a threat to her status as Larry's wife or as his leading lady.

'He'd better be,' Tilly muttered as BeBe gave Larry a dazzling smile before launching into her next number.

CHAPTER TWENTY

Matt had made his own plans for the morning once Kitty and Alice had left for the Pavilion. Days of inaction were proving more than a little frustrating when he wanted to clear his name and be able to return to his own house with his head held high.

'I collected the motorcycle for you, sir, parked her out the back. Little beauty she is.' Mickey handed him the keys to his beloved Sunbeam.

'Thanks, Mickey.' Since he'd been unable to return to his house, he'd been unable to collect his motorcycle himself, tempting though it had been to ignore the inspector's restrictions. At least now he would be able to get about under his own steam.

He donned his long coat, muffler and flat cap and walked out to his motorcycle. Cold pellets of rain bounced off his shoulders as he straddled the bike and fired her up. Within a minute he was on his way to take the ferry across the Dart.

Matt headed up the long hill and on towards Torquay. The cold wind and rain against his face was exhilarating and for the first time in days he felt properly alive. He pulled to a halt outside the police station and jogged up the couple of steps at the entrance.

'Captain Bryant, how may we help you, sir?' The desk sergeant recognised him immediately as he removed his cap.

'I wondered if Inspector Greville might be able to spare me a few moments?' Matt asked. He wanted to find out if there had been anything in Salome or Pearl's belongings which could shed any light on the case.

'If you'd like to take a seat, I'll try his office.' The sergeant indicated the spindly dark wood chairs lined up against the wall.

Matt took a seat as the sergeant dialled a number on the black rotary phone. He listened intently to one side of the conversation as the man spoke to whoever was on the other end of the line.

The sergeant replaced the receiver. 'The inspector can give you a few minutes.'

Matt stood and followed the man towards the inspector's office, along the familiar corridor which he knew all too well continued down stone stairs to the cells where he had been held. He vowed to do what he could to never return there again.

The sergeant rapped on a door, before opening it for Matt to enter. A blueish haze of cigarette smoke greeted him and somewhere in the midst, behind the untidy piles of paper threatening to spill out of the trays on his desk, was Inspector Greville.

'Captain Bryant.' He greeted Matt with a warm handshake and resumed his seat behind the desk. 'Please excuse the paperwork. Now, how can I help you?'

Matt took the seat opposite the inspector and unwound the muffler from around his neck. 'I thought I'd drop in and see if you'd had any luck with Pearl and Salome's property?'

Inspector Greville surveyed him keenly before pulling out his cigarette case and offering one to Matt. He took one himself and lit up after Matt had declined the offer with a shake of his head.

'In fact, something very curious has occurred.' The inspector took a pull on his cigarette and released a thin stream of smoke.

'In what way, sir?' Matt asked. His curiosity was piqued. There was obviously something out of the ordinary from the policeman's reaction.

'We returned to the original lodging house used by both girls. The landlady had parcelled up Pearl's belongings into the girl's trunk. She needed to let the room so had stored the trunk in an outhouse at the back of the property. Salome had already packed her things, as presumably she intended to send for them once she had settled in her new lodgings.'

Matt nodded. So far nothing in the inspector's narrative struck him as strange.

'When my man arrived at the lodging house and asked to see the contents of Salome's trunk, the landlady was quite flustered. She said Miss Donohue's brother had already collected them. A skinny bespectacled man wearing an ill-fitting coat.'

'I was not aware that Miss Donohue had a brother?' Matt frowned.

'Indeed she does, however her brother is only ten years old and resides with her mother and her sisters in Liverpool. You will recall we had made enquiries there? It seems Miss Donohue had left Liverpool a few months ago to tour with some play and had never returned home.'

'I see. Someone must have had the same thought as us then and decided to try and obtain Salome's things.'

'When my man went to the outhouse to check Miss Bright's things, the lock had been broken on her trunk and someone had clearly searched through.'

Matt bit back an expletive. 'Then our murderer may well have obtained whatever it was they were looking for?'

Inspector Greville blew out a final stream of smoke before extinguishing his cigarette in an already overflowing glass ashtray. 'It's entirely possible. Whoever it is seems to be a step ahead of us at the moment. Miss Donohue's mother last heard from Salome a fortnight ago; the girl used to send her some money from her wages. Miss Bright's family live towards Brixham; they didn't agree with her lifestyle and had disowned her.'

'Could the landlady give more detail with the description of this so-called brother of Salome's?'

'This was indeed curious. She said he was about five feet nine, thin-faced with a wispy moustache, brown hair. Softly spoken.'

Matt's frown deepened. 'How so curious, sir? The description could fit many men. You said neither girl had a boyfriend?'

'No, both ladies were unattached. The landlady said she wasn't certain, but she thought there was something not quite right about the moustache.'

'A disguise, perhaps? Then it could be one of the Davenport party. Peter, Sebastian or Laurence Tilney.' His mentally ticked off the list of suspects in his head.

'Indeed,' the inspector commented drily.

'I presume you have looked at their backgrounds?' He knew it would be most unlike the inspector if he hadn't done so. Greville always did things by the book.

'Mr Tilney was an actor when he met his wife. He comes from a good family, nothing really came up in the search apart from a rumour of an affair with another actress when he was directing a film in America eighteen months ago. Mrs Tilney was not amused, and things are rumoured to be quite rocky between them at the moment. But the word is that he's trying hard to keep any dalliances from her, as a nasty divorce would lose him his backers and could end his career.'

'Hmm, that would explain her jealousy regarding her husband. What about Sebastian? Peter's friend?' Matt asked.

'Lots of talk about both those gentlemen and their friendship, especially in theatrical circles. Peter is unhappy that his father is forcing him to take over running the theatres. It seems he wished to pursue his stage career. The other gentleman, Sebastian, has quite a reputation. He had a friendship with a much older fellow thespian who passed away in suspicious circumstances. Fell down stairs and broke his neck. Our friend inherited his house and a generous sum of money. A distant cousin challenged the will, but it didn't get very far.'

Matt raised his eyebrows in astonishment. 'I see. You've been very busy, Inspector.'

'And before you or Miss Underhay enquires, our mutual friend had an alibi for the time his benefactor took his tumble.' The inspector's moustache twitched.

'Thank you, sir, that's been most interesting.'

Kitty was prevailed upon by Larry to remain in the concert hall, perched on a chair at the side of the stage to prompt Tilly with her lines. It seemed that Tilly intended to perform two pieces, beginning with Ophelia's lament from *Hamlet* and then Tennyson's *The Lady of Shalott*, before finishing with a musical piece.

It seemed that Tilly was used to performing for film where her art could be delivered in pieces and re-filmed if needed, unlike a stage performance. The Shakespeare piece was short, and she managed that without a stumble. The poem, however, required a few reminders from Kitty.

They ran through it four times before pausing for lunch. Kitty was relieved to be able to stand and stretch her limbs before collecting the dirty cups and returning backstage to Alice.

She deposited the crockery into the sink and went to the prop room to find the young girl.

'On the last one, miss.' Alice beamed at her from behind a rack of neatly pressed and labelled costumes.

'That's marvellous, Alice. I'm just going to wash up the cups and then we can get some lunch if you like? My treat.'

The girl's thin face flushed with pleasure. 'That would be smashing, miss. I got some things to tell you.' She added the last part in a theatrical whisper.

'Tell me over lunch.' Kitty smiled. 'Tilly Tilney has given me something for you too.'

She left Alice to finish her task while she cleared away the tea things and reset the trolley for the afternoon. She felt as if she had earned a spot of lunch out in the town after coaching Tilly with her lines all morning.

Alice came to find her once her task was complete and they set off from the concert hall back out into the blustery, showery day. Kitty tucked her hand into the crook of Alice's arm, and they held on to their hats as they scuttled across the road into the steamy warmth of Bobby's Café.

The café was busy with other people who were anxious to take refuge from the weather. They had to stand for a moment near the counter until a small table at the rear of the café became available and they could take a seat.

'Cor, miss, it's a right day out there today. More like winter.' Alice shivered and snuggled into her coat as Kitty gave their order for eggs, ham, bread and butter and a pot of tea to the waitress.

'I know. I believe it is meant to improve though over the next few days. Now, tell me what you learned while you were backstage,' Kitty said as she drew off her gloves.

Alice glanced around the crowded tearoom before moving her chair closer to the table and leaning forward to talk to Kitty. 'Well, miss, I was in that room doing the ironing and keeping my ears open like you said.' She paused and glanced around once more. 'Then I heard them two gents again. The ones we met when we came in.'

'Sebastian and Peter?'

Alice nodded. 'Yes, miss. The door banged and I thought, now who's that then? I listened out and heard the one with the dark hair ask the other one, Peter, what was the matter. He said his mother was putting on the pressure for him to marry this girl called Sarah.' She broke off as the waitress approached their table and set down the tea things. She resumed her story as soon as the girl had moved away. 'Anyway, the other one said to him, "What are you going to do?" And Peter said, "I don't know. You know it isn't what I want. In an ideal world you know what I would want."'

Alice paused once more to take a sip of the tea that Kitty had poured for her. Her brow wrinkled as she tried to repeat the conversation to Kitty as exactly as she could. 'The other one, Seb, he said as at least the girl wasn't ugly. He said as Peter just needed to get on, do his duty, give the old bat a grandchild and then he needn't go near the girl again.'

Kitty gasped at the unfeeling cruelty of Seb's remarks. 'Poor Saira, she deserves so much better than that.'

'Peter said at least there wouldn't be any more problems now the girls were dead and someone had done them a favour.' Alice leaned back in her chair as the waitress returned to place their lunch in front of them.

Kitty frowned. 'That sounds as if, however distasteful their conversation may be, that they weren't the ones who killed Salome or Pearl.'

Alice helped herself to bread and butter. 'Unless that Seb done it and the other one don't know.'

'Oh, Alice.' Kitty smiled at her companion. She had to concede though that Alice may well have struck upon something. Seb might be a charmer but he could also be a killer.

The girl swallowed her bread and took another gulp of tea. 'Then I heard the door go again.'

'Oh?' Kitty asked.

'I heard ladies' voices, so I puts down my iron and tiptoes to the door to see who it was.'

Kitty waited for Alice to drain her cup and continue with her story.

'There was an older lady, tall and slim, dressed nice and a younger lady. The younger one had glasses, she was quite plump, and her clothes didn't suit her.' Alice wrinkled her nose.

'That sounds like Genny and her mother, Mrs Davenport.'

'Well, they was arguing. The older lady was ordering the other one about. She mentioned your name, miss.' Alice's bright gaze locked with Kitty's.

'Really?' Kitty said. 'Please don't worry about sparing my feelings if she said something unflattering.'

A red flush crept up the girl's face. 'She was asking the other lady why you were still there, and did you need to be, as both you and Mrs Craven had been poking about asking questions.'

Kitty grinned. 'No surprises there, then. I believe Mrs Davenport wishes the police investigation would cease their interest in her household.'

Alice smiled back at her, relief clearly showing on her thin features. 'She didn't sound a very nice lady. She was carrying on to the other lady something awful. Then that Peter comes out of his dressing room and starts to stick up for her.'

Kitty patted the corners of her lips with her napkin. 'Peter stood up for his sister? Interesting. I got the impression that Mrs Davenport favoured Peter over Genny and this suited Peter quite well.'

'He said,' she paused, her brow furrowing once more before she continued, 'to give Genny a break, that she was always nagging her.'

'Goodness, how did Mrs Davenport take that?' Kitty was surprised. Peter had never struck her as having the backbone to stand up to his mother.

Alice giggled, she seemed to be enjoying her role as a spy. 'Not very well. Shot him down in flames she did. Said, "When you are the one supporting your sister's lame ducks then you may dictate the rules."'

'Hmm.' Alice had learned a great deal while she had been backstage. There were some interesting dynamics at play within the Davenport house. 'Thank you, Alice.'

Kitty called the waitress over and paid their bill. She and Alice refastened their coats and secured their hats before stepping back outside into the wind and drizzle. They hurried back across the road and along the side of the Pavilion building to the stage door.

Genny opened the door to Kitty's knock and they scurried inside, relieved to be out of the cold wind.

'Kitty, thank you so much for helping Tilly this morning with her lines. Would you be able to help with prompting during the performance? Tilly gets dreadful stage fright in front of an audience.' Genny blinked, owl-like, at Kitty from behind her glasses.

'Of course, no problem,' Kitty said. Genny was dressed in crushed cabbage-green velvet today; the colour was unflattering to both her shape and complexion. 'Genny, may I present Miss Alice Miller, she has very generously come to assist me this morning. She has pressed and prepared all the costumes.'

'Oh, thank you, Miss Miller, that is very good of you.' Genny shook hands with a slightly bemused and embarrassed Alice.

'My pleasure, Miss Davenport.'

'There is to be a run-through this afternoon and then a final dress rehearsal of course ahead of the upcoming performance. Miss Miller, could I prevail upon you to assist backstage? Miss Tilney will require some assistance with her costume, and we will need someone to marshal the children for their spot?'

Alice glanced at Kitty, who gave her a barely perceptible nod. 'Of course, Miss Davenport, if you really think I can help.'

Relief shone from Genny's plain face. 'Marvellous. The only person not rehearsing today is Mother.' Her expression clouded momentarily. 'She is indisposed so has returned to the house.' Genny steered Alice along the corridor and started to give her instructions and a timed list of acts.

Kitty grinned to herself and peeled off her coat ready to resume her position at the side of the stage to prompt Tilly once more.

CHAPTER TWENTY-ONE

'You look terribly pleased with yourself,' Kitty remarked when she met Matt the following morning. She was seated in her office trying to deal with the pile of work that had built up whilst she'd been at the Pavilion assisting Genny.

Matt leaned back in his seat opposite her. 'I went to see our friend, Inspector Greville, yesterday.'

'Oh yes?' Kitty asked as she slit open yet another invoice with her small paperknife. Matt told her all he'd learned about Salome and Pearl. Her eyes widened when she learned Sebastian's history.

'I wonder what the thief will do with the trunk and clothes. Presumably they will turn up somewhere soon once he has looked through everything and extracted whatever it was that he was looking for.' Kitty added the invoice she had just opened onto her growing pile of items to book and pay.

'I expect the inspector will be busy searching the bay for it. He seems to have been very active.' Matt absent-mindedly picked up Kitty's favourite dark blue fountain pen from the desk and admired it.

'Alice heard some interesting things yesterday.' Kitty reached over and reclaimed her pen, frowning heavily at Matt as she told him what Alice had overheard.

'This case is so frustrating. Everything points to the involvement of one of the Davenports' party. This mystery man claiming to be Salome's brother could be Seb, Peter or Larry.'

'Inspector Greville is probably checking out their alibis for the time this man turned up and claimed Salome's box from the lodging house,' Kitty suggested.

Matt sighed. 'I asked him, and none of them has an alibi so he can't rule anyone out or in. Seb and Peter were out for a drive collecting some item or other for Mrs Davenport and Laurence Tilney was catching up with his paperwork and telephoning potential sponsors for his new film.'

'The landlady thought the moustache might have been fake so I suppose it could have been any of them. They all have a motive of sorts… but enough to murder two women? And to try to frame you…' Kitty said.

'Well, I'm sure it's nothing personal. I hadn't met the Tilneys before. I scarcely know Peter or Sebastian. The person I know best is Genny and that's only because I've bumped into her a few times and helped her out, carrying parcels and things.' Matt sounded thoughtful.

'But it has to be connected to them somehow, doesn't it? I can't believe that this fake brother of Salome's is a stranger to everyone, is he?' Kitty abandoned her pile of post for a moment. 'I mean, could we be wrong?'

Matt stroked his chin, his expression thoughtful. 'No, someone decided I would make a convenient scapegoat and a stranger wouldn't have done that. It's as if there is a piece missing from this puzzle and I can't make it out.'

'I know, I keep turning it all over in my head trying to puzzle it out. Rather selfishly, I must admit I'll be glad once this wretched concert of Genny's is out of the way. I feel awful that I keep having to leave poor Grams with all my work. Bless Alice, she was so helpful yesterday and Genny's roped her in to assist with the concert too. Thank goodness it's a quiet period so we can spare her from some of her duties at the hotel.'

'I really appreciate everything you, your grandmother, Alice and even Mrs Craven are doing to try and clear my name.'

'Speaking of Mrs Craven, have you updated her with our progress?' Kitty asked.

Matt laughed, 'I believe I should really go and pay her a visit.'

'At least the weather has improved today if you are to walk up the hill.' She reached for her pile of letters once more.

'Ah but I have transport once more, my dear Kitty.' The dimple flashed in his cheek as he dangled the key to his motorcycle in front of her. 'Mickey collected the Sunbeam for me.'

Kitty shook her head in mock despair. 'Rather you than me.' She remembered all too well the ride she had taken as a pillion passenger on Matt's motorcycle when they had trapped a killer at her aunt and uncle's house.

Matt went off, whistling, to call on Mrs Craven, leaving Kitty to finish dealing with her mail.

She opened a few more invoices and added them to her pile. The last envelope on her desk caused her busy fingers to still. There was something about the typewritten address and the envelope itself that seemed familiar. She slit the envelope open carefully and shook the contents onto her desk, opening the single folded sheet of paper it had contained with a shaky hand.

Stop asking questions or you will be next

The letters had been crudely cut from a newspaper and glued to the paper in the same fashion as the previous missive. Kitty gasped, recoiling automatically from the message. Just at that moment there was a knock at the door and before she could recover her wits to hide the note, Alice entered the room.

'Miss Kitty, are you all right?' Alice frowned at her, then her gaze dropped to the letter on top of the desk. 'Oh, what's that?

Is that one of those anonymous letters like in the films?' The girl paled and her eyes widened as she read the brief line. 'Shall I go and find Captain Bryant?' She turned as if to dart out of the door.

'No, Alice, wait!' Kitty called.

The girl halted and turned back around to face Kitty, a puzzled frown creasing her forehead. 'What is it, miss?'

'Close the door and come and sit down for a moment,' Kitty instructed.

Alice obeyed, smoothing her apron across her lap with work-reddened hands as she took her seat.

'I don't wish to say anything about this letter to Captain Bryant.' Kitty held up her hand to silence the protest that she saw starting to form on Alice's lips. 'I will take this letter to Inspector Greville. This is not the first letter of this nature that I've received lately.'

Alice stared at her. 'But, miss, oughtn't Captain Bryant be made aware? You could be in real danger.'

'If Matt learns of the letters, he will tell Grams and then they will conspire to stop me investigating further,' Kitty said.

'But if you're in danger, miss?' Alice pleated the edge of her apron between her fingers.

'Inspector Greville will advise me. I'm not about to put myself at risk, Alice. Besides, you shall be with me. I won't be going to the Pavilion or meeting any of the Davenport party alone.'

Alice appeared somewhat mollified by this statement. 'I want to help you and Captain Bryant, Miss Kitty, but what if something bad happens?'

The same thought had crossed Kitty's mind, but she knew she had to be close to working out who had killed Salome and Pearl. Why else would she receive these notes? Someone was obviously rattled by her asking questions. 'With anything worthwhile there is an element of risk. I shall talk to Inspector Greville and listen to his advice. I promise you; I have no intention of getting myself or especially you, killed.'

'You know as you can count on me, Miss Kitty,' Alice replied and rose from her seat. 'We had best be on our top guard, then.'

'We shall take all precautions.' Kitty managed a smile to hopefully reassure the girl. She would not for the world do anything that might endanger Alice. 'I shall telephone the inspector now. In the meantime, we shall be extremely careful at the dress rehearsal tonight.'

'Very good, miss.' Alice smiled back at her and left Kitty to make her call.

Inspector Greville was unavailable when she telephoned the police station, but the desk sergeant assured her he would pass on her message. Kitty carefully manoeuvred the letter back into the envelope using her letter opener and her handkerchief. The inspector might be able to get some fingerprints from it.

She locked it inside the top drawer of her desk and tucked the key away in the pocket of her cardigan before continuing with her work. She was just coming to the end of her first list of bookwork when there was a knock at her office door and Inspector Greville was announced.

He drew off his hat as Kitty called him in and offered him the vacant seat, requesting her receptionist to send in tea and biscuits. His expression was grave as Kitty explained about the letter.

She unlocked the drawer and carefully passed over the envelope. The inspector opened it with gloved hands and perused the missive.

'It seems someone is concerned about the information you are uncovering, Miss Underhay. Perhaps you can tell me what else you have discovered recently?' He slid the letter back in the envelope and tucked it away carefully inside the breast pocket of his coat.

A maid knocked on the door and carried in the tea tray, setting it down carefully in the space Kitty had cleared on her desk. She waited till the girl had gone before offering the inspector a cup and resuming their conversation.

Inspector Greville munched happily on the hotel's home-made shortbread biscuits while Kitty updated him with everything she knew. It seemed Mrs Greville's diet had gone by the wayside, at least when not at home.

'Thank you, Miss Underhay.' He brushed the crumbs delicately from his moustache with his finger. 'That seems very comprehensive.'

'I have not told Matt about the letters,' Kitty said.

The inspector nodded. 'I see. I wondered if you might have reconsidered.'

'I was concerned he would worry about my safety and suggest I stay away from the Pavilion and the Davenports.' She sighed. 'I want his name cleared, Inspector, and I want this man caught. It is the dress rehearsal tonight and then the concert performance tomorrow night, so time is of the essence. I shall have Alice with me at the Pavilion so shall not be unaccompanied.' She continued to outline both her own duties and Alice's.

The inspector gave her his full attention. 'I can have some of my men at the theatre for the day of the performance. I shall endeavour to get a man inside the theatre for the rehearsal, undercover of course. It has been almost two weeks now since Miss Bright's murder and I would like to see this matter concluded. Do not go anywhere unaccompanied, Miss Underhay, and please advise your maid accordingly.' His tone was grave.

'I have been giving some thought to where the man masquerading as Salome's brother may have disposed of her trunk and the contents,' Kitty said. 'At first, I thought they might try once more incriminating Matt but then I thought, where would I leave something like that where it wouldn't attract attention?'

Inspector Greville gave her a sharp look. 'And your conclusion?'

'Perhaps it might be worth looking at the railway station, in the left luggage?'

'I shall make enquiries, Miss Underhay. Thank you for the refreshments, much appreciated.' He rose from his seat.

Kitty wondered if Mrs Greville was still insisting that he reduce his food intake. 'Not at all, Inspector. You will let me know if there are fingerprints on the letter or if my hunch about the station proves correct?'

He smiled. 'Of course.'

She saw him out and went back to her desk. Perhaps she should have told Matt about the letters, but after their argument at her uncle's home about what she should or shouldn't do, she was still wary. They had moved on from their disagreement and he had opened up to her a little more about his past, but she knew he would not be at all happy about her continued involvement in the investigation if he knew about the threats.

She took lunch with her grandmother in the hotel dining room. They avoided all discussion of the murders and focused their attention on business matters and the plans for the hotel over Christmas and the New Year.

After lunch, her grandmother went to rest for an hour in her salon. Kitty decided to take one of her regular walks around the hotel checking all was in order and to chat with her guests.

As she was making her way back through the deserted residents' lounge, a couple of familiar figures approached her. Matt's mother was dressed as if they had attended church in a smart navy dress and matching coat. The general walked with a silver-headed cane.

'General and Mrs Bryant, what a delightful surprise. I'm not certain if Matthew has returned to the hotel yet. My grandmother is in her salon if you wished to see her.' Kitty smiled a welcome at Matt's parents.

Matt's father made a slight hurrumphing sound as Mrs Bryant's hands fluttered. 'Oh no, Miss Underhay, it was really you we came to see.'

'Oh, very well, shall we take a seat?' Feeling slightly bewildered about why Matt's parents might wish to see her, Kitty led the way to a quiet seating area in the corner of the lounge.

'May I get you both some refreshments?' Kitty asked as the general and his wife arranged themselves in their chosen armchairs.

'Thank you, no, my dear, we have just come from the tearooms at the castle. Such a pleasant spot on a nice day with the views of the river,' Patience said.

Kitty subsided onto the sofa opposite Matt's parents and placed her hands in her lap, wondering what they wished to discuss with her.

General Bryant drew a meerschaum pipe from his pocket and began to fill it with tobacco.

'The weather is much improved today. Yesterday it was almost wintery, but today there is at least a little warmth in the sunshine,' Kitty said in an endeavour to make small talk, at a loss as to what Matt's parents could want with her.

The general focused on applying a light to his pipe.

'Oh yes, we did not venture out at all yesterday, but I wished to attend church this morning.' Mrs Bryant glanced at her husband who was now contentedly puffing away on his pipe.

'Was there something I could help you with?' Kitty asked as the conversation spluttered to an awkward halt once more.

'Well, Miss Underhay, Kitty, this is a little delicate. Your grandmother is of course an old friend of ours so I would not wish you to form the wrong idea about what we are about to say to you.' Patience glanced at her husband once more.

Kitty waited for Mrs Bryant to continue. She had no idea what the general and his wife would possibly wish to discuss with her that could be considered delicate.

Mrs Bryant's complexion had turned a shade of pink similar to the trim on her hat. 'You are aware of course that Matthew had a very difficult time during the war?'

Kitty nodded. She knew very well that Matt had suffered a great deal. She also thought he would not be terribly pleased that his parents were speaking to her about it.

'He was wounded twice. Once quite seriously. That was when he met Edith, his late wife. She nursed him. She was a few years older than Matthew, it was all something of a whirlwind affair.'

'He has spoken to me about his wife. I was unaware of how they met,' Kitty said.

'Edith and Betty, his daughter, were both killed during a Zeppelin raid on London while Matt was away on active service.' Patience fidgeted with the handle of her black leather handbag. The bright sunshine streaming in through the leaded windows highlighted the creases and wrinkles on her face.

'He has told me this,' Kitty said, relieved that at least she could reassure Matt's mother on that score.

Mrs Bryant seemed startled by her statement and looked towards her husband once more. 'Oh, well, I'm pleased he is more able to talk about things now. He has been reluctant to speak about what happened, understandably of course, it was terribly distressing at the time.'

'The war has been over a long time now. High time he pulled himself together. That marriage was most unsuitable. Matthew is too soft-hearted,' General Bryant muttered, his attention still focused on his pipe.

Kitty blinked. She hadn't been aware that Matt's parents had opposed his marriage to Edith.

'Has he spoken much about Edith and Betty?' Mrs Bryant asked.

'He has told me a little.' Kitty wondered where this conversation was leading. She was uncomfortable discussing Matt's past with his parents. It didn't feel right at all to her.

'He was very young, you understand, younger than you are now, and very intense. We are of course delighted that he has made a friendship with you, although there is something of an age gap between you.' Patience lifted her gaze to peep at Kitty and her face heated at the implications in the hint Matt's mother was giving.

'Mrs Milden, Matthew's housekeeper – a most genteel lady – has expressed some small concerns to us that we feel you should, as Matthew's close friend, be made aware of.' Patience paused; the rosy hue of her own cheeks had deepened even further.

'This would be the same lady who went to Inspector Greville and insinuated that Matt was capable of murder?' A cold, hard ball of anger had begun to form deep inside of Kitty.

'Oh, my dear, we know Matthew is most certainly not guilty of those terrible crimes.' Patience looked shocked. 'No, we were pleased that Matthew had begun to settle down and had hoped he could make a fresh start, form a new relationship.'

Kitty wished his mother would hurry and spit out what was on her mind. No wonder her grandmother and Mrs Craven had described Patience as a witterer.

'It's just that now, with these terrible murders and Matthew falling under suspicion, you must see, my dear, that it might be better if he moved away. His business will be badly affected by these allegations. People will say there is no smoke without fire. There must also be a safety concern if he should… well, form a close relationship with someone. The intimacies of sharing well a bedroom with… oh dear. It would take someone mature to… well, deal with his difficulties.' The older woman's hands were trembling, and her cheeks bore two burning spots of colour at the end of her statement.

Kitty stared at Mrs Bryant. 'Matt is a friend, that is all, and I know he is not guilty of these crimes and I intend to prove it.' The hints of a relationship made her feel a little uncomfortable, especially when she recalled the kiss she and Matt had shared. Matt was fourteen years older than her, not an uncommon gap these days. Did he share some of these concerns about the scars on his psyche that the war may have inflicted upon him? Was his mother hinting that they disapproved of a potential relationship between Matt and Kitty?

General Bryant snorted. 'Detective work is no job for a young lady. The police must handle the matter. Let that chap, Greville, earn his keep. Matthew would be better off out of it. I've advised him to return to London with us when we go home.'

Kitty swallowed hard. Her hands had balled into fists and her nails dug into her palms as she strived to maintain her equilibrium. 'I believe Inspector Greville is very close to solving the case. Matt has many friends here and very few people have any belief that he was involved in the deaths of those girls. There seems to me to be no reason for him to leave unless that is what he wants to do.'

'I had hoped that as his close friend you could help persuade him that remaining here might not be good for him. It could trigger a relapse of his health.' Patience's fingers fluttered and fussed with her bag.

'There has to be some truth in the rumours, that's what people will say.' General Bryant emitted another cloud of aromatic tobacco smoke from his pipe as he repeated his wife's words.

'There will always be some who think the worst of anyone,' Kitty agreed. 'However, Inspector Greville has been scrupulous about treating Matt exactly as he would anyone under suspicion of a serious crime. He has ensured that Matt has been kept at a distance and cannot possibly be implicated as being involved, especially with the second murder. All right-thinking people know of Matt's reputation for honesty and integrity. The only person it seems to me who is spreading discord is Mrs Milden. I would strongly urge Matt to rethink his employment of her.' She was proud of the even tone of her voice although she knew her cheeks had flushed with anger.

'You know he has terrors at night? When he may be capable of violence?' Patience asked in a low tone.

'My grandmother and I are sadly very familiar with former soldiers who were left damaged by their experiences during the war. Many of our guests have suffered similarly. Matt has nightmares, that is all, not an uncommon occurrence.' This was true. Mickey had been prevailed upon a few times to discreetly aid some poor soul who had relived an experience during his sleep leading him to wander out of the hotel and even into the river.

Patience gathered her gloves and bag together. 'Very well. We had hoped you would assist us in encouraging Matthew to give this up and return to London. He has a brighter future there. There is an embassy posting which would be perfect for a man of his experience.'

'The choice of what he wishes to do must be Matt's and his alone. I'm sorry to disappoint you but I don't believe I have that level of influence over him and even if I did, I don't believe that it would be right for me to use it.' Kitty stood up at the same time as Matt's parents.

'Give our regards to your grandmother, I'm sorry you are not prepared to assist us.' Patience drew on her gloves and turned to her husband.

The general offered his wife his arm. 'Good day, Miss Underhay.'

Kitty watched them both out before sinking back in her seat with a sigh of relief. Her hands and knees were trembling and her mind reeling from the conversation. Matt had given her no indication that he was considering leaving Devon. What if his parents succeeded in persuading him?

CHAPTER TWENTY-TWO

Matt was shown through to Mrs Craven's drawing room by a uniformed maid, who informed him that her mistress would come through shortly. The drawing room was at the front of the house with a fine bay window. Sunlight sparkled on the sunray design of the coloured glass in the top lights, spilling jewel-coloured rays on the parquet floor and Turkish rug.

He took a seat on one of the tapestry-covered armchairs beside the fireplace and waited for Mrs Craven. The maid had relieved him of his long coat and hat in the hall and despite the sunshine outside, the room had a slightly chilly edge.

Mrs Craven appeared after a moment, dressed in one of her neat navy-blue costumes, pearls around her neck and a diamond brooch on her bosom.

'Matthew, what a surprise. I had the pleasure of seeing your parents earlier today at church. How goes the case?' She took a seat in the chair opposite his and surveyed him keenly.

He dutifully updated her on all that Kitty and Alice had discovered and his own conversations with Inspector Greville. 'I am truly grateful for all the assistance you have given in helping me to clear my name,' he said.

'I owe you a debt and I always pay my debts. I am well aware of how fortunate I was a few months back when you found me after I had been attacked in my own garden by that dreadful man.' She shuddered at the memory. 'Then when I discovered that unfortunate girl in the bunker on the golf course,' she paused and shook her head in sorrow, 'I was determined that justice would be done. I knew you were not responsible. I still consider it most reprehensible that Inspector Greville should have arrested you.'

'I hope the inspector may be closer now to solving the case. I would urge you to be careful, Mrs Craven. This person is dangerous. I have given the same warning to Kitty.'

She gave him a piercing look. 'I understand. Your parents seem to think you are intending to give up your house and may leave Devon?'

Her question took him by surprise. His father had dropped several hints when he had last seen them, but he had not seriously entertained the idea at all. 'I don't know why they would think that. I have no intention of leaving. I want my name completely cleared and my reputation restored. I hope then that my business will recover. Naturally, with the murderer still at large and the reports that have been in the press, I am hardly fighting off clients.' He gave a wry smile.

'I am pleased to hear that you intend to stay. Kitty's grandmother tells me you have had some small breakthroughs investigating Elowed's disappearance?' Her mouth screwed up as she pronounced Elowed's name.

'Yes, we are a little more forward and have traced her to Exeter where it seems she may have been followed.' He wasn't sure how much more they would learn after all this time. The chances of anyone remembering much at the Glass Bottle would be very slim. While they awaited news from Father Lamb, he had asked Mickey to ask his wife for any information she might have regarding the public house before he made a visit there.

'She always kept strange company. Artists, theatre people and those suffragists. Her poor mother suffered a great deal, especially when she became involved with Kitty's father.' Mrs Craven gave a sniff of disapproval.

'Yet her father's family are eminently respectable. Lord Medford is very well thought of.' Matt did his best to defend Kitty's family.

'Unlike some titled people I could mention. Of course, you know Stanley Davenport is angling for a knighthood? For services to the theatre and of course all those good works he gets Genevieve to perform and which he takes all the credit for. Really, Genny would be much the better person than Peter to run the business but Stanley is very old-fashioned. That is why he was so keen to put distance between these murders and his household, especially with the unsavoury rumours around Peter. It would have been very convenient if you had been the culprit,' Mrs Craven said.

'It certainly confirms why Mrs Davenport is so keen to believe me guilty,' Matt replied. Mrs Craven's snippet of information explained a great deal about the Davenports.

He made small talk for a little longer before saying farewell. He needed to ride his motorcycle somewhere open and away from people where he could think. It felt as if all the clues to solving the case were starting to come together but he was missing one key piece to unlock the entire puzzle.

Matt didn't reappear at the hotel before Kitty and Alice needed to leave for the evening dress rehearsal at the Pavilion. She asked Mickey to let Matt know where they had gone and that they were due back some time after ten o'clock that evening.

The letter from earlier had unnerved her a little and she was determined to take what precautions she could to ensure both her own and Alice's safety. She had arranged for Mr Potter to take them into Torquay in his taxi and to collect them and bring them back to the Dolphin once the rehearsal was complete.

She had learned from her previous encounters with ruthless criminals that preparation was key. Accordingly, she ensured she wore her shoes with a low heel in case she had to run and took her stout umbrella which could double as a weapon.

Alice met her in the hotel foyer, having changed from her uniform into a simple crepe de chine frock which Kitty suspected was one of Betty's hand-me-downs. She too wore practical shoes.

'Have you had something to eat, Alice?' Kitty was acutely aware that the girl had not long finished her shift and must be tired.

'Yes, miss, the chef did me poached eggs on toast.' Alice beamed at her.

The light had started to fade as they set off for Torquay and the sun was sinking low over the sea as they travelled down the hill towards the town past the large hotels at the start of the promenade walk.

Mr Potter pulled the taxi to a halt behind the Davenports' large black car. Genny was already out at the kerb waiting for Laurence and Tilly Tilney. As Kitty and Alice joined Genny, a further car pulled up with Seb, Peter and Mrs Davenport inside.

'Oh, there is BeBe and Dickie,' Genny said to Kitty and Alice, waving to attract their attention as the couple crossed the road to join them.

Kitty and Alice greeted the rest of the group as they met up before turning to troop up the marble steps and into the Pavilion via the front doors.

'Right then, everyone, fifteen minutes and we commence the run-through. The children will be here shortly with the am-dram people. We shall do their part early so they may return to the home before it gets late. We don't want them over-tired and fractious for the actual performance,' Laurence said.

'Miss Miller, I'll show you to your place with the amended running order.' Genny bobbed about anxiously from one foot to the other, earning herself a scornful look from her mother. 'Kitty, you have your prompting notes?'

'Of course.' Kitty smiled and went to hang her coat in the cloakroom before taking her seat in the wings.

Laurence removed his jacket and strode about the stage calling instructions to the lighting man in the gallery. In the opposite wing to where Kitty was seated, a youth of around fifteen or sixteen was in charge of raising and lowering the curtain and the painted stage flats which were to be used as backdrops.

For reasons of cost and simplicity there were only two painted backdrops which were being recycled from the opera which had been performed at the Pavilion a couple of weeks earlier.

The other performers arrived and disappeared backstage to get ready. The children also appeared and were rapidly corralled by Genny amidst much giggling to complete their performance first.

Dickie took his place at the piano and flexed his fingers before playing a few notes in readiness for the start of the rehearsal. Once Laurence was happy that all was well, the boy lowered the curtain and Dickie began to play the first song, signalling the curtain to rise once more as it would for the start of the actual performance.

Kitty found it both fascinating and challenging to witness the stitching together of all the separate acts into a credible performance. There were hitches along the way. The children forgot their words and the conjurer's rabbit was reluctant to materialise, but the first half seemed to go well, she thought.

The children were shepherded off while Larry organised the changes to the flats and lights during the fifteen-minute intermission. Alice appeared at Kitty's elbow through the small door leading from the wings to the backstage area bearing a glass of fruit squash.

'Thank you, Alice. Is everything running smoothly back there?' Kitty asked. She had been concentrating so hard on her role she had screened out any sounds coming from the dressing rooms.

'I think so, miss. It's been very chaotic, and that conjuror is a right pest with them animals, what with the doves and rabbits,'

Alice said disapprovingly. 'I'm right glad them young lads have gone as well now.'

'I'm sure you coped brilliantly,' Kitty said.

'All right, places, people, places,' Larry called.

Alice vanished backstage once more, and the second half commenced. Seb and Peter were funny and charming. BeBe sang beautifully and was followed by Tilly, who only required a couple of prompts during her soliloquies. Even Tilly's singing wasn't too off-key and Kitty breathed a sigh of relief.

Mrs Davenport did not appear to have bothered to change into her costume but came out and gave a medley of old music hall songs. Eventually they were all finished, and Larry declared himself satisfied.

Kitty stood up and collected her papers together and stretched. Her back ached and she felt a little numb after sitting on the hard, wooden chair for so long. She bent to collect her empty glass to return it to Alice, deciding she would bring a cushion to sit on for the actual performance.

She glanced around her, Larry was talking to Tilly on the far side of the stage; Dickie was with BeBe, gathering up his sheet music from the piano.

'Miss, look out!'

Startled by the warning shout which seemed to have come from the gallery, Kitty stepped to the side, dropping the glass as she moved. As she did so one of the large sandbags used to weight the pulley system used for the fly mechanism crashed to the floor next to her.

'What the hell?' Larry strode towards her, a furious expression on his face. 'Bill!'

Kitty's knees shook and she sank back down onto her chair. The gawky lad who had been in charge of the ropes came running from the wings at Larry's shout. His ruddy complexion turned ashen when he realised what had happened.

'Who's been messing with me ropes?' the boy asked, his face a picture of bewilderment.

'Kitty, are you all right?' Genny had come out onto the stage with the others at the commotion. 'Miss Miller, a glass of water, please,' she commanded a pale and shaken Alice.

Alice came rushing back with a glass of water, pressing it into Kitty's hand. 'Are you all right, Miss Kitty? What happened?'

'Somebody's cut this rope.' Billy had been examining the sandbag and the rope which normally would have secured it high above the stage.

'Oh, don't be so ridiculous. You must not have secured it properly,' Tilly said.

The lad glowered at her and waved the end of the rope. 'Don't you go throwing your accusations about, missus! It's been cut, see, clean through.'

Kitty felt nauseous. If the bag had hit her, she would have been badly injured or even killed.

Larry stepped forward to confirm the lad's words. 'He's right, there's no sign of fraying or wear. It certainly appears as if it's been cut.'

'Probably one of those wretched children as some kind of practical joke,' Celeste Davenport suggested. 'You know what boys are like with penknives and suchlike. We often had issues when I was performing with youths thinking they were being terribly funny hiding costumes and such hi-jinks.'

'The boys left at the break and they were supervised all the while they was here.' Alice was indignant. 'And why would it drop now?'

'My dear, children are capable of anything.' Celeste stalked off.

'You were lucky, Kitty darling. Probably used one of your nine lives,' Seb said, his face pale as he peeked at Peter.

'I think as we should go home, miss. You look proper poorly.' Alice took the glass from her and set it down, ignoring the broken shards from her earlier glass which were now scattered around her.

'Oh, my goodness yes, shall I see if your car has come for you?' Genny asked.

'I'll go.' Peter walked away towards the main exit.

'My coat is in the cloakroom,' Kitty said. She wanted to stand and leave but annoyingly, her legs felt like cotton wool.

Alice rose from where she had been crouching next to her. 'I'll get my things, miss. Are you all right for a minute?'

Kitty nodded. She wanted to get out of the theatre and away from the Davenports. One of them had sabotaged that rope, whether to scare her or harm her she wasn't sure. Alice bustled back, shrugging on her coat as she came to assist Kitty up from her seat.

'Come on, miss, mind the glass.' Alice walked with her, holding her arm for support. Genny accompanied them, wittering away, as they walked through the auditorium.

'Your taxi is here,' Peter announced.

Genny darted into the cloakroom and retrieved Kitty's coat. 'Are you sure you're all right? What a silly prank for someone to play. I'm sure Mother must be right, and one of those children must have slipped away for a second while we were all so busy.'

Kitty allowed her to continue with her prattle. She was in no doubt that the rope had been cut deliberately and aimed at her. Alice gently but firmly steered her out of the theatre and into the back of Mr Potter's taxi.

'Oh, miss, that was frightening. You need to talk to Inspector Greville, I'm not sure as we shouldn't have called the police there and then,' she said as soon as they had pulled away and were driving off, following the curve of the bay as the moonlight glimmered on the inky sea.

'Perhaps, but they would only have seen a cut rope and I wanted to get away from there as quickly as possible. Someone wants me to mind my own business.' She felt better now she was safely in Mr Potter's car and the Davenports were nowhere near her.

'I think as you should tell Captain Bryant about this, miss. He ought to know.' Alice frowned.

'There is nothing he can do, Alice. I'll telephone Inspector Greville first thing in the morning. Really, you're right, we should have insisted on calling the police tonight, but I don't think they could have done anything. With any luck, whoever did it may be satisfied thinking they have scared me off.' Kitty leaned back against the seat of the taxi.

'Do you think they might try again?' Alice asked in a small voice.

Kitty reached over and squeezed the girl's hand. 'No, I think this was just to scare me off. Anyway there is only tomorrow's performance to go and then it is over. We have to hope that the inspector will have found enough evidence to make an arrest soon.'

She tried to sound confident for Alice's sake. She didn't want to think about what might happen if Inspector Greville failed to catch the murderer. Would Matt even stay? Or would he follow his parents' advice and leave with them?

The closer they got to Dartmouth, the more the fear she'd experienced at the Pavilion was replaced by a cold, hard ball of anger that someone should have made such an audacious attempt upon her life.

After they had crossed the river, Kitty insisted that Mr Potter continue on and take Alice home after setting her down at the hotel. She wanted to ensure that Alice was not walking alone through the dark streets of Dartmouth with a vengeful killer on the loose.

The night porter tipped his peaked cap to her as she entered the hotel. 'Good evening, Miss Kitty.'

The faint sounds of music and people drifted from the ballroom where her guests were enjoying the house band. The familiar sounds and scents of the Dolphin wrapped themselves around her, making her feel safe and secure once more.

'Miss Kitty, a note came for you after you'd gone out.' The evening receptionist handed her a small brown envelope.

Your hunch was correct. Salome's trunk now recovered.
P. G. Greville

'Thank you.' She smiled at the receptionist and slipped the note inside her handbag with her prompting notes. If the inspector now had Salome's trunk, they might get lucky and find some fingerprints or another clue to lead them to the killer.

She collected a cup of cocoa from the kitchen and took it with her to her room. It wasn't until later, once she was safely tucked into her bed with her door locked, that she suddenly wondered what the 'P. G.' stood for in Inspector Greville's name.

The following morning, a sharp rap on her bedroom door woke her from a fitful sleep.

'One minute.' She slipped out of bed and shrugged on her wrapper before unlocking her door and risking a peek.

'Alice, come in.' Alice was on the landing bearing a tray of breakfast things.

The girl obeyed and carried the tray to Kitty's table before opening the curtains to let in the weak autumnal sunshine. She was dressed in the same neat outfit she'd worn yesterday – the navy crepe de chine which was slightly large and looked a little too old for her. However, it had been neatly pressed, and the girl had taken care with her appearance.

'I brought you some breakfast up, Miss Kitty. Mrs Craven is sending the car for us in an hour.'

'What? What time is it?' Kitty glanced at her beloved cuckoo clock and groaned. 'Oh no, I've overslept.'

'And no wonder, after yesterday. You have your toast and a cup of tea now, miss, and I'll fix your hair,' Alice said placidly.

Kitty groaned again. She had forgotten that Mrs Craven had arranged for them to go into Torquay before lunch. They were to collect the remaining outstanding donations and money from ticket sales and take them to the theatre. Genny would then ensure everything was organised, ready for the evening performance.

Kitty intended to call at the police station to make Inspector Greville aware of the events of last night. She hastily swallowed the cup of tea which Alice had poured for her.

'I was thinking when I got home last night,' Alice said, picking up a comb and gesturing to Kitty to sit on the stool in front of the dressing table, 'that we could rule some people out now.'

Kitty sat down and picked up a slice of toast, ready to submit to Alice's ministrations. 'Yes, I see what you mean. Dickie never left the piano so he couldn't have cut the rope and Larry was always opposite me on the other side of the stage.'

'Well, then that's two of them. Everyone else was here, there and everywhere though.' Alice's deft fingers began to restore some order to the waves in Kitty's hair.

'Whoever cut it must have taken their chance when I moved. Everyone knew where I would be seated for the prompting. That means it had to be someone in the theatre at the time. It couldn't have been one of the children – not that I ever believed that anyway.' Kitty crunched on her toast and winced as Alice caught a knot in her hair with the comb.

'Sorry, miss,' Alice apologised.

'I need to call in and update Inspector Greville this morning, but I don't wish to alarm Mrs Craven. You know she has taken a keen interest in the case.' Kitty licked a crumb from the corner of her mouth.

'I can distract her for you, miss, like they do in the films.' Alice's expression, reflected in the dressing table mirror, brightened.

'We may have a chance whilst we are collecting the remainder of the ticket monies,' Kitty said.

Alice took a step back. 'There you go, miss, mind you don't knock your hair getting your frock on. I'll clear these things and meet you in the lobby.' She gathered up the breakfast tray and hurried away to leave Kitty to finish dressing.

Mrs Craven, courtesy of Mr Potter and his taxi, was prompt as usual. Kitty hurried down the main staircase with seconds to spare. Alice was next to the reception desk waiting for her.

'The car has just pulled up, miss.'

'Thank you, Alice.' Kitty wondered where Matt was; she was a little surprised he hadn't left a message for her after going to see Mrs Craven yesterday. Then again, she hadn't told him that someone had tried to kill her. She made sure the receptionist knew where she was going in case her grandmother or Matt needed to find her and followed Alice outside to the waiting car.

Mrs Craven was pointedly studying the tiny platinum and diamond studded watch on her wrist as Kitty scrambled breathlessly into the seat next to her. Alice joined her and closed the door.

'We have a lot to get done today before the performance.' Mrs Craven settled her capacious black patent handbag onto her lap. 'Now, when we get to Torquay, we have a number of establishments to visit. They have donated financially or have offered prizes for a raffle during the intermission.'

'Has Genny provided you with a list?' Kitty asked. She intended to offer to visit the ones nearest to the police station.

Mrs Craven twisted the gilt fastener on the top of her bag to open it and retrieve the list. She passed it to Kitty.

'I take it we are to divide and conquer, so to speak, if we are to get around all of these?'

Mrs Craven glanced at the list. 'I suppose it would be easier if you and Miss Miller were to take the organisations Genny has listed that are offering prizes. Miss Miller can assist you to carry them.'

Kitty raised an eyebrow but bit her tongue. Alice stayed silent, her attention apparently given to the passing scenery.

'At least the weather is holding now and remaining fine,' Mrs Craven remarked. 'It shouldn't take the two of you very long to collect the outstanding items and deliver them to Genny at the theatre. With luck, if you don't dawdle you should have time for lunch before being back at the Pavilion in time to begin preparing for the evening performance. Oh, and Mrs Davenport is very kindly offering supper back at her house after the performance for all the artistes and helpers.'

'How very kind of her.' Kitty couldn't think of anything she'd like less, and Alice's expression appeared to share the same sentiment.

Mr Potter set them down in the town centre and Mrs Craven issued them with the portion of the list she wished them to visit before she set off briskly in the opposite direction.

'Are we going to the police station first, miss?' Alice asked.

Kitty sighed as she studied the list. 'Yes, I think we must. Let's hope the inspector is free to see us as it may take us some time to complete Mrs Craven's list.'

The two women made their way towards the police station. Kitty sensed Alice's reluctance to enter as they arrived at the front steps.

'It's quite all right, I've been here several times now,' Kitty reassured her as they went inside.

The desk sergeant recognised her. 'Good morning, Miss Under-hay, miss.' He nodded at Alice who immediately blushed and partly hid behind Kitty. 'I'll let the inspector know you're here.'

'Thank you.' Kitty led Alice to the by now familiar dark wood chairs and waited to see if the inspector had time to see them.

'If you'd care to follow me,' the sergeant said as he replaced the telephone receiver back on the handset.

Alice looked nervous as the sergeant led them along the corridor to the inspector's office.

'Miss Underhay and another young lady to see you, sir.' The sergeant pulled another chair up ready for Alice and left them to talk to the inspector.

The office appeared to be disappearing under stacks of paper and Kitty found her fingers itching with the urge to tidy them all up.

'You received my note, Miss Underhay?' Inspector Greville asked after he'd greeted them both.

'Indeed. It was waiting for me when I returned to the hotel last night,' Kitty said.

The inspector's moustache twitched. 'Yet, I have the feeling that it wasn't that which has brought you here this morning.'

'Somebody tried to kill Miss Kitty at the theatre last night,' Alice blurted, her cheeks a fiery shade of scarlet.

Inspector Greville leaned back in his chair, a grave expression on his face as he glanced first at Alice, who looked as if she wished to sink through the floor, and then at Kitty.

'Someone attempted to drop a sandbag – one of the weights for the pulley system for changing the scenery – on my head. They cut through the rope,' Kitty explained. She told the inspector some of the conclusions that she and Alice had drawn after the incident.

'You were very fortunate, Miss Underhay. This is a very serious incident. I shall send a constable to take a look around and talk to this Bill fellow.' The inspector continued to survey them.

'I would have reported it last night, but quite honestly, I was rather shaken.'

'Hmm, I don't suppose a few hours will make much difference in the case of an event such as this. I'll make sure everyone is questioned.' He rummaged under a sheaf of papers to retrieve the telephone and issued a stream of instructions into the receiver before hanging up.

'Did you learn anything of use from Miss Donohue's trunk?' Kitty asked, feeling somewhat better knowing the inspector was taking her report of the incident seriously.

'No fingerprints other than Salome's and the landlady's. Nothing in the contents. They had clearly been searched though, and in a hurry, I would say,' Inspector Greville replied.

'Did anyone at the station recall anything?' Kitty asked. She had not expected there to be anything in the trunk that might help them, the murderer would have seen to that.

'A gentleman deposited the trunk, no clear description.' Greville suddenly leaned forward across his desk, causing Alice to shrink back in her chair. 'I'm in two minds about this concert. This may be a warning to you, Miss Underhay, but it may also have been a serious attempt to kill you. And if you return then I suspect there may be another.'

Alarm showed on Alice's thin features. 'I told Miss Kitty as she was lucky last night.'

A frisson of fear skittered along Kitty's spine, but she held her nerve. 'We have to catch this man, Inspector, and it's obvious that he must be amongst the group at the theatre. There is only this evening's performance to go and then I believe the Davenport party intends to return to London in the next few days.'

'What are the plans for this performance?' the inspector asked.

Kitty glanced at Alice. 'We are currently collecting the outstanding raffle prizes and ticket sales money from a few businesses in the town. We have to return them to the Pavilion to Genevieve Davenport. Mrs Craven is collecting items also. I believe we are then checking that everything is ready for the evening, setting up the raffle and so on before breaking for lunch. We are due to return to the theatre at six to prepare for the evening performance. Alice will be backstage assisting with the children and making sure the performers have the correct costumes and props. I will be in the wings at the side of the stage where I am to prompt. At the end of the performance I shall assist Alice to pack up all the costumes and props before we leave.'

The inspector nodded at her run-down of the day's schedule. 'Very comprehensive, Miss Underhay.'

Kitty felt slightly sick every time she thought of having to resume her seat in the wings, but she was also determined that she would catch whoever had tried to kill her. 'I doubt the person who tried to harm me would try the same method again. But I admit, I don't like to think what they would try next.'

Inspector Greville leaned back once more. 'Either way, you need to be on your guard. I have arranged for officers to be at the theatre. If there is any sign of trouble or danger, I want you and this young lady,' he nodded at Alice, 'to be out of there.'

'I got a whistle in my bag. I saw it in the films where they blow it, so the police come running if something happens,' Alice announced proudly, taking Kitty by surprise.

'Good thinking, young lady.' The inspector smiled at Alice, sending colour flooding into her face once more.

'Stay alert, Miss Underhay. Please, if you value your safety, do nothing and say nothing that might provoke this person to action. If they think they have frightened you off from poking around then you may be safe.' The inspector frowned.

'I promise I shall be careful,' Kitty assured him.

Alice nodded agreement as the two of them took their farewells with the inspector. He saw them back along the corridor to the reception area.

'If there is anything at all amiss, send word immediately.' The inspector looked at his desk sergeant. 'I shall advise my staff that they are to find me and send aid straight away.'

'Thank you, Inspector. Come, Alice, or Mrs Craven will be on the warpath and I am more frightened of her sometimes than this murderer.' She smiled at the inspector and she and Alice left the station to resume their errands.

CHAPTER TWENTY-THREE

Matt waited until he saw Kitty and Alice exit the police station before making his way across the street and up the steps into the reception. Kitty was up to something and he was determined to discover what was going on.

'Captain Bryant.' Inspector Greville was standing with the desk sergeant in the waiting area. He noted that the inspector appeared unsurprised to see him.

'Inspector.' He shook Greville's hand and the inspector led him along the corridor to his office.

Once he was seated the policeman asked, 'What can I do for you?'

'I saw Miss Underhay and her companion leaving the police station. Have there been any new developments in the case?'

Greville opened his cigarette case and offered one to Matt. Matt accepted and took a light, waiting for a reply. The inspector lit his own cigarette and took a drag at it before answering.

'I take it you haven't spoken to Miss Underhay today?'

Matt blew out a thin stream of smoke. The small room made him uncomfortable, reminding him too closely of the cells in the floor below. 'No, I missed her when she returned from the theatre last night and she didn't go to the dining room for breakfast this morning, but I know Kitty, and there is something afoot.'

The inspector looked at him through the faint blue haze of cigarette smoke now starting to fill the office. 'There was an incident at the theatre last night. Miss Underhay came to report it this morning.' He told Matt what had happened at the Pavilion and updated him on the discovery of Salome's box.

Matt listened with a growing sense of anger, mixed with concern. He knew from the hotel staff that it had been late when Kitty had returned to the hotel, but she could still have tried to find him. Perhaps that was why she hadn't been at breakfast, perhaps she hadn't wanted him to find out.

'There is more,' the inspector added and produced the letters that Kitty had received from a drawer in his desk. 'No fingerprints, cheap paper, nothing to identify the sender.'

Matt was stunned. 'Why did she not say anything?' Did she not trust him? Was this to do with their argument at Enderley Hall where she had insisted on her right to be treated as an equal partner with no concession to her sex?

'I think that is a discussion you need to have with Miss Underhay. However, she indicated that she feels very strongly that your name should be publicly cleared.' The inspector exhaled and extinguished his cigarette in the glass ashtray on his desk.

'What arrangements are in hand for her safety?' Matt asked, putting out his own cigarette in the same fashion.

'I've arranged for some of my men to be in the theatre tonight. I have dispatched some of my constables to question the witnesses to the incident and to look at the ropes and sandbag. Miss Underhay's companion is carrying a police whistle to summon aid if needed and Miss Underhay herself is adamant that she will not take any risks.'

Matt groaned involuntarily at the latter part of the inspector's statement. Both times before when Kitty had assured him that she would be careful and not take any risks she had almost succeeded in getting herself killed.

'I want to be there tonight, inside the theatre, Inspector.'

Greville looked at him. 'I cannot prevent you, but I advise against it.'

'I shall not get in the way of any of your men or impede your investigation, but I cannot continue to stand back and allow Kitty to bear all the risks.' Matt met the inspector's gaze without a blink.

Inspector Greville picked up a pencil and drummed it absent-mindedly against the edge of his desk. 'It would be better if no one in the Davenport party catches sight of you. That could be the thing that makes them desperate.'

'Because it would give them one more opportunity to fix the crimes on me?' Matt asked.

'And they know of your friendship with Miss Underhay,' the inspector said.

'Can you get me inside the theatre gallery? Where the lighting man sits, up at the top?' Matt had attended many performances at different theatres and had a good understanding of their general layout. He guessed that from the stage no one would look up directly at the gallery where the lighting man sat, and if they did, they would be unlikely to see him. He, on the other hand, would have a good bird's-eye view of the stage and auditorium.

Greville appeared to consider the idea. 'I believe Miss Underhay to be in more danger than she thinks, so very well, I will see the Pavilion manager and make arrangements.'

Matt released a sigh of relief. 'That's Kitty for you. She always underestimates the risks and doesn't take kindly to being reminded of them.'

Inspector Greville smiled sadly and shook his head. 'That's all modern young ladies these days. Even Mrs Greville is the same way. Though, I wouldn't have her any other way.'

Genny was in the Pavilion box office when Alice and Kitty arrived carrying an assortment of raffle prizes and the remainder of the unsold tickets and collected monies. She was dressed in a particularly

ugly shade of mustard-yellow crushed velvet and wore her usual
distracted air.

'Oh, Miss Underhay and Miss Miller, thank you so much.
Millicent has just delivered the things she's collected.' Genny
waved her hand at a pile of goods in a cardboard box standing on
a small side table.

Alice added the items they had collected to the box while Kitty
delved into her bag for the money and tickets.

'No trouble collecting these, I hope?' Genny asked anxiously,
peering at them through her spectacles.

'No, not at all. There aren't many tickets remaining. Everyone
appears to have done very well with their sales,' Kitty remarked.

'Everyone has been remarkably generous. The orphanage
Christmas fund should do very well out of this,' Genny said.
She squinted at Kitty. 'Are you recovered from last night? Such a
horrid thing to happen and so frightening. The police have been
here already asking questions.' Her round, pleasant face wore a
concerned expression.

'A night's sleep always helps, doesn't it? I have been to see Inspector Greville, though I doubt he will be able to do anything. That's
probably why the police have called. No doubt it was a prank of
some kind that went wrong.' Kitty tried to brush it off. 'Now, how
can we assist you?'

Alice and Kitty helped to arrange a table in the foyer to display
the raffle prizes whilst Genny completed counting the money from
the ticket sales.

'Oh, that does look splendid. Are you going for lunch now? I
believe Millicent has gone back to the house to dine with Mother.'
Genny admired their display. The businesses had been generous;
toys, wine, chocolates and some fancy goods adorned the table.

'Yes, I promised Alice lunch at one of the cafés. You are welcome
to join us if you like,' Kitty offered. She always felt a little sorry for

Genny. The girl appeared somewhat lonely and without friends, plus Celeste was never very kind to her.

Genny's face lit up and her eyes sparkled. 'Really? Oh, that is terribly kind of you.' Then her face fell, and the sparkle faded. 'I have to go back to the house, though. I need to keep an eye on Mother.'

'That's a pity. Then we shall have to make a luncheon date when this is all finished,' Kitty said.

Genny cheered up at her suggestion. 'Yes, that would be lovely.'

'Will you be all right if Alice and I go for our lunch now?' Kitty felt a little uncomfortable at leaving Genny alone in the theatre with money and goods.

'Oh yes, perfectly. The manager and the lighting man are inside. Peter and Seb should be calling in too when the police have finished speaking to them. They can give me a ride home,' Genny said.

Kitty and Alice left her to finish off and walked back down the steps of the theatre ready to cross the road.

'Just in time, miss. There's Mr Peter and his friend now.' Alice nudged her arm as they scampered across the street, drawing her attention to Peter's car gliding to a stop near the theatre.

'Yes, I am in no hurry to see either of them.' Kitty shuddered and tucked her hand in the crook of Alice's elbow. 'Come, I promised you ham and eggs at the Cosy Kettle.'

The Cosy Kettle was popular amongst the older, well-heeled residents of Torquay. Kitty had lunched there several times before with her grandmother and her great aunt Livvy. The tablecloths were delicate pink damask overlaid with lace and the waitresses wore smart, dark grey uniforms.

The restaurant was quiet as the main lunch rush was over by the time they arrived. Alice beamed as they were shown to one of the best tables near the window. 'It's proper posh in here, miss,' she whispered to Kitty as she opened her menu and peeped shyly over the top of its leatherette cover.

'We deserve a treat.' Kitty gave their order to the waitress.

Alice gazed out of the window, a small frown puckering the centre of her forehead. 'Is that Captain Bryant's motorcycle, miss?' she asked as a Sunbeam drove slowly along the street before halting in front of a shop further down.

Kitty followed Alice's gaze as the rider dismounted and entered one of the shops. Her pulse speeded at the glimpse of his tall, rangy figure. 'It certainly looks like Matt. Oh dear, I hope he doesn't see us. I don't really want to tell him anything about last night or the letters until after tonight's performance is completed.'

'I think as you should have told him, miss,' Alice ventured.

'I shall tell him as soon as this performance tonight is done and out of the way. I know Matt; if he knew about the sandbag then he would want me to pull out of the investigation or even worse, do something that might place him in danger of the noose. Remember, this person, whoever it is, has gone to some trouble to try to implicate Matt.'

The waitress returned with their order, placing two steaming plates of golden-yolked eggs and thick slices of ham before them.

Alice waited until the girl had gone. 'At least the inspector knows about it all. I shall feel better knowing as there's police in the theatre tonight.'

'Yes, that is reassuring. Do you really have a police whistle, Alice?'

The girl nodded vigorously, her auburn curls bouncing under the brim of her hat. 'Oh yes, miss. My uncle Bert give it me, for when I'm walking home and it's dark or if a lad was to get too fresh, if you get my meaning. I have to blow it and then someone will likely come to help me, or it'll scare them off.' She fished inside her bag and showed it to Kitty. 'You have it with you tonight, miss.'

'Your uncle Bert is a man of good sense, Alice.' Kitty smiled.

They took their time over lunch, enjoying the cosy, genteel ambience of the café. Kitty couldn't resist taking regular peeps through the window at Matt's motorcycle, only relaxing with a tinge of regret when he'd gone.

After their late lunch they window-shopped for a while, dawdling along the high street peering at the various delights in the shops. Kitty refused to admit to herself that she wished to defer the return to the Pavilion for as long as possible. The incident the previous night had affected her more than she cared to acknowledge.

Gradually however, the sun disappeared beneath a growing blanket of cloud and a cool breeze started to blow in from the sea.

'We should get back to the concert hall. Genny will have another list of tasks for us, no doubt,' Kitty said, taking a last lingering look at a very pretty pair of patent heels in a shop window display.

'It was nice that you invited her out, miss. She seems a nice lady and her family treat her something terrible,' Alice observed as they made their way back towards the seafront.

'I can't help thinking that if Peter and Seb are somehow involved in this terrible business, poor Genny will take it very hard. She already has enough on her plate with her mother,' Kitty said.

Alice nodded sagely. 'That Mrs Davenport likes a tipple. She had a silver hip flask on her last night and she fair smelled of liquor by the end of the show.'

'Oh dear, no wonder Genny felt she needed to return home for lunch.'

The lights were on inside the Pavilion as they approached, illuminating the decorative leaded glass of the windows. Kitty took a deep breath and led the way as she and Alice re-entered the building.

They hung their things in the cloakroom ready to start work. Alice took the silver-coloured whistle from her bag and pressed it into Kitty's hand, taking care no one was around to witness the exchange. 'Here, miss, keep it in your pocket. I don't reckon as I need it as much as you. Besides, I've got other tricks up my sleeve if I need them.' Alice patted her pocket with a smile.

Kitty slipped the whistle into the side pocket of her jacket and silently blessed Alice's uncle Bert for his forethought. She decided not to ask Alice what other items she might have concealed about her person.

'Miss Underhay, you came. Are you recovered? Are you still all right to prompt this evening?' Larry approached them as soon as they walked back into the foyer. He was dressed for the evening already in formal evening wear and white tie. Tilly accompanied him, swathed in sable and diamonds with a dainty hat perched on her blonde curls.

'Of course, but I shall be very careful about where I sit,' Kitty reassured him even though her heart was beating faster at the thought of sitting in the wings.

Tilly turned to Alice, who was wide-eyed at Kitty's elbow. 'Miss Miller, would you be terribly kind and give me a little help with my costume? The fastener at the back is very tricky to do on one's own.'

'My pleasure, Miss Tilly.' She turned lobster-red with pleasure at the request and Kitty bit back a smile. Alice had loved the photograph Tilly had signed for her and was fully prepared to become her devoted slave.

Genny had also changed into a purple satin bias cut evening gown that did little for her figure or her complexion. Kitty felt rather underdressed; it was a good thing she was not expected to be front of house.

'The artistes are starting to arrive, and the children will be here shortly. Kitty, please would you assist Miss Miller backstage for an hour or so until it's time for everyone to take their places?' Genny already looked harassed.

'Of course, just let me know what help you need, and I'll be happy to help you,' Kitty said.

'Thank you so much. Millicent will be here shortly and has agreed to manage the raffle. The Pavilion staff will look after the box office.' Genny glanced around her with a distracted air.

'I'm sure it will go beautifully,' Larry assured her.

Kitty noticed that a large poster advertising Larry's upcoming film, starring Tilly, had appeared in the foyer along with a table of flyers. She could only assume this was in readiness for the signing event at the end of the show. She accompanied Alice and Tilly through the auditorium to the backstage area.

There was an air of suppressed excitement and adrenaline in the dressing room area with the constant arrival of various performers and their bags and baggage. Chatter and laughter filled the air as they battled for time at the mirrors and space in the dressing rooms. Kitty was soon swept into the mix, helping people find their costumes and ready their props. Seb and Peter both greeted her but to her relief they were too busy preparing for their performance to have time to chat.

Mrs Davenport had not yet arrived, and Kitty wondered if her non-appearance was what had contributed to Genny's general air of anxiety. When the party of children from the orphanage arrived already dressed in their costumes, Kitty collected her prompting notes. She left the children under Alice's supervision and went through to the wings to check her seat was ready.

Thankfully, the evidence of the previous night's incident had been removed and she was somewhat cheered to see the lad in charge of the ropes busy checking everything. His expression immediately became more guarded as she approached, and she suspected that he thought she might blame him for the sandbag falling.

'Good evening, Billy. Thank you so much for checking every-thing over, I shall feel so much safer.' She smiled at him, anxious that he should see she did not blame him in any way for what had happened.

He appeared to relax a little. 'Got to be safe, miss. That weren't no accident though, last night. I showed the policeman this afternoon when he came to see me.'

'Yes, I thought as much. I know you take good care with the scenery and flats.' She looked up at the mass of ropes and pulleys looped high above her head.

'I've been up the ladder and checked them all out. You'll be perfectly safe tonight, miss.' He folded the stepladders he'd been using and stowed them safely just off stage near her chair in the wings so they would be out of the way of the performers.

'Thank you, Billy.' She checked her chair would be out of sight of the audience when the curtain was raised and placed her prompt sheets ready. Out in the auditorium, she could hear the audience starting to take their places.

Dickie entered the side of the stage looking debonair in his evening attire. 'Are you all right, Miss Underhay?'

'Yes, thank you. Are you and BeBe all set for tonight?' Kitty asked as Billy scuttled over to the far side of the stage, ready to take his cues from Larry.

'Yes, thank you. There is a rumour that Larry has a friend who scouts talent for films coming from London tonight as his guest. It's probably nonsense, but of course it would be nice if BeBe got her break.' His plain, round face lit up at the idea that his wife's talents might be recognised.

'You are both very talented.' She remembered it was supposed to be unlucky to wish them good luck, so refrained.

Dickie flashed her a smile and went to take his place at the piano. Kitty took her seat and waited for Laurence to give Billy the nod to raise the curtain. The small group of musicians in the auditorium began to play and the noise of the audience dropped to a few people coughing and some shuffling of feet.

Laurence brushed the lapels of his jacket with his hands and nodded to Billy to raise the curtain. He strode to the centre of the stage as the music stopped and introduced Mr Davenport.

Kitty watched with interest as Mr Davenport took to the stage, resplendent in evening attire and top hat. A dapper man, short in stature with a waxed moustache, he reminded her of the ringmaster at a circus. In a loud, booming voice he thanked the audience for their support of the orphanage, shamelessly taking full credit for all of Genny's hard work, and reminded them to attend the foyer after the show to meet Tilly and obtain her autograph.

CHAPTER TWENTY-FOUR

Matt stood at the back of the gallery at the top of the theatre auditorium. He had seen Kitty take her place, but to his frustration found he couldn't see far enough into the wings to keep an eye on her. Mr Davenport waffled away for five minutes before the show commenced.

Inspector Greville had placed a uniformed officer outside the theatre and two men in evening dress inside. As a former soldier, Matt wasn't usually given to hunches or a sense of foreboding, but he had a growing sense of unease about these murders. His military training had given him some skills in predicting an enemy's moves and it seemed likely that this particular villain would try again. It could be tonight, and it could be that Kitty was in the firing line.

The first half of the programme seemed interminable to Matt. He noted a man, who he assumed to be a police officer, standing at the side of the auditorium with a view of the stage. This at least gave him some reassurance.

The intermission was to last twenty minutes with usherettes selling sweets and refreshments. Mr Davenport had announced in his opening address that Tilly would be signing autographs for donations in the foyer after the performance. This seemed to have created a buzz of excitement, combined with a surge in people purchasing tickets for the raffle, to be drawn at the end of the concert.

Matt itched to get backstage to check on Kitty and Alice, but he knew if he were recognised then it could push the murderer into the very thing he wished to avoid. Instead, he was forced to bide his time and observe what he could from the gallery.

Kitty was glad of the intermission to stretch her legs and check on Alice. Backstage was crammed with people and smelt of perspiration, stage make-up and hair oil. Alice was busy organising the children ready to go on for the second half. She managed a reassuring wave at Kitty from the far end of the corridor.

Unable to reach Alice through the crush or make herself heard over the babble of noise, Kitty turned to retreat back to her seat in the wings.

'Miss Underhay, are you recovered from your ordeal?' Celeste Davenport blocked her way to the stage. Kitty thought she caught a faint odour of stale liquor.

'Oh yes, quite, thank you. The show seems to be going well, doesn't it?' Kitty said politely.

'Yes, Stanley is very pleased. It should help enormously to boost his profile. He's being considered for a knighthood, you know.'

Kitty privately thought this seemed more than a little unfair, considering it was all Genny's hard work and not her father's. 'How lovely, you must be very proud,' she said.

Celeste gave a thin-lipped smile. 'Yes, it will certainly rankle some of those who have always looked down on us theatre folk when they have to address us by our titles.'

Kitty wondered if she had any particular people in mind. It would certainly add to Peter's motives for wishing to avoid any potential scandal, knowing his father's knighthood held so much meaning for his parents. A cold shiver danced along her spine.

'I must get back to my place, the curtain will be rising again soon. I'm looking forward to your performance.' Kitty began to edge past her.

'Then I shall make certain it's unforgettable.' Celeste gave a brilliant smile and moved into her dressing room, allowing Kitty access back into the wings.

The strange encounter left Kitty feeling uncomfortable and on edge as she made her way back to her seat. She checked the ropes above her head before sitting down once more. Celeste had obviously been drinking and she wasn't even in her costume, whatever it might be, ready for her performance. Kitty hoped for Genny's sake that Celeste was not about to embarrass herself in front of the cream of Torbay's society.

She had noticed a man during the first half of the show stationed near the door on the opposite side of the auditorium. She could only assume from his build and the position he assumed that he must be one of Inspector Greville's men. That gave her some comfort as she gathered her papers and found her place, ready for the curtain to rise once more.

She forced herself to concentrate as Larry gave the signal and Billy raised the curtain on the second half of the show. There was a lot more for her to do during this second half. The children were stage-struck so her prompts were required to keep them on track and Tilly, as usual, required several hints.

Finally, Laurence announced: '… the return to the stage, after an extended absence, of Miss Celeste Porter.' A single spotlight shone down on the centre mark and Celeste strolled out to the accompaniment of Dickie's piano.

Kitty gasped in surprise. Gone was the neurotic, tipsy socialite from backstage and in her place was an effete, moustached young man in top hat and tails, twirling a cane as she sang 'Burlington Bertie'. She froze in her seat as all kinds of suspicions began to arise in her mind.

The spotlight tracked Celeste as she walked up and down coaxing the audience into singing a medley of the older, well-loved music hall songs, finishing with 'Come into the Garden, Maud'. She sang with feeling and produced a rose from her lapel which she presented to a young girl seated in the front row.

Tilly's applause had been warm, but Celeste brought the house down with the audience calling for an encore. Larry escorted her back to the stage where she sang 'Show me the Way to go Home' to more rapturous applause. Kitty suspected that Tilly would not be happy with Celeste stealing her limelight. She hadn't realised that Celeste was so adept at male impersonation.

Billy brought down the curtain as the cast assembled on stage for a final bow together with Larry tactfully squiring his wife on one arm and Celeste on the other. Billy raised the curtain for their final bow then lowered it once more along with the heavier fire curtain and the show was over.

The cast dispersed backstage whilst Genny and Larry went out in front of the curtain to announce the winning raffle numbers. Kitty stretched and rolled her shoulders, relieved the performance had gone without a hitch. Her mind raced as the puzzle began to slot into place. She had to talk to Inspector Greville as soon as possible. Dickie collected up his sheet music, placing it in a black leather case, a large grin stretched across his face.

'Larry did invite that agent and he wants to talk to BeBe and me. This could be our big break.'

'Oh, Dickie, that's marvellous.' Kitty was delighted for them. BeBe deserved an opportunity and Dickie was a very talented musician. On the other side of the curtain she could hear the hustle and bustle of the audience exiting the auditorium. She fidgeted with impatience as she made small talk for a moment with Dickie as the theatre emptied.

'Shall we see you later, at the Davenports? Celeste was rather marvellous, wasn't she?' he asked.

'Maybe, I need to speak to Alice first as I'm not sure of her plans.' Kitty really didn't want to spend more time with the Davenports. Her priority was to talk to the inspector about her suspicions.

Dickie grinned and rushed off, whistling. Kitty prepared to follow him only to realise, much to her annoyance, that she was missing an earring. Since they were a recent gift from her cousin Lucy, she was anxious to find it. She knew they had both been in place when she'd taken her seat. It took her a few minutes searching about the floor near her chair and over by Dickie's piano before she spotted it, glinting in the dim light. She retrieved it and refastened it on her earlobe.

The auditorium had fallen silent and the hubbub from backstage had also died away. Kitty walked out of the wings towards the backstage area. To her surprise, the small door that was usually wedged open to allow the cast to enter the wings was now closed.

She frowned. Dickie hadn't been very far in front of her and she hadn't heard the door shut. She rattled the handle, only to discover the door seemed to be locked. The hairs at the back of her neck prickled in alarm and she turned to hurry across the stage around the scenery to the opposite wing, hoping that door was open.

Kitty saw the door was closed and twisted the handle, gasping in alarm as the limited lights which had been lighting the stage suddenly went out plunging the area into darkness. She thumped on the door, hoping someone was still backstage to hear her. Where was Alice? Drat the darkness! If she could see a little, she could raise the fire curtain, or fight her way under it to get out via the auditorium.

'Hello, can anyone hear me? Open the door!' She tried shouting but the empty blackness seemed to swallow up the sound. Somewhere on the other side of the stage she heard a scraping noise.

'Hello?' For a fleeting second her hopes rose that someone was unlocking the side door.

The eerie, soft sound of someone singing to the tune of 'Daisy, Daisy' drifted across the stage. 'Kitty, Kitty, where are you? I've come looking, what are you going to do?'

Kitty held her breath and edged further back away from the door, hoping she was going towards the curtains. It was so hard to work out where she was. There was little comfort in knowing her notion about Celeste was correct. She kept her fingertips against the wall, not wanting to lose her place in the darkness. Her heel caught against something and she froze, her heart thumping against the wall of her chest.

'Found you!' A hand clamped itself firmly across her mouth, preventing her from screaming. The faint stale scent of alcohol reached her, confirming the identity of her assailant, even as something cold and metallic was pressed against the side of her neck.

'Now, Miss Nosy Parker, I'm going to move my hand from your mouth but one squeak out of you and my knife here will slit your throat as easily as it cut that rope last night, understand me?' Celeste's throaty voice murmured in her ear.

Kitty held her breath as Celeste took her hand from her mouth then promptly caught hold of her arm, forcing it up her back. The knife remained at her throat.

'Now we're going to take a little walk.' Celeste urged her forwards in the darkness and Kitty wondered how on earth the woman could possibly know where they were in the inky darkness.

'Walk faster, there is not much time,' Celeste hissed.

She forced her to a halt and Kitty could only assume they had reached the far side of the stage near her prompting chair. Her pulse whooshed in her ears and she wondered if Celeste was acting alone, or if Peter was assisting her.

There was a scuffling noise and a click. A small side light came on and Kitty saw she was right, and they were in the wings. The stepladder that Billy had folded up and placed to one side had been opened out. Above her head, a coil of rope had been pulled down and fashioned into a noose.

'What are you doing?' Kitty croaked. She could hear the distant sound of doors opening and closing and the low hum of voices. Knowing people were so close only made her predicament worse somehow.

'You don't know? You haven't guessed?' Celeste whispered. 'Well, you are going to kill yourself, obviously.'

'Why would I do that?' Kitty asked, trying to stop her voice from shaking as the flat of the knife blade was pressed more firmly against her throat.

'Oh, it's all right, I've taken care of everything. You're so distraught, you see. Your lover is leaving you. Oh yes, Millicent Craven told me that Captain Bryant is moving away. Dear Millicent, she so loves to be of use to people, doesn't she?' Celeste gave a peculiar little giggle. 'Now, do come on, we haven't much time. I've a party to host and your maid will be looking for you when she realises the note that I sent her is a forgery.' She gave Kitty a little push towards the steps.

'Why did you kill Pearl and leave her on the golf course? Was this all about Peter? Is he involved in this too?' Kitty asked. She had to keep Celeste talking in the hope that someone would come to her rescue.

'I'm so disappointed in you, Kitty. Of course Peter isn't involved. I was sure you had it all worked out, that's why I warned you off. Poking around, asking questions and snooping. That girl had photographs of Peter and that depraved friend of his, taken at some party in London. Disgusting pictures. I couldn't let those get out with Stanley under consideration for a knighthood. No, I had to protect my family. We haven't worked hard all these years for nothing. It's not Peter's fault; he was led astray by that wicked boy. She wanted money, I heard her at the party asking Peter. She would have bled him dry.' Celeste pressed the flat of the knife blade deeper against Kitty's neck. 'Come along and don't be difficult. It would be so much easier for you to kill yourself. I really don't want to spoil my costume with your blood.'

'Why did you leave Pearl on the golf course? And what had Matt done to make you try to incriminate him?' Kitty tried to edge away only for Celeste to twist her arm further up her back, making her wince with pain.

'Wretched golf club committee kept blackballing my membership. I wish I could have seen the smug smile being wiped off Millicent's face when she found that girl. Always looking down at me.' She mimicked Mrs Craven's voice. "*I was mayoress, you know. We met the queen. I'm a member of the golf club.*" Pah.'

'And Matt?' Kitty asked. The noises backstage had ceased again.

'I saw them go to his door. It was easy to persuade Pearl to come with me to sit in my car for a little chat while her friend went to get more drink. It struck me that he would have no alibi, so I got Pearl to show me what they had scavenged and used the bootlace to kill her. Then I drove her to the eleventh tee and threw her out before hiding the travel rug in Captain Bryant's outhouse. It was nothing personal but obviously I needed someone to be arrested.' She spoke so matter-of-factly, Kitty was stunned.

'And Salome?'

Celeste laughed. 'She thought she was so clever, taking the photographs from Pearl's trunk before I could get them. I tracked her down though and promised her money. She thought it was Peter who had killed Pearl, so she didn't suspect me at all. I have some sedatives from the doctor, and I put them in her drink. She went for a bath thinking I would let myself out. It was easy to sneak back. I just grabbed her feet and pulled her under the water. She didn't put up a fight, but then she didn't have the photographs with her.'

'I suppose that's when you had to go back to her old lodgings and convince the landlady you were her brother and take the box,' Kitty said.

'Once I had the photographs, I burned them. Peter thinks I still have them, of course.' She giggled again. 'A little leverage to ensure he marries Saira and stops associating with Sebastian and his kind.'

Kitty suppressed a shudder.

Celeste's face was close to Kitty's. 'Don't tell me you feel sorry for that nasty little pair of blackmailers? Tut tut, now hurry up, up the steps you go.' She once more pushed Kitty towards the stepladder, forcing her to use her free hand to hold the steps as she climbed up a few rungs.

'Once you're out of the way there will be no more loose ends. Captain Bryant will have already left for London and poor Kitty… well, the dead can tell no tales.' Celeste had been forced to move the knife from Kitty's neck to her stomach as Kitty had ascended a few of the steps. 'Now slip the rope over your head.'

Kitty glanced upwards to the loop of rope dangling above her head. Her arm ached from where Celeste had wrenched it back behind her. 'I can't reach it; I need to be higher.' For once in her life Kitty was thankful she was quite petite. If Celeste would just permit her to go up another couple of steps…

'Hurry up!' Celeste hissed and waved the knife at her.

Out in the auditorium Kitty heard someone calling her name. Adrenaline kicked in and she went up another couple of rungs. Celeste's attention was momentarily deflected by whoever was calling and Kitty spied her chance.

She gripped the sides of the stepladder and kicked out at Celeste's hand, sending the knife spinning off into the darkened stage area. Celeste gave a shriek of rage and grabbed at her. Kitty wobbled and kicked out at her assailant, hoping not to fall.

'Help, on the stage!' Kitty called at the top of her voice as the ladder gave one final shudder and she toppled back onto Celeste.

She fumbled in her pocket to retrieve Alice's police whistle as Celeste clawed at her arms and face. Kitty rolled, trying to shake Celeste off, as her fingers closed around the cool metal whistle. She managed to get it to her lips and blew as hard as she could as Celeste's strong fingers closed around her throat.

Dark spots danced before Kitty's eyes and she dug her nails into her attacker's hands as fiercely as she could to try to force her to loosen her grip. Celeste was astride her now, her alcohol-laden breath in Kitty's nostrils as they grappled. In the distance, she thought she heard Matt's voice. Then there was a rattling, rustling and banging at the curtain edge and the pressure was suddenly gone from her throat and Celeste's weight from her stomach.

Kitty rolled onto her side coughing and retching, and the main lights came back on. Her eyes streamed with tears as she was gently helped into a sitting position. Alice was next to her, anxiety and fear written into her expression. Matt knelt at her other side, his strong arms supporting her so she could breathe.

Inspector Greville and a uniformed officer were locking handcuffs around Celeste's wrists ready to lead her away.

CHAPTER TWENTY-FIVE

'Kitty, my God, Kitty, are you all right? Can you stand?' Matt supported her to her feet and steered her to the chair she'd used whilst prompting the performers.

'I'm all right.' Her voice came out sounding much croakier than she had anticipated. Her arms and legs were shaking, and chills seemed to be enveloping her body.

'I've asked the Pavilion manager to telephone Doctor Carter. He should be here shortly.' Inspector Greville's face was grave.

'I'm so sorry Miss Kitty, it's my fault. I had a note to meet you in the foyer. I should have known better.' Alice sniffed, her lower lip trembling as her eyes filled with tears. 'I run into Captain Bryant in the crowd and we couldn't see you anywhere. Then it was all chaos in the foyer as this man tried to snatch at Miss Tilly's diamond brooch and the police arrested him.'

Kitty coughed, trying to clear her throat, conscious of Celeste glowering at her, and was thankful the officers were holding her securely. 'Celeste sent you the note. She wanted me to hang myself. I saw her on stage and realised she was involved.'

Matt, Alice and Inspector Greville all looked up and saw the prepared noose. Alice gasped.

'I was in the lighting gallery for the whole of the show until just before the end of Celeste's performance. I met Alice in the foyer and she showed me the note. Then that chap you dismissed for stealing suddenly appeared from nowhere and snatched Tilly's brooch and the place erupted.' Matt glanced at Celeste who scowled at him, hatred burning in her eyes.

'It was all her,' Kitty said. 'Everything. She did it for Peter and for her husband. She wanted to be Lady Davenport.'

There was a banging from the door in the wings. The door opened and Genny stared at them, her eyes round and owl-like behind her spectacles as she took in the scene before her.

'Mother? The car is waiting for us. What's going on?'

Celeste said nothing. Genny entered the wings and Matt tightened his grip protectively around Kitty's shoulders.

'Mother?' Genny asked, stopping in her tracks when she noticed the handcuffs securing her mother's hands behind her back.

'Miss Davenport, I regret to inform you that your mother is now formally under arrest for the murders of Pearl Bright and Salome Donohue, and for the attempted murder of Miss Kitty Underhay.' Inspector Greville's tone was firm but kind as Genny swayed a little on her heels.

'I don't understand?' Genny looked at her mother.

'You never understand anything, you just stand around bleating like an unattractive sheep. There is nothing to understand. Please give my apologies to our guests,' Celeste snapped.

'But surely there has been some mistake?' Genny blinked.

'The only mistake is that both my children are a huge disappointment to me. One is depraved and the other a do-gooding man-mad frump of a spinster,' Celeste retorted.

Kitty watched as Genny's pleasant features crumpled for a moment before she collected herself, sucking in a deep breath. 'I'll telephone Father, he has already gone on ahead.' She turned and walked away without a backwards glance.

'Hello, anyone around?' Dr Carter appeared through the side door, his round cherubic face beaming at them. 'Miss Underhay, in a scrape again?' He dropped his bag down next to Kitty and gave her a brisk but thorough examination. 'No real harm done, although you will have some bruising I fear.'

'Thank you.' Kitty managed a hoarse whisper as the doctor turned his attention to the injuries Kitty had inflicted on Celeste.

'Superficial scratch marks.' The doctor closed his bag.

Inspector Greville nodded his head and the policeman led Celeste away. As soon as she was out of sight, Kitty released a shuddering sigh.

'Alice, will you accompany Kitty back to the Dolphin please?' Matt asked.

Alice nodded. 'Yes, sir, I'm not letting her out of my sight.'

The fierceness of her tone brought a smile to Kitty's lips even though she still felt shaken and teary.

'I'll need a statement from you, Miss Underhay,' Inspector Greville said.

'Of course.' Kitty wished her voice was less scratchy.

'Tomorrow, after she's rested.' Doctor Carter exchanged a look with the inspector.

Inspector Greville grunted his assent.

'Now, shall I give you ladies a ride back to Dartmouth? I presume you have your motorcycle?' Doctor Carter turned to Matt.

Kitty hoped Doctor Carter would drive a little more cautiously if he only had herself and Alice in the car. 'Thank you.'

'Yes, my bike is parked outside,' Matt said. He helped Kitty to her feet. 'I'll walk you to Doctor Carter's car.'

Alice scrambled to collect their coats and bags, assisting Kitty to fasten her buttons when she realised that she was shaking too much still to manage them herself. Kitty was glad of Matt's support as they made their way out of the theatre and outside into the cool night air. She hadn't expected to still feel so wobbly.

Doctor Carter opened the rear door of his large black car and Alice slipped inside.

'I'll be over first thing in the morning, I need to attend to a few things here first. Father Lamb was in the foyer, he has some more information for you about your mother. When that chap attempted to rob Tilly, it threw everything into confusion. Now go back with Alice and get some rest and I'll tell you everything tomorrow.' Matt helped Kitty into the car, his dark blue gaze locking with hers as he assisted her into her seat. 'So much for being careful. I swear you'll be the death of me, Kitty Underhay. Good night, old girl.' His lips brushed hers and he closed the door swiftly before she could reply. Doctor Carter started the car engine as Matt stepped back onto the pavement.

She craned her head as best as she could to watch Matt walking away, the taste of his lips still on her mouth, sending butterflies fluttering in her stomach. As the car picked up speed, she settled into her seat and caught a smile on Alice's face.

'I don't reckon as how Captain Bryant will be going back to London now after all,' Alice observed.

Kitty brushed her fingertips against her lips. 'I hope you're right, Alice,' she murmured. 'I do hope you're right.'

A LETTER FROM HELENA DIXON

I want to say thank you for choosing to read *Murder at the Playhouse*. If you enjoyed it and want to keep up to date with all my latest releases, just sign up at the following link. Your email address will never be shared and you can unsubscribe at any time.

www.bookouture.com/helena-dixon

If you read the first book in the series, *Murder at the Dolphin Hotel*, you can discover how Kitty and Matt first met. Their next adventure was *Murder at Enderley Hall*. I always enjoy meeting characters again as a series reader which is why I love writing about Kitty and Matt so much. I hope you enjoy their adventures as much as I love creating them.

I hope you loved *Murder at the Playhouse* and if you did, I would be very grateful if you could write a review. I'd love to hear what you think, and it makes such a difference helping new readers to discover one of my books for the first time.

I love hearing from my readers – you can get in touch on my Facebook page, through Twitter, Goodreads or my website.

Many Thanks,
Helena Dixon

nelldixonauthor

@NellDixon

www.nelldixon.com

ACKNOWLEDGEMENTS

My thanks as always go to the wonderful people of Dartmouth for allowing me to fictionalise parts of their beautiful town. Their help and assistance is greatly appreciated. Special thanks to Matthew Gill and everyone at Churston Golf Club. Matthew very generously gave us a golf buggy tour and provided lots of helpful information. Plus, the fisherman in the bay is all Matthew. My thanks also to everyone in Torquay and Paignton for their help with memories of the seaplanes and the beautiful Pavilion in its heyday. I very much hope that the Pavilion will be reopened one day and come to life once more.

Special thanks to my husband and daughters for their assistance in collating all the research information and photographs and accompanying me on my adventures around the bay.

Lots of love to the coffee crew, Phillipa Ashley and Elizabeth Hanbury for the plotting, handholding and moral support, not to mention the coffee. Lots of coffee.

This book wouldn't exist either without a whole team of fantastic people, my agent, Kate Nash, my fabulous editor, Emily Gowers, my patient and meticulous copy editor, Jennie Ayres, and my invaluable proofreader, Shirley Khan, the talented cover designer, Debbie Clement, and everyone at Bookouture. Thank you.